Title: If Anything Happens to Me

Author: Luanne Rice

On-Sale Date: September 17, 2024

Format: Jacketed Hardcover

ISBN: 978-1-338-73953-4 || Price: $19.99 US

Ages: 12 and up

Grades: 7 and up

LOC Number: Available

Length: 320 pages

Trim: 5 1/2 X 8 1/4 inches

Classification: Young Adult Fiction: Law & Crime /
Family / Siblings / Action & Adventure / Mysteries &
Detective Stories

---------------- *Additional Formats Available* --------------

Ebook ISBN: 978-1-338-73954-1

Digital Audiobook ISBN: 978-1-5461-3687-3 || Price: $24.99 US

Library Audiobook ISBN: 978-1-5461-3688-0 || Price: $74.99 US

Scholastic Press
An Imprint of Scholastic Inc.
557 Broadway, New York, NY 10012
For information, contact us at:
tradepublicity@scholastic.com

IF ANYTHING

HAPPENS

TO ME

IF ANYTHING

HAPPENS

TO ME

LUANNE RICE

SCHOLASTIC PRESS / NEW YORK

Library of Congress Cataloging-in-Publication Data available

ISBN 978-1-338-73953-4

10 9 8 7 6 5 4 3 2 1   24 25 26 27 28

Printed in the U.S.A. 128

First edition, September 2024

Book design by Maeve Norton

FOR AIMEE FRIEDMAN
BRILLIANT WRITER, BELOVED EDITOR

one

I hadn't visited my sister in thirty days, but today was June 9, and I always showed up on the ninth of the month.

I felt guilty for staying away so long. To make it up to her, I packed a basket of wild strawberries into my backpack, picked a bouquet of sweet peas—her favorites—and headed out.

It was late afternoon, and a steady breeze had picked up. It made me think of sailing. Eloise and I should have been on a boat, feeling the breeze in our hair. We should have been taking this picnic to Dauntless Island instead of having it in the woods where I was meeting her.

I walked through town. We live in Black Hall, one of those postcard-pretty New England villages with sea captains' houses, rose gardens, and white picket fences. Stately maple trees lined the streets. The deep yellow sunlight burnished everything, made the town even more beautiful. I passed our high school. As of yesterday, we were out for summer vacation, so no one was there. In September I'd be a junior. And Eloise was just one year behind.

I wished I'd left earlier in the day, but honestly, I'd been finding reasons not to leave the house. I wanted to see her, but I also didn't.

Eloise would be disappointed. She could read my mind, and I could read hers. She'd be hurt that I only came to see her once a month. She would have preferred it be more often; she would have liked it to be every day. I could hear her voice, predict what she would say when I stood in front of her.

Seriously, Oli? Where have you been? I could see her little frown, her furrowed brow, the familiar expression she wore when she was frustrated.

You know, I've been busy, I would reply.

Doing what?

Um . . .

Exactly—um. *Come on, Oli!*

You should know better than anyone, Eloise. We're . . .

TGWTMR, she would say, her expression softening, a smile entering her voice.

Yep. The Girls With Too Much Responsibility, I would say, and we would crack up laughing, and everything would be okay again.

Our grandmother used to tell us: "You'll have many friends in life, but only one sister." And she was right—I felt it in my bones, that I would never love anyone as much as Eloise.

People sometimes thought we were twins at first glance, because we were the same height and had similar features. But Eloise's hair was blonde, and mine was more reddish in color. And while my eyes were blue, Eloise's were hazel—the same color of the green leaves overhead, touched by the magical late-day golden light.

You can trust the universe, Eloise liked to say.

In response, I'd give her my best skeptical raised eyebrow. "You sound like Dr. Hirsch," I'd say. Dr. Hirsch was the therapist we used to see.

"Well, she's right!" Eloise would insist. My sister was sunshine and optimism, and she believed that everything worked out in the end. I was shadows and hesitation, with a hard shell. This was the best way—protect myself from ever getting hurt, let things roll off my back.

Our parents had died when we were very young, so long ago that only I remembered them—Eloise didn't at all. But I knew she *felt* their leaving—the emptiness that filled our house after they were gone. So it made perfect sense, our need to hold tight to each other.

I reached the arched stone bridge that led from Main Street onto a footpath into the Braided Woods, and my whole body tensed. In spite of the almost-summer air, the temperature seemed to drop, coating me with frost.

Eloise and I would come here to go birding, either just the two of us or with our nature club from school. We had been avid birders since our dad got us started when we were little. These woods were the perfect place to see migrating warblers each spring and fall, to listen for barred and great horned owls at dusk and search for their pellets in daylight, to spot red-tailed hawks hiding in the foliage as they watched for prey.

We had actually come to these woods with our nature club the

3

morning of October 9: the same day it happened. Later that day, Eloise had disappeared.

Exactly eight months ago.

My sister had been gone that long.

We told each other that we were best friends, not just sisters, and that we would always stay close. We would probably go to the same college. Definitely live in the same town after graduation. It was our promise, and she had broken hers. I knew it wasn't fair of me to feel that way—she hadn't meant to go away forever. It wasn't her fault.

But the fact was, she wasn't here with me anymore. The best *I* could do to keep my vow was to stay true to the ninth. Every month since October 9, rain or snow or shine, I'd been there.

November 9

December 9

January 9

February 9

March 9

April 9

May 9

Now June 9

People might think me strange for bringing strawberries and flowers. They'd say: *What does Eloise care, what good are they to her?* Well, I knew she would love them, so that was why I brought them. Just like I brought apple cider, Christmas cookies, pine cones, roasted chestnuts, clementines, lemon cake, valentine hearts, and

4

lilacs on some of the other ninths. I packed up her favorite treats, things I was sure she would like, and carried them right here, into the Braided Woods.

This was where I visited her.

Not the cemetery, with its tall oaks and weeping willows, its centuries-old gravestones. For twelve years, ever since our parents died, our grandmother took me and Eloise there to leave flowers on their graves. It is a place full of history, with some of the tombstones dating back to the 1600s and crumbling with age. While Gram tended the grass and plantings, Eloise and I would make grave rubbings of the angels and epitaphs carved into the ancient sandstone and shale, and think about the people and their lives. Believe it or not, those were happy times for us.

Now that Eloise was buried there, next to our mom and dad, I never wanted to go back. It was too hard, too final, seeing her name and the dates of her life engraved in that gray stone.

Here in the Braided Woods, where her life was stolen from her, she seemed more alive somehow. As I walked along the narrow path, the trees closing in around me, I could feel her breath in my own chest. I was following the footsteps she took that October day.

The police found little clues, as surely as if she had left a trail of breadcrumbs: a long blonde hair caught on a bayberry bush, a little fuzz from her blue fleece jacket stuck to the rough bark of an oak tree, the footprints of boots in the spongy soil.

Nature had left clues as well: a sprinkle of pollen, bits of yellow leaves that seemed to have turned to gold dust. A downy feather the color of the sea at dawn.

But they still hadn't caught who did it.

I thought about my sister's case all the time. *Case:* such an insignificant word for the most important thing on earth, my sister's murder.

At first the detective assigned to the case would visit my grandmother regularly, to fill her in on the investigation. Once Detective Tyrone realized that Gram wasn't exactly retaining the information, she would still stop by, just to check on us, but not say very much.

I explained to Detective Tyrone about Gram's Alzheimer's, and I asked her to report the case's progress to me instead. I knew how to talk to Gram, how to get through to her, in the hit-or-miss language of the wind trying to get through the drafty walls of a beloved summer cottage. But the detective didn't take me seriously. As much as I liked her, she seemed to be looking beyond me, as if I had nothing to offer the investigation. She was young and kind, but she gave me a sad, indulgent smile that said *you're just a kid, you can't handle this.*

That drove me out of my mind. Can't handle *what,* Detective? I wanted to scream. The small details, the tiny threads of information, the dead ends, the wrong turns of your stupid investigation? Grilling our friends, wasting all that time when you should have been finding an actual killer? Because those details were *nothing* compared to having to handle the fact Eloise was gone.

6

The whole thing made me want to jump right in and do what the police couldn't: solve Eloise's murder. I was constantly trying to put this huge, terrible puzzle together, and it made me realize that I wanted to become a detective when I graduated.

Eloise used to tease me that I knew a little about a lot of things.

"You go from curious to obsessed in ten seconds flat," she'd say, and I could only shrug, because she was correct. My current and overwhelming obsession was needing to learn who had taken my sister away from me, and why.

There were no leads. Some nights, one name would shimmer through my dreams. I refused to let it come to the surface while I was awake. It would be even more unbearable to think that someone my sister had known, someone we had hung out with, could have done this to her.

I looked around the woods. That person could be here now, waiting for another girl to come along. But I was not afraid. I was not even sad. One thing for sure, I wouldn't cry—I never cry. I am tough. If bad things happen, once you start crying, you might never stop. Other than feeling wound too tight, I was numb. I might as well have been floating, as if I had left my body, just as Eloise had left hers.

When I approached the clearing, I slung off my backpack. There was the spot up ahead, the rock crevice where hikers had found her body, buried under dirt and fallen leaves, two days after we reported her missing. This was her real grave—the place where she took her

7

last breath and turned from a human into a ghost—nothing like that manicured area in the cemetery.

Some people might find this place creepy. I didn't. I walked slowly to the disturbed ground—it was a narrow furrow, the earth softer than everything around it. The killer had dug leaves and dirt out of the rock ledge, placed Eloise inside. After they found her, yellow crime scene tape had surrounded the perimeter. There was still a scrap of it wedged under a stone. I felt a knife in my heart because it reminded me once again of how the investigation had dwindled away.

I looked up. A shaft of that lovely fading sunlight came through the trees' canopy. Yep, picnic time. I was hungry for those berries. My sister would be, too. I took the basket of strawberries out of my backpack and placed them, along with the bouquet of sweet peas, on the ground.

"Hi, Eloise," I said out loud.

Since she died, she had spoken to me through nature—the sound of the breeze, stones tossed around in the waves, the rustle of seagrasses at the beach, the call of the owls. The ospreys had returned from their winters down south, and I heard Eloise in their exuberant, high-pitched cries. I didn't expect to hear her actual human voice, but then:

"Help," she whispered. "Help me."

The words were not clear, but garbled, as if they were coming through a tunnel. I wasn't startled—I had lost my mind after I lost

8

Eloise, so expecting weirdness, terribleness, cruel tricks was just part of my life now.

I had gotten pretty good at turning the worst into the normal, so I said, "I want to go back in time. I would help you. I would do anything for you."

"Then dig me up!" she said, her voice rising to a muffled yet outraged shriek.

Here was how I know I had gone around the bend and completely lost it: I saw the dirt moving. I was staring at the fissure in the rock ledge where Eloise's body had been found. Just like then, it was filled with leaves and branches and mud. But now the dirt was heaving, tossing, as if the ground were alive. I leaned closer and saw her left hand reaching up from the depths of the crevice.

I fell to my knees, grabbing her hand with one of mine, frantically digging and scraping with the other. Her fingers were scored with cuts, the skin dirty and cracked, her fingernails torn and broken. I let go of her hand to dig deeper, my arms windmilling like mad, scooping dirt and mud, until I was looking straight into her face.

But it wasn't Eloise's face. It was someone else, a girl with short dark hair, there in the same grave where the murderer had left my sister. She lay perfectly still. Her forehead and cheeks were caked with dirt that shimmered in the late light, as if it were flecked with bits of real gold.

"Help me," the girl said.

She put her arms around my neck, and I hauled her out of the ground. It took all my strength because she was covered with leaves and mud, but I did it as if she was as weightless as air. She tried to stand, but her legs buckled. She was like a baby deer walking for the first time. She faltered, all knees and elbows, got up, fell down again. She coughed, choking on debris. I crouched and brushed dirt from her eyes and mouth.

"We have to hurry," she said, voice rasping.

"Who are you?" I cried. "Who put you here?"

"Hurry, now," she said, and I could tell from the panic pouring off her that we didn't have time for questions. I lifted her to her feet. I put my arm around her shoulders and helped her take the first few steps. Then she was okay. Or at least okay enough to walk fast, and then we began to run.

Two

As soon as we got out of the woods, I realized I had left my backpack behind, along with the strawberries and flowers. My cell phone was in my bag.

"Wait here," I said to the girl. I felt electricity running through me. "I have to go back."

"You can't!" she cried.

"I need my phone. We have to call 911."

"No police!" she said.

I stared at her. Did she have any idea what she looked like? What had she been through?

"You need an ambulance," I told her. "And the police—"

"Didn't you hear me?" the girl said. "I said no police. There's a reason."

"What is the reason?" I asked.

She gazed down at the ground, and when she looked up at me, her eyes were blank. "I don't know," she said.

She wasn't making sense. I chalked that up to the fact I had just pulled her out of a hole in the ground, and her thoughts probably weren't tracking all that well.

I was going to have to take charge here. I glanced around. My heart was racing. I felt the shock of danger, and a shiver ran down my spine. Whoever had left the girl in my sister's grave could still be around. I had to think clearly.

We were on the village outskirts, on a lane with pretty houses, the kind you would expect to find full of nice, happy families. But one thing about having a sister murdered in your own hometown— everyone was guilty until proven innocent.

I spotted a FOR SALE sign at the end of a driveway. The yard was overgrown, and there were some newspapers on the front porch, which made me think the people had already moved out.

A red barn stood behind the house. I ran to it, discovered that the door was unlocked, and hurried the girl inside, into an old horse stall piled high with musty bales of hay. Swallows had nested in the rafters. There must have been eggs because the adult birds were swooping in and out, trying to chase us away. Farm implements like shovels, an axe, and a pitchfork leaned against the splintery wall. I made the girl sit down on a hay bale.

"Hide here. I'll be right back," I said.

"Don't leave me!" she said.

"Count to a hundred, I won't be long," I said, closing the door behind me. I tore down the lane back to the Braided Woods. I had never run faster. When I got to the spot where Eloise and this girl had been buried, I couldn't find my backpack.

Terror can do that.

I walked around the clearing, and there was my backpack, right where I had left it, nestled in the roots of a tall spruce tree. But as I picked it up, I saw something glint on the ground. I bent down and picked it up—a tiny gold charm, about a half inch in diameter, with an enameled white figure etched on the front: It looked like a ghost girl.

I turned the charm over in my hand, saw microscopic etching on the back, and my neck prickled: Who had dropped it? The girl I'd just found in the grave? Her attacker? *Eloise*, all those months ago? No way—I would have known if my sister had something like this. Besides, the police would have found it. Right?

I was holding my breath, as if I were in my own private horror movie, and I forced myself to breathe. I had to get back to the girl. I shoved the charm into my pocket, grabbed my backpack, and raced back toward the barn.

The door's rusty hinges creaked when I pushed it open, and as I stepped into the horse stall, I heard a terrified shriek. The girl was standing there with wild eyes, holding the pitchfork waist-height, thrusting it forward.

"Hey!" I said, jumping back.

"Sorry," she said, lowering the pitchfork. She wiped her sweaty forehead with the back of her hand. "I wasn't sure who it was."

I was completely freaked out by the sight of those long, sharp, curved tines pointed straight at me. I fumbled inside the outer pocket of my backpack and pulled out my phone, ready to call the police.

The girl had the speed of a feral barn cat and leapt toward me, yanking the phone from my hand. Her violence shocked me.

"Don't you listen?" she asked. "You are *not* going to call anyone."

"You're not thinking straight," I said, taking a step back to get away from her rage. "This is an emergency. You get that, right? You were buried alive. Who did this to you? You could have died!"

"I know," she said, her tone dropping a few notches. She shook her head and her expression softened. She reluctantly handed me my phone. "I'm sorry."

"So am I," I said. "Listen. My sister—she was found in that exact same spot where I found you. Her body. She was killed."

"Sister," the girl whispered, and as soon as she said the word she began to shake uncontrollably.

"Eloise," I said. "That's my sister's name."

The girl didn't reply, just stood there.

I stepped toward her, put a hand on her shoulder, wanting to help her stop trembling. "You're okay now," I said. "You're safe."

"I don't think that's true," she said.

I took a deep breath. "If you're not safe, that's all the more reason to call the police," I explained. "They've been trying to find out who killed my sister." I held out some hope that this horrible situation could breathe life into my sister's cold case. "And not only that, we should get you to the emergency room—"

She interrupted me midsentence. "Have you ever had something that's not really a memory? Just a picture in your mind, and you're not even sure where you saw it before, but you know you did? Because I can see two words, just the words, like in a black-and-white photograph."

14

"What words?" I asked, thinking of that name that kept shimmering in my mind.

"No Police," the girl said, gazing down, as if reading it from an invisible page. She wrapped her arms around herself, like she was trying to keep from breaking into pieces.

"Who told you that?" I asked. "Who said 'no police'?"

"I don't know," she said. "But you're not calling them." She sounded angry and glared up at me. "Got it, Eloise's sister? What's your name, anyway?"

"Oli Parrish," I said. "What's yours?"

No answer. She just held herself tighter. She looked away again, frowning, staring at the ground. Her silence felt rude.

"I rescued you, remember?" I asked a little harshly. "You can tell me."

"Remember?" she asked and laughed slightly, in a high, shrill tone.

"That's what I said. You were in that hole? I pulled you out?" I asked. "A few minutes ago? Did you forget that?"

"No, I didn't forget that," she said. "What a miracle."

"A miracle? That I rescued you?"

"No. That I remember." Now she wasn't just shaking—she was wobbling. I thought she might fall over or pass out, so I put my arm around her shoulders and eased her back down onto the bale of hay.

"Put your head down, between your knees," I said, remembering that old direction from my therapist, Dr. Hirsch. She had told me to do that when I got really upset and started to hyperventilate. "Take deep breaths."

15

The girl did what I said. I stared at the back of her head. Her brown hair was tangled and matted with twigs, sticky with blood. When she calmed down a little, she looked up at me.

I remembered the gold charm. I dug it out of my pocket, held it toward her. "Is this yours?" I asked.

She glanced at it, shook her head. Her face was streaked with grime, and I saw that along with the cut on her head, there were scrapes on her cheek and above her eyebrow.

I crouched down beside her, so I could look into her brown eyes.

"Still dizzy?" I asked.

"I'm fine," she said. I shouldn't have even bothered asking, because she was so obviously not fine.

"We can't stay here," I told her. "You've made it clear you don't want me to call the police. I don't know why—I think that's a mistake—but I'm not going to argue with you right now."

"Thank you," she said.

"There is one thing I really need to know, though. You've got to tell me, okay?"

She watched me with this incredible sadness in her eyes, as if, without even hearing the question yet, she already knew I wouldn't like her answer.

"What's your name?" I asked again.

She took another deep breath. Sitting there, she stared at me for a long time. I thought she was going to hold her breath forever, but then she exhaled hard and bent over almost double, so her head was touching her knees. She shuddered and said something in a voice so low I couldn't understand.

"What?" I asked, leaning close to her, straining to hear.

"I don't know," she whispered.

Had I heard right? I was about to ask her to repeat what she had said, but then she lifted her head, looked into my eyes, and spoke clearly.

"I don't know my name," she said, her voice rising in despair.

Three

The girl's answer turned my heart into a jackhammer. That plus the photograph in her mind—*No Police*. What did it mean? I could barely breathe. I knew that the girl-with-no-name needed help, but considering everything, I decided to hold off on calling Detective Tyrone. I had to think, but not here in this musty barn just down the lane from the Braided Woods.

"Come home with me," I said. "We'll figure out everything there."

I led the girl-with-no-name out of the barn. Her nervousness was catching. Her gaze darted around, as if she felt anyone could be an enemy. I understood. It took me back to those first weeks after losing Eloise, when I would look into every face and wonder if that was the last face my sister saw. I still felt that way sometimes. So I chose a route where we were less likely to see people.

We cut through backyards, down a quiet road, onto a dirt path along the marsh. As we walked, I thought back to the start of the murder investigation, how the police had questioned everyone, even our friends.

Even me.

I thought of all the alibis, how we'd had to supply the police with details of our movements that day Eloise went missing. At first, that made me frantic, because it was obvious the police were wasting time. It seemed clear that a stranger had killed my sister, not someone we knew. I kept hammering that thought through my mind—and I kept saying it to Detective Tyrone. A stranger, maybe from our town. Someone who had spotted Eloise that last day and followed her into the woods.

At the edge of the marsh, I saw an oriole nest, shaped like a teardrop, dangling from a branch overhead. Two snowy egrets and one great blue heron fished the shallow waters. I had to harden my heart, because birds made me think of Eloise and if I thought of Eloise now I would cry. And I never cried.

The girl beside me was pale. She kept up with me, but every so often she tripped over her own feet. Once, she grabbed my arm to steady herself, as if she was too weakened to proceed. I looked into her eyes to see if her pupils were dilating right—I knew how to check. I slowed my pace so the girl wouldn't feel too taxed.

"The cut on your head looks bad," I told her. "It's full of dirt. We can wash it off at my house, but you might need stitches."

"At least I'm waking up," she said. "I think someone drugged me. My legs feel like rubber."

That gave me a cold feeling—after Eloise died, the coroner discovered that she had been given a muscle relaxant and sedative. In fact, those drugs were the cause of her death. They had stopped her respiration.

That fact had been one of the reasons for that name, the one I kept pushing away.

"Who drugged you?" I asked the girl, afraid to hear her answer.

"I don't know," she said, her voice sounding wobbly again.

We passed a shingled house with white shutters next to the creek that fed into the marsh. I heard the screen door squeak open, and a woman stood aside to let a black cat dash into the yard. I pulled the girl into a shadow, until the woman went back inside. The cat strutted toward us.

"Oh!" the girl exclaimed, sounding happy. It was the first time I'd seen her smile. She bent down and held her hand out to the cat.

"Hey, there," she said. "Beautiful kitty."

She scratched the cat under its chin. Doing this appeared to relax her. The cat leaned into her hand, basking in the affection. The smile didn't leave the girl's face until the cat stretched and stepped away. She watched it stride out of sight. Then the worried look returned to her eyes, and we started walking again.

We made it to Hubbard's Point, the cozy little beach community where my grandmother lived—where Eloise and I had lived since our parents died.

It was only June, so most of the summer cottages were unoccupied, waiting for the July influx of vacationing families. But we lived here year-round. It felt so special, to have this beautiful place to enjoy before the crowds arrived.

When I saw my house, I grabbed the girl's hand to pull her along. We had a garden that my grandmother had planted long before I was born. The narrow stretch of earth was full of late-spring flowers— purple, yellow, and pink blossoms on tall stems surrounded by spiky leaves. They had bloomed most brightly a week or two earlier, and now they were drooping, nearly dead. The girl stopped short and stared at them.

"Come on," I said. "Let's get inside."

"What are they called?" she asked, as if the faded flowers were hypnotizing her. I ignored her question and tugged at her hand.

The spell cast by the garden seemed to be broken, and she came with me.

Our house was small, but it was perfect. Some of our neighbors had a lot of money. You could tell by their cars, their boats, their expensive beach toys. My grandparents had built our place when they were young, so it had been there forever and hardly changed at all. Others had bought cottages like ours and torn them down to put up houses that were bigger and fancier. It was typical of my grandmother's sense of humor that she called our little place "The Palace." And it was, to me: enchanted, magical, fortified not by walls, but by the love inside.

Usually, I would have been proud to bring a friend over, show her around and introduce her to my grandmother and her home health aide, Noreen. But this was a different situation. I didn't want Gram to see a girl bleeding and caked with dirt, and I was afraid that if Noreen caught sight of the girl, she would feel duty bound to call for help.

So I hustled the girl across the porch, through the hallway, and upstairs. I heard the TV going—Noreen and Gram were watching a cooking show—so I felt reassured they hadn't heard us come in.

I steered the nameless girl into Eloise's room. That action didn't take much thought—I didn't ponder all the things that would hit me like a ton of bricks just a few minutes later.

"Can I take a shower?" the girl asked.

"You'll wash away evidence," I said.

"Evidence . . ." she said as if she had never heard the word before.

Ever since Eloise's death, I'd been obsessively reading books and watching shows about crime and detective work. I made the girl sit on the edge of the bed. I used my phone to take photographs of all her injuries. Then I ran downstairs to the kitchen and came back with a few Ziploc bags. I plucked dead leaves and a dull gray feather out of the girl's hair, and put these items in one bag.

What kind of bird had the feather come from? It looked like pewter, but when I held it to the light, I saw that it was tinged with blue, but not as bright as those on bluebirds and blue jays. At first, I dismissed it, figuring it had just drifted into the leaves in the crevice from a bird up above. But then my heart clenched. The feather was the color . . . the color of the sea at dawn.

I took a nail file from Eloise's dresser and ran it under the girl's dirty fingernails, then dropped the file and the scrapings into another Ziploc bag. I stared at the dirt: Were those glints of gold dust? They sparked something deep in my memory that I couldn't quite get to.

"What are you going to do with those?" the girl asked, glaring at the bags.

22

"Give them to the police," I said. Then, in response to the glowering look in her eyes, I added, "When the time comes."

"The time will never come," she said.

"What are these gold specks?" I asked, holding up the baggie to the light. I peered at them, trying to read their message.

"Who knows?" she asked. "It doesn't matter. No one else is going to see them."

"Aren't you curious?" I asked, and I realized I was asking myself that more than the girl. "It might help you remember what happened. Or where you came from, who you are."

"I'm trying to remember," she said. "But one thing is for sure—you are not handing that 'evidence' to the police. Now I'm wondering if I can even trust you."

Arguing with her, or trying to reassure her, seemed futile. But that didn't matter. This was between me and Eloise. I knew I would stick the Ziploc bags into my backpack when I got downstairs. I went into Eloise's bathroom and turned on the shower. I stood there with my hand under the stream, waiting for it to get hot. Our house is old and we get our water from a well, so neither the temperature nor the pressure is reliable.

"Come on," I called to the girl, gesturing for her. "The hot water doesn't last long—you have about seven minutes."

The girl slipped off her filthy jeans and shirt. Still in her underwear, she came into the steamy bathroom, and I handed her a travel-size bottle of Molton Brown shampoo. She probably had no idea how special that was; Eloise and I had stocked up on tiny hotel bottles during the last vacation we'd taken with Gram, before the Alzheimer's got so bad, at an amazing seaside hotel in Watch Hill, Rhode Island.

The girl shut the bathroom door, and I heard the shower curtain rings clattering across the metal rod.

I wondered who she was, what had really happened to her, and how it all connected to Eloise. I grabbed a notebook off my sister's desk and wrote things down:

Braided Woods

buried but still breathing

black cat

mesmerized by dying flowers

gold dust (October pollen, bits of yellow leaves)

pewter-blue feather (the color of the sea at dawn)

no police—why?

should I call Detective Tyrone anyway?

yes I should

or maybe I shouldn't

what do this girl and Eloise have in common?

I stared at the list. I had the feeling that if I could figure out the answer to that last question, I'd be on the way to solving my sister's murder. The reality of that hit me with a thud. I had never needed to know something more. The items on my list felt like deadweight, pressing down on me, because they seemed so disparate—how could they fit together and give me the truth that the police had so far been unable to provide?

I picked up the Ziploc bags, trying to see if those little tiny gold flakes were really precious metal or just bits of leaves, particles of pollen. And that soft gray-blue feather. Were these clues to finding the girl's attacker, or traces of nature? I knew with everything I had that these were the elements that tied my sister and this girl together. I put both bags into my back pocket.

Those were my thoughts as I sat on Eloise's bed for seven more minutes, waiting for the girl's hot water to run out. During that time, I stared at the photo Eloise had taped to her mirror. It showed the two of us with our birding friends, including the boy Eloise had a huge crush on.

And, standing next to him, the one I did.

I heard the girl turn off the shower. She came out wearing my sister's fluffy white robe that I hadn't been able to put away, which still hung on a hook on the bathroom wall. She had washed the dirt and blood off her skin, but I could still see her cuts and bruises.

I went to the linen closet, where one shelf served as a medicine cabinet, and returned with hydrogen peroxide, Neosporin, and a box of Band-Aids. The girl perched on the chair by the desk where Eloise had always studied, and let me dab the cut on her head, dress it with the antiseptic, and cover it with Band-Aids.

"Stitches," I said. "Pretty sure you should get them."

"No," she said. "Police are always at ERs. I told you already."

"I know," I said. "'No police.' But you're going to have a scar."

She shrugged as if that was the least of her worries. She seemed exhausted. Her eyelids fluttered. I gestured at the pillow. That was all it took. She pulled back the covers and tumbled into bed and was asleep before I could even say "Get some rest."

I stared at the girl, her head on my sister's pillow. I knew that sometimes truth was revealed during deep sleep. Answers came in dreams. I hoped that when she woke up, she would know who she was.

And I hoped she would be able to tell me who had hurt her.

The same person, I was sure, who had killed my sister.

four

My grandmother was sitting alone in the living room, watching a Bobby Flay cooking show. That was Noreen's doing. My grandmother had never watched TV during the day in her whole life. Before she began to have dementia, she would have been gardening, volunteering at the art museum, reading, or writing her memoirs.

"Hi, Gram," I said, giving her a big hug.

"Hello, Eloise," she said, smiling.

I nearly corrected her, but I didn't. I wanted her to have a moment where she believed Eloise was still with us, still on this earth.

"Where have you been?" Gram asked.

"I've been with the birds," I said. "Studying nests, and flight, and migration."

"Flying north or south?" she asked.

"North, of course," I said. "Because it's almost summer, and that means I'll be heading up to the Canadian forest to see them."

"Of course," she said.

My grandmother, Ida Gibson, had started writing her memoirs a few years ago. She had led a fascinating life, full of adventures to Machu Picchu and the Galápagos Islands, Tierra del Fuego and Patagonia, Baffin Island, Corfu in Greece, Juan-les-Pins in France. She had taught at American schools in France, Canada, Chile, and

Greece, and used those locations as jumping-off points for her travels. She had lost her only son—my dad—when the boat he and my mom were on went down in a gale. She had raised her granddaughters, Eloise and me. She had buried my sister, and now the only place we could visit everyone was the graveyard.

I wondered if Gram would be able to write again, or whether the clouds in her mind would forever keep the words from coming. Whether the trauma she felt would keep her memories locked inside forever.

Was trauma the reason the girl upstairs had lost her memory, too?

The TV droned on. My grandmother began to doze. I went into the kitchen where Noreen was heating up some soup.

"How is she today?" I asked. "Anything different?"

"She's fine," Noreen said. "No changes. You don't have to worry, Oli. I take good care of her."

I had my doubts about that. Noreen was also a dog trainer, and she brought her incredibly adorable golden retriever puppy, Zoey, to the house. I saw her playing with Zoey more than she paid attention to my grandmother. But, then, I had the mentality that I was supposed to take care of everyone. It was the older-sister, girl-with-too-much-responsibility syndrome.

When my parents died, it was a huge shock, one that had dulled slightly but never really went away. Losing them, and not having them anywhere in the world, had, well, unhinged me.

In the early years following their deaths, I found myself doing things that were very un-Oli. I faked sore throats and missed a lot of school. Before we moved into Gram's cottage full-time, I would sit in our basement, in my dad's woodworking shop, just so I could smell the sawdust—it reminded me of him. Or I'd sit in their old room and rummage through their drawers. I'd go through my mother's side of the closet and stand in there, between her dresses and jackets, and pretend she was hugging me.

Those were comforts, but as I got older, I also tempted danger. I'm not sure why, but sometimes I think it was because death had touched our family and I wanted to prove it wouldn't touch me. I climbed onto our roof to peer into the brick chimney to look for chimney swift nests. I swam nearly a half mile out to North Brother Island—farther than was safe, with my muscles aching and lungs burning—to count the gulls' eggs and hatchlings.

I guess it was about families: parents and chicks. Eloise and I were baby birds whose mother and father had abandoned the nest. Not by choice, obviously, but still, they were gone. I tried to be more than an older sister to Eloise. I tried to be her parent.

And now, as Gram regressed, our roles were reversing, and I knew I was trying to be her parent, too.

I helped myself to a cup of soup and stepped over Zoey, curled up on a rug next to the stove. I hadn't realized how hungry I was. I sat in a chair facing the yard. The sun had set, night was falling, but light from a streetlamp illuminated our border of bright blue hydrangeas.

The sight of the flowers, combined with the lingering scent of that Molton Brown shampoo from upstairs, brought memories of last summer suddenly flooding through me.

five

That stay at Ocean House, where we'd gotten the little bottles of shampoo, swirled with sorcery. It was as if I was under a spell, but not one cast by a sea witch: It was cast by me, for the secret reason we were there.

On the drive over, my emotions made me feel I was flying, or at least floating on air. Neither Eloise nor my grandmother knew why I had suggested we stay there. I had steered us to that hotel for a reason known only to me and one other person.

Gram was already fading, forgetting words, but she was still healthy enough to drive, to have fun with us. Eloise and I had been at our best—wildest. Meaning that Gram saw us at our polite granddaughter-best, and we saw us as our true selves.

We stayed in a suite. It had two bedrooms and a large terrace. Everything felt so cozy—the sofa was soft rose-red, there was a fireplace, the bookcases were full. Gram napped in an armchair, a book open on her lap, but I grabbed Eloise's hand and pulled her onto the wraparound terrace.

Waves crashed on the long, white sand beach down below, just past the lawn and a thick border of cream-colored hydrangeas. Hydrangeas had been my mother's favorite flower. I had seen them on the Ocean House website, and as soon as I showed the photo to Gram, she was sold on this destination.

She liked that the hotel put out yellow chaises and blue-and-white-striped umbrellas on the beach—it reminded her of a vacation she'd taken at Juan-les-Pins in the South of France. You could get lemonade, or iced tea, or anything off the menu. Down the beach, to the right, was the lighthouse. Perched above it all was a big white house where everyone knew Taylor Swift lived—or at least spent the Fourth of July most years. We could see the house from the terrace.

Gram had thought the proximity of Taylor's house would be a big draw for me and Eloise. But even though we loved her music, we figured there were enough fangirls gawking at her house, and besides, we weren't into celebrities. There were other wonders for us to be in awe of.

"Look," I said, pointing up.

"What?" Eloise asked.

A magnificent tower rose above the top story of the yellow hotel. What looked like a filigreed wrought iron railing rimmed the very top, and I could see that a raptor was perched on the railing, silhouetted against the blue sky. Even though I had never seen one before, its shape was unmistakable: a merlin. And I must confess: I had known it would be there. I'd been told it hunted from its perch at the top of the hotel.

A merlin is a small, swift falcon. Even its name carries magic, with echoes of Merlin, the wizard. This bird, for me, also connected to something like love. There was no question that I had to go up there. And of course I wasn't going to leave Eloise—she would want to be there, too, and not just because of the raptor. I couldn't wait to surprise her.

"Come on," I said.

"Up to the tower?" she said, following my gaze. "Are we allowed?"

"I know someone," I said mysteriously.

She didn't answer. I hurried her through the suite, past dozing Gram, into the hotel's hallway. This was a very grand place where adults spoke in hushed tones. That suited me fine. I liked slipping through spaces, almost as if I were invisible. That was one of my superpowers—disappearing into thin air. I was quiet, and I never wore anything fancy, and if I didn't want to be seen, I could just walk through a crowd and no one would notice me.

All I had to do was find the way up to the tower. I was intent on seeing that merlin, but there was another reason—it felt like a romantic destination. If I could get up there, I'd find some kind of enchantment, maybe like Merlin's cave where spells could be cast, where sadness and worry drifted away.

Eloise and I climbed the stairs until we got to the top floor and found a door with an oval plaque marked TOWER SUITE. I leaned against the heavy door with my shoulder and it opened right away.

"Should we really go in?" Eloise asked.

"We should," I said, smiling. Although I sounded confident, I had butterflies in my stomach.

We walked into the suite, and it was every bit as astonishing as I'd been told, with walls of gleaming wood, like the inside of a ship.

I glanced around—I didn't see anyone's luggage or belongings. No one was in sight. But my heart skipped because I knew who had left the door unlocked for us.

There were bookcases flanking the fireplace, with cozy chairs gathered around. A table with an antique chess set nestled between two arched windows that overlooked the town and harbor. Windows on the other walls looked onto the sparkling blue ocean and out toward the lighthouse. The sound of waves hitting the beach matched the crashing feeling in my heart.

We went upward to a balcony—the Crow's Nest—a secret nook with books, a ship's log, and a wide daybed with big, comfy pillows. Every step felt like an adventure. From there, a steep spiral staircase with finely tooled balusters—they reminded me of the precise woodworking my boat-building father had done—led up to a trapdoor in the ceiling. I knew that it opened to where the merlin was perched—and much more. I'd been told how private this was, how very few guests climbed through the door. Only someone with a special key could open it.

I knew who had that key.

Eloise followed me up the tall spiral staircase. My heart pounded again, and it wasn't from the effort of climbing: It came from the excitement sizzling all through my body. I didn't even think about this trapdoor being locked. I just knew the enchanted tower had been left open for us.

And it was, and we stepped out into the bright sunshine, onto a widow's walk. Many old New England houses had them—a place up on the roof where, long ago, wives would stand with a telescope, watching the horizon for their husbands' ships to return. Some never would, and the wives became widows.

A flagpole rose in the middle, an American flag rippling in the summer breeze. My gaze went straight to the merlin. The fierce little raptor was about twenty feet away from us, peering intently at some prey down below. It had blue-gray wings, a blue back, and a speckled white breast.

"It's not afraid of us," Eloise whispered.

I nodded, full of anticipation.

"Oli?" It was a boy's voice, and my heart sped up.

I looked over my shoulder, and there he was: Matt Grinnell.

Matt, with his blue eyes and brown hair, who made me blush just to look at him, who made my heart race just to hear his voice. I felt my cheeks get hot, and I saw that his were flushed, too. We grinned at each other.

"You came," Matt said. "You convinced your grandmother?"

I nodded. "It wasn't hard," I said. "She liked the hydrangeas."

"What are you doing here?" Eloise asked. Matt was in my grade but he, Eloise, and I were all part of the same nature club.

"My family comes here every summer," Matt said.

"And he knows everyone who works at this hotel," Chris Nicholson said, turning around. He was smiling at all of us but his gaze was focused on Eloise. Chris and Matt were best friends, and in the same nature club with us.

"Hi, Chris," Eloise said, and her blushing cheeks gave everything away. She'd had a crush on Chris since the spring. The way he smiled back made me wonder if he felt the same about her.

Chris was very cute, with perfect teeth and short blond hair. Girls mooned over him, but not me. He was too professionally handsome for my taste. He talked about going to Harvard as an undergrad and also for medical school. I didn't doubt that he could make those dreams come true. His grades put him near the top of our class, and he could afford to go anywhere he wanted: His parents were both executives at Denzer—a major pharmaceutical company.

"The hotel gives guests tours, including the tower when the suite's not occupied," Matt said. "So I always take the tour, because it's so cool up here. Devon, one of the managers, brought us up to the tower. He knows we're birders."

"Tell them the rest," Chris said.

"I might be able to get a job here this summer," Matt said. "There's a naturalist who takes guests out on a boat, and into a salt pond near Weekapaug, and Devon says I'll be able to help with bird identification."

"That's amazing," I said.

"That would mean he wouldn't be at Hubbard's Point," Chris said with a teasing tone. "You wouldn't like that, would you, Oli?"

It was my turn to blush again.

"So you two planned to meet here?" Eloise asked, glancing from me to Matt. She knew how I felt about Matt, of course, from our sister talks. But she'd be able to guess anyway, from the fact I always seemed to drive past his house on our way home, pretending it was random.

And it was obvious that Chris could tell I liked Matt, too. Maybe I wasn't as good at hiding my feelings as I thought I was.

I would explain to Eloise later that Matt had told me all about his family vacations at Ocean House, how the manager had taken him to this tower before. And how the look in his eyes had been an invitation, a dare, to meet him there.

"He was just sharing a bird-watching spot," I said to Eloise as we stood on the roof.

"Yeah, I wanted to show you the merlin," Matt said.

I listened to see if there was anything in his voice to let me know it was more than that, but it sounded as if it was just what he said: sharing a birding opportunity with friends.

"The merlin's cool, right?" another voice asked.

I turned to see Fitch Martin, another boy from our nature club, climbing up from the staircase below.

"Hi, Fitch," I said, and Eloise waved.

Fitch was cute, too: tall and skinny, with unruly dark hair and black-rimmed glasses. Sometimes I thought he wore those glasses because they made him look even smarter than he was—which was very smart. His shirt was always untucked, sometimes buttoned wrong. He was intense about academics, and proud of his membership in the Agassiz Foundation, a scientific organization funded by his family. Both he and Chris were officers of the Future Doctors Club. Matt, Eloise, and I were happy to just be in the nature club, along with my close friend, Adalyn Banda. I was sorry that Adalyn couldn't be there that day.

Fitch came to stand beside me and Matt, looking up at the sky. Eloise and Chris had moved off to the side, standing so close to each other their shoulders were touching. They were talking quietly. Between the two of us, Eloise was the one whom boys liked the most. She had a bouncier personality, flirty eyes, a sweet way of laughing that made boys lean in and want more.

With all the activity, the merlin had flown from the railing and was perched on top of the flagpole. I felt a slight pang that Matt wasn't standing close to me, the way Chris was to my sister.

"Hey, check this out," Matt said. He had set up a large scope, pointing it toward the lighthouse. The tide was out, and a narrow strip of sand ran along the seawall. "Look at the sanderlings. There have to be at least fifty."

I looked through the scope, and he was right—many of the little brown shorebirds darted along the frilled edge of the waves, teasing the foam and pecking the sand for food. When I stepped back, Eloise took her turn.

As Eloise, Chris, and Fitch discussed the sanderlings, Matt and I watched the merlin again. And as if Matt had read my mind, saw my wish, he leaned slightly against me. Shoulders touching.

It felt as if something between us was starting to unlock.

My reddish-blonde hair was long, in a braid. He tugged it lightly and I turned and saw him grinning. One of his bottom teeth was crooked, and I thought it gave him the cutest smile I'd ever seen. He was still holding my braid, but then he let go and traced my shoulder with one finger. In spite of the summer heat, his touch gave me goose bumps all over.

"You could get sunburned if you stay up here too long," he said.

I felt embarrassed. Some girls tanned, but I stayed pale. Every single freckle showed, and it made me feel self-conscious. The sun would turn me crimson if I didn't spread gallons of sunscreen all over.

"I'll go in soon," I said, looking into his eyes. They were blue, like mine, but they had gold flecks around the pupils. *But I don't want to go. I just want to stay here,* I thought. My breathlessness kept the words trapped inside. We stood there, not saying anything. It was almost as if my silence had made him turn quiet, too. I wished he would lean even closer to me, and then he did.

Our foreheads touched. I closed my eyes. I could almost feel his kiss, but it didn't happen. Instead, the merlin flew away, and we broke apart.

Eloise called us to the scope to look at the sanderlings again, and we joined her, Chris, and Fitch. My heart was pounding as I replayed the moment Matt had leaned his forehead against mine. The almost-kiss that was so close, my lips still tingled.

Back in my kitchen, almost a year later, I shook off that summer memory and stood up. I took my phone out of my pocket. I had Matt's number, and I thought about calling him. But it was already late. I wondered again if I should call the police, but then I remembered my promise to the girl upstairs. So I put the Ziploc bags into my backpack, said good night to Noreen, and went to my room to try to sleep.

six

I usually wake up by 6:30 a.m., but I was so exhausted from the day before, I slept past 9:00. My mind was fuzzy, with threads of yesterday weaving through as I slowly woke up. At first I thought I had dreamed up the nameless girl, but when I ran to Eloise's room, there she was—wide awake, sitting up and propped against the pillow, staring into space.

"Good morning," I said.

"Hi, Oli," she said.

"Did you remember anything?" I asked. "About what happened to you before I found you yesterday?"

She frowned. "I'm not sure," she said. "Little things, maybe. I didn't sleep that well, and I had weird dreams. They felt like memories, but not exactly."

"What did you dream about?" I asked.

"Cats," she said. "A lot of cats. And a little hawk—I think it was a hawk. And owls. So many, flying overhead, with yellow eyes that looked fake. Like plastic eyes in toys. In dolls."

I shivered at that last part. It sounded like a horror movie.

"What else?" I asked.

"Girls our age, wearing long white dresses that looked like columns," the girl went on. "And a blue van, driving around . . ."

"What about your name? Your family?" I asked. "The person who hurt you? Did any of that come back to you in your dreams?"

"No," she said, shaking her head. "But there was someone driving the blue van. He didn't seem real. He was like a ghoul, in a black cape and a hood pulled over his head, almost covering his face. But when I looked closely, he didn't *have* a face. There was nothing in there."

"Sounds like a nightmare," I said.

"It must have been," she said. "It was too terrible to be a memory."

"Why don't you get dressed?" I said to the girl. I handed her a stack of Eloise's clothes from her dresser. I hadn't been able to give away any of my sister's belongings yet, and now I was very glad I'd kept her things. "I'll go downstairs and make breakfast."

"Oli, I don't want to be rude, but if there are other people in the house, I don't want to see them."

"Believe me, my grandmother and Noreen had nothing to do with your attack," I said.

"I believe you, but even so . . ." she began, staring off into the distance. "How do you know when someone's good or bad?"

"I used to be able to tell," I said. "I'm not sure I do now." Losing Eloise had changed that.

"Same for me," she said. "This isn't an actual memory, just a sense. But I feel as if the person who took us was nice at first. Someone easy to trust. And then the bad things happened."

"'Us'?" I repeated.

"What?"

"You said the person took *us*. Was someone else with you?" I asked, my pulse picking up.

"I don't know," she said. "I didn't mean to say that. Nothing is clear, Oli. It's all a blur. Those owls and those girls in the dream seemed more real than anything I can actually remember." She looked around my sister's room. "It's nice here. I can think better than I could before."

"What are you thinking about?" I asked.

"That black kitty we saw," she said, her brow furrowed. "There was something about her that reminded me of . . . my old life. I think my family had cats. And those flowers in your garden, the ones that were so wilted . . ."

"What about them?" I asked.

"What is the name of those flowers?" she asked, and I recalled that she had asked me that before. I pictured the garden, and I could see the delicate purple, yellow, and pale pink blossoms, the sharp leaves.

"They're one of my favorites," I said. "They're beautiful—different colors, from pale yellow to dark purple. Eloise and I planted bulbs every fall, and the flowers come up each spring. They're called . . ."

The girl gasped.

"What?" I asked.

"Irises. That's what they are," the girl said, her eyes widening.

I paused, waiting for her to say more. "Do you have irises at home, in your family's garden?" I asked after a minute.

43

She didn't answer, just gazed ahead. It seemed as if the effort of trying to remember had worn her out.

"You said you didn't sleep well," I said. "Why don't you stay here and rest? I'll bring breakfast back up here."

"Thanks, Oli. I'm sorry." She closed her eyes.

"Don't be," I said.

I ran downstairs. Gram and Noreen were watching TV in the living room, so I knew the girl and I were safe from discovery for now.

I looked in the refrigerator. I pulled out some strawberries and a container of Greek yogurt. Noreen and my grandmother had already had their coffee. A lot of kids my age don't drink it, but I love coffee. It makes me feel older; it goes along with my feeling parental. I put on another pot. While waiting for it to brew, I stepped out onto the porch. It was a beautiful, sunny day, and I felt a pang. I wished I were on the island instead of here.

There was a tiny island, just about a quarter mile off the rocky coast. Dauntless Island was perfect for beach picnics, crabbing and fishing, swimming and stargazing at night—lying on the sand and looking up at the sky. Every summer Eloise and I went out there to see the osprey nests.

I felt a small blip of resentment—toward Eloise for changing everything, and toward the nameless girl upstairs for throwing my whole day into turmoil. I didn't like feeling that way, so I pushed it aside. I'd become good at that—burying emotions and certain other things, like that name I really didn't want to think about.

I set a tray with breakfast things and headed back upstairs.

The girl had gotten out of bed and was dressed in Eloise's shorts, T-shirt, and sneakers. I started to hand her a cup of coffee, but then I noticed her wide smile and bright eyes.

"Iris," she said.

"Yes, the flowers."

"No, me!" she said. "Iris. That's my name! Seeing that garden unlocked my name."

"That's fantastic," I said. "Hi, Iris. Do you remember your last name?"

She shook her head. "My mind is so fuzzy. There's so much else I can't remember. It's as if everything is hidden from me—behind a wall or something, blocking me from seeing."

"You said you saw those words: *No Police*," I said.

"I know, it's as if they are on a sign—but not just words." She closed her eyes tight, and I could tell she was trying hard to bring something else to the forefront. "Paintings of girls. Three of them. They're tall, beautiful, wearing long white dresses."

"Like brides?" I asked.

She shook her head. "No. More like classical statues. Old-fashioned, like pictures you would see in a history book. Or a museum. Three girls in separate paintings, standing side by side. Wearing matching long, pleated gowns."

"Like the ones in your dream?" I asked.

"Exactly. They're sisters," she said, and suddenly she got so excited she jostled the tray and spilled some coffee. "Sisters—I have a sister!"

I felt shocked. How could she just be realizing that now? How was it possible to forget having a sister? "What's her name? Where is she?" I asked.

Iris closed her eyes tight, and I could see she was concentrating as hard as she could. "In a room where they—where *he*," she said, correcting herself, "kept us. We were prisoners. Those pictures . . ." She trailed off.

"Pictures of what?" I asked, my heart pounding. We were getting somewhere.

"The girls in white dresses," Iris said. "They were right there, the paintings of the girls, on the walls, in the place we were being held. Where she still is . . ."

"She?"

"My sister," Iris said. She blinked hard, as if coming out of a trance. "Hayley. That's her name."

"Hayley, your sister. She's still a prisoner?"

"Yes," Iris said. She held her head between both hands, began walking in circles, as if movement would jostle the memories, make them come back.

"Where is he keeping her?" I asked. "And who *is* he? Where did he take you from, Iris? Where are your parents, the rest of your family?"

"I don't know," she said, putting her hands over her ears. "I don't know!" Then staring at me, she added, "He was nice at first. I liked him. I do remember that."

"Did you go with him willingly?" I asked.

"I don't think so," she said. "I would have, at first. He seemed like someone I could trust. But then he changed into a monster."

"Iris, we have to call Detective Tyrone," I said firmly. "We need to find out who did this to you. And that will help find my sister's murderer. It has to be the same person, right? To put you in the same grave where she was buried? He must have thought you were dead— that he had killed you, like he killed Eloise."

My mind went white hot with rage, terror, grief. Who was he? How could he have taken Iris and her sister? And Eloise?

"I played dead," Iris went on. "I remember that part now. It wasn't hard because he'd given me those drugs, knocked me out. He thought I wouldn't wake up, but I did." Slowly she touched two spots on either side of her head. I could see faint pink circles under her fingertips. "Sticky," she said softly. "It feels like glue."

"Who would put glue on your head?" I asked.

"Him," she said. "He did."

"Why? What does he look like?" I asked.

"I can't see him," she said. "His face is a blur."

"Think, Iris. It's in there, you just have to bring it up."

She squeezed her eyes tight, trying to remember. Then she opened her eyes. "I can hear his voice. I can't get it out of my mind."

"You'd recognize it if you heard it again?" I asked.

"Yes, definitely."

"That's good," I said. I wondered what his voice sounded like, and I thought of the terror it must have caused Eloise. "Iris, we need to call the police. To rescue Hayley. To get her away from him."

"Oli," Iris said. "I can still see the words I told you about: *No Police*. And now I know why. He said that to us over and over. That if we tried to escape, and if one of us ever managed to, and told the police about him, he would kill the other. If you call the police, my sister will die. Please, Oli."

I took that in. Iris seemed clear now, levelheaded. I thought of Dr. Hirsch and what she had told me about trauma reactions. I knew it was possible to block out the worst—violence, terror—and I realized that that was why Iris had so much memory loss. But her emotions were intact. She was positive that whoever was holding Hayley would murder her, and her certitude convinced me.

I knew he was capable of it, because he had done it to Eloise.

"I'm going to find my sister myself," Iris said.

"How can we do that?" I asked.

Iris stared at me. "You said 'we.'"

"Of course I'll help you," I said. "Did you think I wouldn't?"

Something Iris had said before made me think there had been more than one kidnapper.

"You mentioned the room where *they* kept you," I said. "So it wasn't just him? There was someone else?"

"I'm picturing someone in a white dress," Iris said. "Or maybe I was thinking of the paintings of those girls." She paused. "If only I could remember *when* he took us, and how. I feel as if we were in the back of a truck, or a van, or something. And he took us somewhere strange. It wasn't a normal room." She sighed. "It's still blurry."

"We just need a clue of where to start," I said. I was trying to put together everything we knew so far, even the barest hints.

He was nice at first.

She thought she could trust him.

But then he took them, Iris and her sister.

Held them in some room with paintings.

He knocked Iris out with drugs.

There was a sticky substance on her head.

He turned into a monster.

She played dead, and he buried her.

I suddenly felt terror, as if I had seen him transform into someone evil, just the way Iris had. The way my sister must have.

Who had turned into a monster and killed her?

Who had dropped a gold charm and a blue-gray feather?

How had the gold dust gotten there?

The name I didn't want to think about flashed through my mind, over and over.

"I have an idea," Iris said, interrupting my thoughts.

"What?"

"Tell me one thing about the day Eloise went missing. Not the whole day, okay? Just one incident that stands out. Or one word! Even if you think it has nothing to do with her being taken. Just something that really sticks in your mind. Something that made you really nervous, and you didn't like the way you felt. Or . . . something you loved. That the two of you loved."

I gave her a look full of skepticism.

"Oli, maybe there's something in common with the day Hayley and I were taken. It might jog my memory," she said.

"Like whoever took you has a signature?" I asked. "Something he can't help doing that will tell us who he is?"

"Exactly," Iris said.

Then I felt excited, because the possibility of uncovering the murderer's identity was the first bit of hope we'd had so far.

The only thing was, I knew how painful it would be to remember that horrific day when my sister disappeared.

"Tell me," Iris said.

I didn't have to think very hard because everything about that day was emblazoned in my heart.

seven

"Birds," I said, picturing the early-morning quiet, the net in the thicket. "We went birding with our nature club that morning." Matt, Fitch, Chris, Adalyn, Eloise, and me.

Eloise and I had woken up before dawn, when it was still dark and cold, the grass and leaves tinged silver with an early frost. Matt, Chris, and Fitch were waiting outside our house in Matt's Jeep. Matt drove us to the highest elevation in the seven hundred–acre Braided Woods. We met Adalyn in the parking lot, then trekked down a narrow trail into a hollow that spread into the grasslands.

Adalyn was beautiful, with golden-brown eyes and wavy dark hair that she wore pulled back in a thick ponytail. We'd known each other since fourth grade, when her family had moved here from Ohio, and we'd become friends right away. Adalyn was an unlikely birder—she wasn't really into nature. She didn't like walking through narrow trails where there might be mud, or branches that would brush up against her, or bugs or snakes. She loved pretty things, had impeccable style, dreamed of being a fashion designer. She'd joined the nature club to be a good friend to me, but also because she had a slight crush on Fitch. The two of them walked side by side that morning. I ended up walking next to Matt, and Eloise next to Chris.

I tripped over a root, and Matt grabbed my hand just long enough to steady me. I felt my heart flip. He looked at me with those gold-flecked blue eyes and smiled before he let go of my hand.

Chris and Eloise were talking softly, as they had up on the roof of Ocean House a few months before. Chris carried an expensive Swarovski telescope that probably cost as much as some of the old used cars our classmates drove.

The six of us came to the blind our group had built to hide in while watching a net. The net was made of threads that formed inch-squared openings that would catch but not harm the birds, and was assembled in a fifty-foot-long curve—like a giant badminton net. Chris set up the telescope on a tripod, through which we could watch far-off birds and other wildlife.

October 9 was toward the end of fall migration, when birds flew down from northern Canada, stopping in New England on their way to a warmer climate. That autumn was especially exciting because it was an irruption year—when certain species not usually seen on the Connecticut shoreline arrived in impressive numbers.

We were spotting white-winged crossbills, evening grosbeaks, redpolls, and red-breasted nuthatches. None of us had ever seen crossbills before; they fed on the seeds of closed spruce cones, and we heard them up above, their bills clicking as they cracked open the cones.

As we stood in the blind in the gray predawn light, I saw Eloise lean close to Chris, the two of them taking turns looking through the telescope. He pointed it toward the sky. She pressed her eye to the scope and I knew she was looking up at Venus glowing beside the morning moon—the last quarter, suspended above the horizon just before sunrise. He was whispering to her. She laughed and nodded, and I heard her say, "Definitely."

I turned away from them. I faced the net and could see that it had caught several birds. A storm the night before had caused a "fallout"—more migrants than usual, landing to rest and feed during their long flight north.

Adalyn, Fitch, Matt, and I got to work. We documented every species. Adalyn took pictures on her phone. Fitch kept an ongoing list in his tablet, making meticulous notes of all his observations. Matt prepared the bands to gently press around the birds' legs. His delight was obvious, the way he beamed at me when I pointed out a late migrant, a very unusual bird for our area: a Louisiana water thrush.

Matt stood beside me as I carefully removed a male black-throated blue warbler from the netting. The four-inch beauty rippled and felt impossibly delicate. I held him steady while Matt wrapped a narrow band around his leg and documented the number. In the future, if another birder found the warbler, it would be possible to track where he had been, and the distance traveled.

"Isn't it amazing?" Matt asked softly. "Holding life in your hands?"

I nodded, momentarily unable to speak.

Chris and Eloise came over then. Chris checked the warbler for any signs of injury or disease, for lice or other parasites, for general health. The bird's head and back were bright blue, fading to blue-gray closer to the tail and in the wings. He sported a black mask and had a white breast. After Chris recorded the description, we let him fly away. Matt and I glanced at each other, exhilarated from holding the bird, contributing to research, and, especially, standing so close together.

The six of us traded back and forth, partnering for different birds, taking turns holding and recording. When it was time to pack up and go, my sister and I walked a little way off the trail to look up at a roosting great horned owl. Owls were Eloise's favorite. She and I had come here one night last month, to hear a male and female calling to each other from pines on opposite sides of the clearing—a duetting pair. By winter they would mate, and by January the female would be sitting on eggs.

"What were you and Chris whispering about?" I asked Eloise.

"Wouldn't you love to know?" she asked, with a sweetly wicked glint in her eyes.

"I would."

"He asked me if I'd come back here with him tonight," she said. "To hear the owls calling."

So that's why she'd said "definitely."

"I don't think you should do it," I said.

"Why not?" she asked.

I was silent; I couldn't answer that. It was just a cold feeling that rippled through me, that something could happen to her. It was the month of Halloween, and maybe that's what made things feel scary, as if the woods we loved could turn dangerous, as if malevolent spirits might come drifting down from the treetops.

"I'll be safe with Chris," Eloise said. "You and I came here at night, and we were fine."

"That was September," I said.

"You sound so superstitious," she said, and I could tell she was impatient, annoyed at me for not wanting her to go out on a school night with the boy she liked. "Are you jealous?" she asked.

"Why would I be?"

"Because Chris asked me and Matt didn't ask you?"

"Of course not," I said, my face flushing. But what if she was right?

"Sometimes I think you don't even like Chris," Eloise went on. "Or trust him. You think he's too handsome and popular to want to go out with me."

"That's not true," I said. "It's just that you're my little sister, and I'm protective of you."

"Well, I don't need you to be," she said, sounding upset.

I gave her a hug to let her know I loved and trusted her. But I still had that uneasy feeling. In a way she was right; I wasn't sure about Chris. For one thing, I thought she was jumping in too fast with him. My crush on Matt had lasted forever, and in a weird way, that made it more exciting. Whatever was happening between us had been simmering a long time. But her question did linger in my mind: Was I jealous about Chris asking her to go owling that night when Matt hadn't asked me?

The terrible thing was that my premonition was right.

The day of that birding excursion was the last time I saw my sister.

That afternoon, when she wasn't on the school bus home, I texted and called her over and over, but got no answer. I texted everyone—our nature group, Eloise's friends from her grade—to ask if she was with them. She wasn't.

And, it turned out, she hadn't shown up at school that day at all.

She hadn't even been on the late bus that morning.

That's when I knew something terrible had happened. When I got home, I ran into the house, but Eloise wasn't there. Neither Gram nor Noreen had seen or heard from her since she'd left to catch the bus that morning.

I called the police, and two patrol officers came over. The officers asked me, Gram, and Noreen a few questions, and they learned that Eloise wasn't the type to go running off. So they called Detective Tyrone.

She was very calm. She had wide brown eyes and dark brown hair, and she wore a navy blue blazer that made her look very official. We stood in the kitchen while Noreen tidied up and Gram dozed in the living room.

The detective watched me with a neutral gaze as I started to lose it.

"You have to find her!" I shouted. "It's dark, it's been dark for over an hour, and Eloise is missing! She must be hurt, lying somewhere. She'd call if she could!"

"Breathe, Oli," Detective Tyrone said. "You can't help Eloise if you pass out."

So I did—I breathed.

"Tell me about the day," she said. "Were you and Eloise getting along? Did you have a fight?"

"No," I said. Why was she asking me that? But I thought of the blip of disagreement Eloise and I had had, over her going out with Chris, and the detective noticed the look in my eyes.

"A little fight maybe?" the detective asked.

"Not really," I said. "Just sister stuff. And we hugged—no one was mad."

"You sure it wasn't more than that? Maybe she was upset at you and took off?"

"Why are you asking me these things?" I wailed with frustration.

"It's just procedure, Oli," Detective Tyrone said. "We have to talk to everyone, even family members—people who love Eloise."

"But I don't know where she is," I said, my voice wobbling from the terror building inside me. "Can't you stop all this now and look for her? Please, go out and find her!"

"We are looking for her, Oli," the detective said. "Pretty much the whole force is out. But the more you can tell me, the better chance we'll have of finding her. Let's start at the beginning. When did you last see her?"

"Here, at home, this morning," I said. "We were getting ready for school. We were rushing because we didn't want to be late. We'd been out earlier . . ."

"Out where?"

"In the Braided Woods," I said. "Birding."

"And what about after that? Did you go to school together?"

"No," I said. "We had different class schedules. I went on the early bus, and she was going to get the later one."

"What about after school?"

I shook my head. "No. She didn't come home."

"Tell me more about birding," the detective asked. "Who was with you?"

"We went with our friends. We always do—it's our nature group."

She asked me their names, and I gave them. But when I got to Chris, I felt a huge jolt, and Detective Tyrone noticed.

"What is it, Oli?" she asked.

"Nothing," I said. I really didn't want to tell. It seemed completely far-fetched that Chris could have been in any way involved with Eloise disappearing. Or what if he was—not in a guilty way, but in a romantic way? Maybe the two of them had made a plan to run away together. But no, Eloise would never do that without telling me. She would never make Gram and me worry.

"You had a reaction when you said Chris Nicholson's name," Detective Tyrone said.

I blurted it out: "He asked Eloise to go out tonight. To look for owls. And that . . . that's what our fight was about. I didn't think she should go."

"Why not?"

I shrugged. "I was just being protective."

"Do you and your sister ever like the same guy? Was that what happened? You didn't want her going with Chris because you like him?"

I glared at the detective. Could she be more wrong? "No," I said. "I like someone else."

"Okay," she said, looking into my eyes as if she could read whether I was telling the truth or not.

She asked me a few more questions, but I hardly heard them. I felt too panicked, knowing time was ticking by, it was nighttime, and Eloise was out there somewhere.

But by the next morning, Eloise still hadn't been found. Detective Tyrone asked everyone who knew Eloise to come to the police station, just outside town. Gram, Noreen, me. Our teachers. All our friends from school.

Individually, we had to go into an interview room and sit at a table across from Detective Tyrone and another police officer. We had to give our alibis—where we had been when Eloise had disappeared—so the police could check them.

The last time Eloise had been seen by anyone—by Gram and Noreen—was when she left the house that morning to catch the late school bus. Which she never caught.

Everyone had an alibi.

My friends and I had been at school, or on our way there. Same with nearly every student or teacher at the school; anyone who'd been absent that day had a good excuse. Gram and Noreen had been at doctors' appointments all day, and our neighbors had all been at work. After school, I had hurried straight home to see if Eloise was there. Adalyn's mother had picked up Adalyn and taken her to get her hair cut. Fitch's mother was on a business trip. His sister was sick and she needed help, so he went home to be with her. Matt's family had boats, and since it was October, it was time to haul them and get them ready for winter. He had been down at the dock with his dad and brother.

Chris had a paper due, and he worked on it at the library. The librarian confirmed that. He had repeatedly tried to contact my sister, but she never replied. The police examined his cell phone. It provided location data—showing that he was at the library, then he went straight home. And all his unanswered texts and calls to Eloise proved what he'd told them.

So Chris had ended up not meeting Eloise that night. If only he had, or if we had all stayed together, she might still be alive. Her killer wouldn't have gotten to her—we could have protected her.

Detective Tyrone asked us all if we would be willing to give DNA samples. She said it was because forensic evidence was always left behind during crimes, and DNA could help identify the criminal. That scared me because at that point, I wanted so badly to believe no one had taken or hurt Eloise, that she had somehow left on her own, that no crime had occurred.

Both Chris's and Adalyn's parents were against them giving DNA at first. But Detective Tyrone said that it was very important, because it would let her exclude them as suspects—they would be off the list. Eventually we all let them swab our mouths, to collect saliva, and the samples were sent to the police lab.

One day later, Eloise's body was found in the Braided Woods. And there was no DNA evidence found on her. No match.

And the case went cold.

"Birds," Iris repeated, bringing me back to the present. I shivered, shaking away the memories of those terrible days—and that moment when we got the call from the police that Eloise's body had been found.

I looked at Iris. I thought I saw a flicker of memory in her brown eyes. I waited for a few moments, but she didn't say anything more.

"Did anything come up?" I asked her.

"Dead owls flying overhead," she said, then shook her head. "But no. That's not a real memory. Just something from my nightmare. Because dead birds can't fly. Right?" She looked at me, but I didn't say anything. "Oli, I think it's real. I think there really were dead birds up above. Every time I looked, they were there."

It sounded completely bizarre.

And something was haunting me. That blue-gray feather I'd found in Iris's hair. It was the same color as the back and wings of the black-throated blue warbler our nature club had found the morning of Eloise's disappearance. I thought about how Chris's parents worked for that pharmaceutical company, and how easy it would have been for him to get the substance that had drugged my sister and Iris. Plus he had invited Eloise to go owling in the Braided Woods, the same day she had died.

Were those clues? Or just coincidences?

I wanted them to be coincidences.

But his was the name that kept swirling and shimmering through my mind.

Chris

Chris

Chris

I told myself: It couldn't be him. I'd seen how tender he was toward Eloise. There was no way someone we knew could have murdered her. And Chris had an alibi—his phone data proved it.

But

What if

What if

What if he had written those unanswered texts to my sister after he had killed her? What if he had invented an alibi and gotten someone to lie and back him up? He had that handsome boy way about him; his smile could melt hearts—and he knew it.

I tried to push these thoughts of Chris away. But they wouldn't leave. They lodged in the part of my brain that held instincts and suspicion.

"Do you remember anything else?" I asked Iris.

"No," she said. "I can't get hold of the thread." She tilted her head. "A thread! Or a string . . . something about a string."

"You're doing great, Iris," I said. "Letting little bursts come through. Your name, Hayley's name. The paintings of those girls. Someone in a white dress. Cats. Birds. A string. It seems like your memory is starting to come back."

"I hope so," she said.

Something occurred to me then. "What if we drove around, starting where I found you?" I asked. "Then we'd work our way out, in wider circles. We might see things that could help you remember more."

She nodded, resolute in a way that showed me she thought it was a really good idea. "Do you have a car?" she asked.

My grandmother's old Volvo was parked in the driveway outside our house. I had my license, but the car battery was dead and one of the tires was flat.

"I do, but it isn't running right now." I paused. The perfect solution came to me. I gave her a smile. "Don't worry, though. I know someone who can help."

eight

Hi Matt

As soon as I sent the text, my heart literally began skipping beats as I waited to hear back. His reply came quickly.

Hey Oli.

Are you busy? I wrote.

No reply for a whole minute. Then he wrote:

w Chris and Fitch at the blind.

OK never mind, I wrote.

What's up?

Suddenly the whole idea of telling him seemed impossible. I both wanted to tell him everything, and also hide it from him—because how could a normal boy deal with anything this bizarre and dreadful? How could I, for that matter?

It's OK. Hope you see some good birds, I wrote.

Won't be much longer. Call you in about 30 mins.

Sure, I wrote.

He sent a smiling emoji.

I double-checked that the ringer was on and put my phone in my pocket. My heart kept doing that weird skittering thing, and I knew it would keep doing that for the entire half hour, till he called—although, considering he was birding with his friends, it might be longer. It was easy to lose track of time when you were bird banding. I knew how into it we all got.

The nature club had stopped meeting after Eloise died. The group, as we'd known it, had drifted apart. We were all still friends, but we didn't get together the way we used to.

And I had mostly stayed off social media since Eloise died. Tried to avoid the internet entirely, even. I couldn't stand what people were saying on there—some blaming our family for not paying enough attention to Eloise, others showering me with phony, even saccharine, sympathy.

"Who were you texting?" Iris asked.

"A friend," I said. "Matt Grinnell. He has a car so he could drive us around. Iris, we have to do something. You have to remember. It's the only way we'll find Hayley, and solve the mystery. We have to go searching for your memory."

"Go searching for my memory," Iris repeated. "That sounds so weird."

It is, I thought. *It's all weird.* I wondered what we were getting into. *Should I even bring Matt into it?* I wondered. We were looking for a killer, after all. I decided I would tell him everything, give him the option to say yes or no.

I suggested to Iris that we head downstairs to wait, and Iris followed me cautiously. Out the kitchen window, I saw Noreen playing with Zoey—that sweet young golden retriever that she had been training—in the side yard. Noreen kept hinting that Zoey would make a great companion for my grandmother—an emotional support animal.

"Who is that?" Iris asked, sounding nervous.

"My grandmother's caregiver," I said. "But as you can see, she's mostly into caring for her puppy. She won't even notice us here."

Iris was quiet, keeping watch on Noreen. She sat down at the kitchen table while I paced around. I couldn't wait to get started. We had to be detectives dedicated to our sisters, searching for life-and-death answers.

After Eloise went missing, the police had come here looking for clues. They had taken certain things for evidence—my sister's journal, some photos, and the scarf she had worn birding that morning. But they had left a lot behind.

Her jean jacket was hanging on the back of the door. A pair of rubber boots, tufted with dry mud from tromping through the marsh, stood neatly in the corner. The linen towel she had used to dry dishes—that was her job—was hanging on a rack above the sink. Laundry was one of my chores, but I hadn't had the heart to wash the towel since October. It reminded me of her. I had warned Noreen not to touch it.

I double-checked my backpack to make sure I'd packed the Ziploc bags yesterday. I took a couple of extra empty ones from the cabinet, just in case we needed to gather more evidence.

"I'll be right back," I said to Iris.

"Where are you going?" she asked, sounding alarmed.

"Just in the other room, to see my grandmother."

She nodded and went back to watching Noreen and Zoey.

Gram was still dozing in her chair in the living room, her memoir notebook open on her lap. She cared so much about finishing it, and I would do anything to help her. Gram liked to write in longhand, and almost never used her computer or phone.

She always kept a notepad in the rolltop desk. We used it for grocery lists and other reminders. I reached for the notepad now, found a pen, and in big dramatic letters printed *IF ANYTHING HAPPENS TO ME . . .*

Then I wrote Gram a short note about how I'd found Iris and believed that she had been left for dead by the same person who had killed Eloise. I explained that we were going in search of her sister Hayley.

I signed it *"With love, Oli."*

I heard my grandmother stir, and I walked over to sit beside her.

"What is that you're writing?" my grandmother asked.

"It's just for us," I said. "Don't show Noreen."

"Who?" she asked.

"Your aide."

My grandmother chuckled. "The lady with the cute puppy."

"She leaves you alone too much," I said. "I'll find someone better to be with you when I get back."

"Where are you going?" she asked, a look of worry crossing her face.

"North, remember?"

"Yes, darling. With the other birds." She paused and peered at me with her bright blue eyes. "Are you a bird?"

"I'm a girl. Who sometimes wishes she was a bird," I whispered.

The voice of a cheerful chef spilled from the television, droning on about how to prepare panna cotta with balsamic strawberries. I hugged Gram and left the room, walked into the kitchen, and opened the freezer.

We kept a box of frozen peas there that was really our own private safe full of cash—about a hundred dollars. We all contributed—Eloise and I from summer jobs and babysitting, Gram from her Social Security. We called it our "rainy day money," for impromptu things like trips to Paradise Ice Cream, movies on the beach, or books from the Book Barn, and we figured the freezer was the perfect place to hide it from burglars. What robber would look in a box of frozen peas?

Not even Noreen knew about it. I would have felt guilty for taking the money, but with Eloise gone and Gram unable to go out, I figured no one would miss it right now. I jammed the cash into my jeans pocket, then sat down at the table. Iris was still looking out the window.

Eloise's and my bird photographs hung on the wall. My sister was so much better at photography than I was. I stared at one she had taken at the blind, of a red-breasted nuthatch caught in the net.

My phone buzzed, and I saw Matt's name on the screen.

"Hi, Matt," I said. My voice cracked between *hi* and *Matt*.

"Oli, what's wrong?" he asked.

I wanted to start as lightheartedly as I could, just asking for a ride, thinking that Iris and I would tell him, as we drove around, the whole story.

But hearing his voice broke something inside me. Tears came but didn't fall, and I tried to swallow down a sob.

"I need help," I said.

"Tell me where you are," he said. "And I'll be right there."

So I did, and he was.

nine

"You okay?" Matt asked as I opened the front door of his Jeep. He'd just pulled into my driveway.

I don't like crying in front of people. It embarrasses me and makes me feel like the center of attention. Eloise was the one who bubbled over; she wore her feelings on the outside, and people loved her for it. I was shyer, kept most things to myself. So in the time it took Matt to drive here, I made sure I was back to my usual calm self.

I nodded and went straight to introductions.

"Matt, this is Iris," I said. "And, Iris . . ."

"Nice to meet you," they both said at the same time.

Then they laughed awkwardly. Obviously something was wrong; Matt knew it, and Iris and I certainly did—but I was glad the ice was broken. I got into the passenger seat next to Matt, and Iris got into the back seat.

I felt Matt looking at me, waiting to hear what I'd meant by *I need help*. My mouth was dry; it was hard to talk.

"I guess Oli told you what's going on," Iris said. "She wants to call the police, but I said no. And I don't want you to, either."

"The police?" Matt asked, sounding shocked. "I thought we were done with them. They grilled us pretty hard already."

"No, she means because of what happened to me," Iris said. "I'm sure Oli filled you in."

"No," Matt said. "She didn't."

The Matt-ness of the situation had me tongue-tied. It's one thing to call a friend for help. It's another when it's the boy you like. Matt put the Jeep into reverse and pulled onto my street. "Where are we going?" he asked.

"I'm not sure," I said. "And that's what this is all about. The reason I called you."

"Not being sure?" he asked.

"Yes," I said. "We're going on . . . a sort of scavenger hunt."

"Like in a game?" he asked.

"Anything but a game," I said.

"We're searching for my memory," Iris said. "And for my sister."

"Okay, that's either mysterious or creepy or both," Matt said. "Can you tell me more, or am I supposed to guess?"

We hit the main road. I pointed toward the Braided Woods. "Let's start there," I said. "Where I found Iris."

"Found her?"

"Buried," I said, and again that closed-throat, stinging-eyes feeling came over me. "In the same place as Eloise."

"Whoa," he said, looking in the rearview mirror at Iris. "Buried?"

"Yeah," she said.

"Why? Who did it?" Matt asked.

"That's what we need to find out," I said. "It must be the same person who killed Eloise. He kidnapped Iris and Hayley—her sister. And he still has Hayley."

"Okay, you need to start at the beginning," Matt said, a hint of disbelief in his voice. "This is bizarre. Where is your sister now?" he asked Iris, glancing in the rearview mirror. "Shouldn't we call the police so they can go get her?"

"Iris can't remember where her sister is," I said. I explained the whole traumatic reaction thing, and the fact that little bursts of memory were starting to come back to her. "We thought that if we started in the place where I found Iris, and drove around from there, she might see things that turn out to be clues."

Again, I saw Matt looking in the rearview mirror at Iris. He glanced at me, concern in his eyes. He was here with me: I felt it in my heart. I stared at his hand and wanted so badly for him to reach across the front seat and hold mine.

"You have a gash in your head," he said over his shoulder to Iris. I saw what he saw—the Band-Aids had come off, and the dried blood looked scary. "A head injury isn't anything to fool around with—it might be part of why you can't remember. We should take you to the ER."

"That's not goint to happen," Iris said. "They'd call the police."

"The person who took her said he'd kill Hayley if the police got involved," I explained.

Matt drove in silence for a minute, taking that in, as I had, probably wondering whether to override Iris and—now—me. "Well, if we don't go to the ER," he said eventually, "we should have Chris or Fitch check her out."

High school kids obviously weren't doctors, but the strange thing was, Matt had a point. They were both at the top of our class, into science and medicine. But I didn't want to see Chris.

It was too hard, for two major reasons. We had barely spoken since Eloise died. I'd see him in the hall at school, and he'd turn away. Or I'd turn away. Of course he reminded me of her, of what she had wished would happen with him.

But also, mostly, I couldn't stop thinking that he might be her killer. Was that the reason he was avoiding *me*? Because he knew he was guilty and couldn't look me in the eye?

"Let's call just Fitch," I said. "Not Chris."

"Who's Fitch?" Iris asked.

"Another friend," Matt said. "He's our age, but he's basically a doctor-in-training."

I nodded. Fitch had known since sixth grade that he wanted to be a doctor. His sister, Abigail, who was a year behind us in school, had a rare disease, and he wanted to find a cure. Their parents were divorced and their mom was a famous neurologist who traveled all over the country to give talks.

"Really?" Iris asked, sounding skeptical.

"Remember what happened with Tuck?" Matt said to me, and I told Iris the story.

Last September, three weeks before Eloise went missing, our nature group went up Mount Crawford for the hawk migration. Tuck Barlow, a friend of Adalyn's who'd tagged along, tripped and fell. He hit his head, said he was okay, but Fitch made him stay still while he looked into his eyes to see if his pupils were dilating properly. That was how I'd learned to do that, too.

"Fitch could see that Tuck had a concussion," Matt explained to Iris now. "We got Tuck straight to the ER, and the doctor said he had a pretty bad head injury. He seriously could have died if he wasn't treated." He glanced back at Iris again. "Fitch could take a look at you. Just in case."

"Oli already checked my pupils," Iris said. "When she first found me."

"Still," Matt said. "Let me at least call him to look at your cut."

"Please, Iris?" I asked. "It wouldn't hurt." What I really wished was that she would let us take her to a clinic, somewhere she could have tests, but I knew that was not going to happen. Seeing Fitch would be something of a compromise.

"Okay," she said, sounding reluctant. "But I know I'm fine."

You didn't even know your own name, I wanted to say. But I didn't because Matt was already calling Fitch on the Jeep's Bluetooth.

You have reached 203 . . . The automated voicemail picked up.

"Hey, Fitch," Matt said. "Oli and I have a question for you. Call me when you and Chris finish banding."

In spite of everything else that was going on, my whole body shimmered when I heard him say "Oli and I," our names together.

"They're still banding?" I asked.

"Yeah," Matt said, looking over at me. "I would have stayed, but you said you needed help."

He had chosen to come to me instead of staying with them. I had to look out my window so he wouldn't see how what he said had affected me.

We drove into the Braided Woods, toward the crevice. Iris gasped in recognition when she saw the spot, so we pulled over and all three of us got out of the Jeep. We walked around, searching for any kind of clue that would jog her memory. I stared down at the ground, looking for gold specks, like the ones I'd collected in my evidence bags. But I didn't see any. It seemed possible that the wind had blown them away.

Iris wandered ahead of Matt and me.

"Where is she from?" Matt asked, taking advantage of the fact she was out of earshot. "Not from school . . ."

"No," I said. "Definitely not. She says she has no idea."

"Doesn't know where her family is?" Matt asked, with the same disbelief in his voice that I had initially felt. "But she remembers Hayley?"

"Yes," I said.

"If she was with whoever hurt Eloise, she must live near here."

"She doesn't know *where* she lives," I said.

"What does she say about the person who took her?" Matt asked.

"She knows it was a guy, but she can't remember his face."

"How are *you*?" Matt asked, stepping closer to me. "This must be terrible for you, Oli. Here where Eloise . . ." His words filled my imagination with images of my sister, what she had gone through right here, within sight of where we were standing. A tremor went through me, and he noticed. We were standing so close to each other. He started to put his arm around me, and I leaned into him. I felt his warm breath on my cheek.

Iris let out a loud, frustrated sigh. "Nothing," she said, walking back to us, and Matt and I stepped apart. "Or, at least, nothing before you found me here, Oli."

"We'll keep trying," I said. "Don't give up hope."

"Right, we're just getting started," Matt said as we all climbed back into the Jeep. My heart was still thudding from what had almost happened between us.

"I keep thinking of cats," Iris said. "Maybe I was a cat in another life."

"Or you have one in your real life," I said.

"Yes," she said and paused, as if she was remembering something from far away. "But I think it's more than just one . . ." She squeezed her eyes shut. "A lot of cats. One of them was named Maisie." But that was as far as she got.

My stomach growled. It was almost lunchtime. I figured Iris could think better if she had something to eat, and that was true of me, too. I asked Matt to stop at the Big Y. Iris stayed in the car while Matt and I ran inside to get sandwiches from the deli counter, snacks, and juices.

After Gram got sick, Eloise and I had come to the Big Y once a week to shop. We'd push the cart up and down the aisles, getting all the things we needed, the way parents did. As the oldest, I always remembered to get staples like paper towels and dryer sheets, dishwashing detergent and light bulbs, healthy meals, brain food like salmon for our grandmother—to slow the progression of her Alzheimer's. Eloise was in charge of getting snacks, like cookies and fruit. We were a team: the Parrish sisters. The Girls With Too Much Responsibility.

But never did I picture myself at the Y with Matt Grinnell. I kind of wished some kids from school would see us—see me with him— and while we were waiting in line to get rung up, I spotted Gisele St. John at one of the other registers. She was tall and willowy, a year ahead of us, and I didn't really know her. Of course she and everyone knew that I was the girl whose sister had been murdered, so she said an awkward hello to me. Then she waved at Matt.

"How's it going, Matt?" she called.

"Good. How about you?"

She smiled. "Awesome. Looking forward to that boat ride you promised. When are we going?"

"We're still getting the boats ready for summer," Matt said. I found myself feeling ridiculously jealous. She was tall, she was beautiful, and she and Matt had made plans for a boat ride.

After I'd paid for our food with the cash from the freezer, Matt and I walked toward the exit.

"I didn't actually ask her," he said to me.

"You didn't?" I asked. "Seems as if she thought you did."

"Well, she's friends with Fitch's sister. I asked him, and he asked if we could take Abigail and Gisele, too. He said the salt air would help Abigail, but actually, I think he likes Gisele."

That made me feel bad for Adalyn, who had a crush on Fitch. Or maybe she didn't anymore. Adalyn got over crushes quickly, and I realized that I hadn't spoken to her in ages. After Eloise died, I backed away from pretty much everyone. At first, people texted, trying to get me to do things, but when I stopped answering, they stopped asking. I was a little worried that I'd hurt their feelings, but when your sister dies, everything changes.

"Fitch might like Gisele, but Gisele likes you," I said to Matt as we walked outside.

He looked amused. "That bothers you?"

"Well, no, I mean . . . I don't blame her, but . . ." I said. Now I was stammering, and it made him grin.

"I'm only doing it for Fitch. He'll try anything to help Abigail," he said.

I didn't know Abigail well, but everyone knew she was sick. Last spring there had been an incident on a school field trip where she'd had a seizure and had to be taken to the hospital. It was serious, and ever since then she'd been homeschooled.

"Is Abigail okay?" I asked.

"Not really," Matt said. "Her condition is serious, and apparently it runs in the family. Some of their ancestors died of it. Fitch said she's really depressed, and has been totally shutting herself off from friends. And Fitch's upset that their mom isn't doing more to help Abigail, but she's wrapped up in other things."

"That's horrible," I said. I understood the dynamic of shutting off from friends. And I felt a connection with Fitch, too. I knew how it felt to worry about a sister.

We headed to the Jeep, and Matt's phone buzzed. A voicemail had dropped in. There'd been no cell reception inside the Y, and he had missed a call from Fitch. He played the message on speaker.

Hey, what's going on? What's your question? I'm in the middle of some research, trying to figure something out, but I'll pick up if I can.

Matt called again—still no answer, so he texted:

We want you to check on a friend who we think might have a concussion. Can we stop by?

We climbed into the Jeep. Fitch could get obsessed when he was focused on science, so I knew it might be a while before he told us we could come over.

"Ready to continue the scavenger hunt?" Matt said as he handed Iris her sandwich and a bottle of iced tea.

"Right. Searching for my memory," Iris said, staring blankly into space.

"You have to eat," I said. "You need your strength."

"I'm not hungry," she said.

"Do it for your sister, if you won't for yourself," I said. "Your brain needs food to start remembering where to find Hayley."

She shrugged and reluctantly began to unwrap the sandwich. I'd known it would work: the mention of Hayley's name. It was a major thing we had in common: Like me, Iris would do anything to help her sister.

Ten

After we finished eating, we continued our scavenger hunt for Iris's memory. Matt drove slowly, giving Iris a chance to scan the scene. We passed the barn where I'd hidden Iris when I'd gone back to the grave for my phone. Then we were in the countryside. There weren't many houses, but there was lots of open space—woods, meadows, ponds, and farms.

Iris stared out the window.

"Anything look familiar?" I asked.

"No."

Matt kept driving, expanding the circle. Now we were making our way through neighborhoods. At first we passed estates—mansions you could barely see from the road, surrounded by tall hedges, with long driveways. Some had gates. This was where the rich people lived. They belonged to the country club—which we also passed— and many sent their kids to boarding school instead of Black Hall High. Fitch and Abigail lived here in a big stone house on a hill. Chris lived next door to them.

I looked over at Matt. "Does Chris ever talk about what happened to Eloise?" I asked, my stomach clenching. "Like the investigation?"

"Only that he hopes the cops find the person soon." Matt glanced at me. "We all hope that."

I wanted to ask him more, but I felt uncomfortable—Chris was our friend. I didn't want to seem suspicious. So I focused on our route. Now we were driving through a swirl of streets lined with smaller, regular-sized houses. The yards were not big, and I saw two tree houses and a jungle gym, some above-ground pools, and bikes in the driveways. Kids lived here. Families.

"Do any of these neighborhoods remind you of where you live?" I asked Iris.

"No," Iris said, frowning. "Not at all. Why do I feel as if I didn't grow up in a house?"

"In an apartment, then?" I asked, surprised. There weren't really any apartment buildings nearby.

"I don't think so," Iris said.

Strange. Had she been raised in the wilderness? Was that why I found her in the woods? I felt it would be rude to ask that.

"If not a house," Matt said, "where?"

"I'm trying to think," Iris said. She bowed her head for a second. "What does any of this matter, anyway? I don't care where I came from—I just want to find Hayley."

"I know," I said, trying to be patient. "But since we don't have any idea where she is, you remembering where you were taken from could make a big difference. We're not just looking for your home. We're hoping you see something that will lead us to her."

"Okay," she said. "Let's keep going."

We drove through the small village of Black Hall, past the old white church, the chocolate shop, the magical art gallery that gave out the best candy at Halloween, the library, our high school, the inn and restaurant, and the wonderful museum where artists had painted panels in the dining room. Iris kept shaking her head— nothing. From there we crossed from our town into Silver Bay. We hit a red light, and while we were stopped, a familiar blue Prius pulled right next to us.

"Adalyn!" I called, rolling down my window. I had just been thinking of her, and feeling slightly guilty that we hadn't talked or gotten together in a long time.

I would have expected her to smile, but she didn't. She looked really upset and worried.

"Are you okay?" I asked.

"Not really," she said.

I frowned. Had something happened to her that somehow connected to Iris? To Eloise?

I glanced at Matt. "I have to talk to her," I said.

"We'll pull into the boatyard," he said, gesturing at the marina about a hundred yards up the road.

"Meet us there," I said to Adalyn.

We parked side by side next to one of the docks. I jumped out, ran to Adalyn, and hugged her. I felt a pang over how I'd been avoiding her, over how much I had missed her.

"What's wrong?" I asked.

"I feel like the worst sister in the world," she said. "I was supposed to be feeding Thea's kitten while she looks at colleges with our parents, and guess who escaped? Yep, you got it. The furry baby is gone. My sister will kill me. And she'll be back any second. They called to say they'll be home this afternoon. And no cat."

"Oh no," I said. "No wonder you're upset."

"Upset would be a step up. I'm a wreck. I've been driving around for over an hour, looking for the little thing. Where do kittens hide? What if she got taken by a fox or a coyote?"

"Don't think like that," I said. "Be positive. Maybe she'll come back on her own."

"But what if she doesn't?" Adalyn asked, despair in her voice. But then she glanced at Matt's Jeep and managed a smile.

"Really?" she asked.

I blushed because I knew exactly what she meant. Matt. She was completely aware of how I felt about him. "Yeah," I said.

"How did this come about?"

"Well, I needed a ride."

She laughed and raised her eyebrows. "Hello, I have a car. Why didn't you call me? Don't answer that, I already know."

I was sure she did. "It's not like Matt and I don't hang out sometimes."

"Yes, but in our nature group. You and Matt without us—this is progress!" She paused. "Chris is helping me look."

Chris?

"Where is he?" I asked, feeling sudden dread.

"He's cutting through backyards," she said. "Looking up in trees, under bushes."

I nodded, but my insides hurt. The mention of Chris sent me spinning. Eloise had liked him so much; I wondered if he was getting close to Adalyn. She hadn't mentioned it, but maybe that was because she knew it would be a tender subject. I almost felt like warning her, spilling my doubts about him.

Adalyn caught sight of Iris in the back seat. "Who's that?"

"I just met her," I said. "You won't believe this . . . I found her . . ." I stopped myself. I trusted Adalyn, but if she was hanging around with Chris, telling her about Iris was the last thing I should do. Then I had a brainstorm. "She seems to know a lot about cats. Maybe she'll have advice about where Thea's kitten could have escaped to."

I waved to Iris, and she rolled down the back window. She was eyeing Adalyn a little suspiciously, but I managed to skip introducing her and Adalyn by name, in case Adalyn mentioned anything to Chris. Iris looked relieved, and Adalyn was too distracted to notice. She told Iris about the missing kitten.

"They like to hide," Iris said. "That's the big thing. In closets, basements, under buildings. Under parked cars. In alleys."

It interested me to hear her rattling off these ideas—she really did know about cats, so that was something to add to my list. And something about the places she named stuck in my mind—I wasn't sure why.

"Where were you when the kitten ran away?" Iris asked Adalyn.

"My house is over there," Adalyn said, pointing at the familiar white Cape I'd spent so many happy times in over the years, since fourth grade. "I opened the front door to get the mail when Esmeralda dashed outside and disappeared."

"Can you show me where you last saw her?" Iris asked. "I might get a sense of her."

Another mystery, another search.

"We'll meet you at your house," Matt told Adalyn.

We parked in the Bandas' driveway. When Adalyn got out of her car, Iris got out of the Jeep and together they headed toward Adalyn's front door. I was curious about the fact that Iris was willing to be seen out in the open with Adalyn when she had been so cautious all along. I figured it must have to do with her love of cats.

Matt stayed in the driver's seat, scrolling through his phone. I got out of the Jeep and started to follow Iris and Adalyn when I heard a boy speak my name.

"Oli."

I turned to see Chris, and I stiffened. He stood a few feet away from me in Adalyn's yard, hands in his jeans pockets, sunlight glinting on his blond hair. It was hard for me to look at him, and this was the closest he had come to me in months.

I froze, waiting to see how he would react to Iris. If he was the one—Eloise's killer, Iris and Hayley's kidnapper—he would freak out at the sight of her. But when Iris passed by him with Adalyn, he barely glanced at her. He didn't seem to recognize her at all. He was only focused on me.

"How've you been?" Chris asked.

"I'm fine," I said. "How about you?"

"Fine, too," he said.

I stared into his eyes and saw something I hadn't expected: true sadness. Like me, he was lying about being fine. Even though I'd seen him with friends at school, laughing and talking like things were normal, at this moment I felt grief pouring off him. Maybe bumping into me was as hard for him as it was for me.

"I keep thinking I'll see her again," he said quietly. "Especially times like now, seeing you. Because you two were so often together."

"It's the same for me, Chris," I said. "She always . . ." *Wanted to be with you*, I thought but didn't say.

"I'm so sorry, Oli," he said.

"For what?" I asked, almost afraid to hear what he was going to say.

"That I didn't realize how serious it was when I didn't hear back from Eloise that last day," he said. "I figured she'd gotten tired of waiting for me to finish my paper, and went to see the owls on her own. Or got someone else to go with her."

The police had floated those theories, too. "She didn't go to the woods on her own," I said. Eloise didn't have her license yet, and she hadn't taken her bike.

"I know that now," Chris said. "I'm just telling you what I

wondered that night." His eyes glittered with tears. "I don't talk about it. I don't talk about her. And I stay away from you. I can't see you. It's too hard, Oli."

"What's too hard?" I asked.

"To see how you feel about me. If I'd been there, I could have stopped what happened to her, I could have saved her."

For a few seconds I couldn't reply, but then the words came pouring out. "It's true, Chris. I thought that, too. I was really angry at you at first."

"I was angry at myself," he said.

"I even wondered . . ."

"If I was involved?"

I nodded, my heart pounding. I couldn't believe I'd admitted it, but now that I was actually talking to Chris, I felt like I could be honest with him. "I'm sorry for thinking that."

He looked down. "I don't blame you. We all suspect everyone, even each other. Because how can we know? I hardly sleep, trying to think of clues, what we might have missed, wishing I had been there with her. Wishing you didn't hate me."

"I don't," I said. "I never did. I was just upset." I paused. "Chris, we don't know who did this to her. If you had been there, you might have been killed, too."

He grimaced. "I would have fought whoever it was," he said. "I would have saved Els."

Els. Hearing him call her that made me take a deep breath. It showed how familiar he was with her, giving her a nickname I had never heard before.

"Oli, what do you think would have happened?" Chris asked. "With us—Els and me?"

That question was too hard to answer or even contemplate. I knew what she wanted, but that's the thing about someone being gone: You don't get to see the story unfold. I never got to see my sister and Chris getting together, holding hands, being a couple. I felt sad that Chris never got to see— or feel—any of that. Most of all, it broke my heart to know that Eloise was missing out on all of it.

On life.

"She liked you," I said, and that was all I could get out.

"I know she did," he said. "And I . . . well, multiply that however you want, and that's how much I . . ."

He stopped talking, and then he turned and walked out of the driveway. He got into his car and started it up. Matt called his name but either Chris didn't hear or couldn't speak. He just drove away.

The conversation with him made the air all around me shimmer. It made me see Chris in a different way, and suddenly I felt as if Eloise had just left. As if she had walked behind him, invisible, and gotten into his car with him. I told myself they were going for a ride, that she had heard what he had said, that she was happy to know that he liked her, even more than liked her.

Els.

My dream of my sister and Chris was interrupted by Iris running back to the Jeep. She opened the back door and grabbed what was left of her sandwich. She pulled out the sliced turkey and went to kneel next to the front steps of Adalyn's house.

Adalyn was walking around the house, calling "Esmeralda, Esmeralda," but Iris was totally silent. She peered under the deck. Then she dangled a turkey slice, and I heard her whispering, "Here, now. That's a girl, good girl."

A tiny tiger cat scooted out from the darkness, into Iris's arms, and began hungrily chomping on turkey.

"Thank you so much!" Adalyn cried as Iris handed her Esmeralda and the rest of her sandwich. "How did you know she'd be under there?"

"I think I'm part cat," Iris said, smiling.

"You saved me. You're definitely the cat whisperer," Adalyn said.

"You'd better get her inside," Iris said. "She's quite the little adventurer."

I gave Adalyn a quick hug and she ran up the steps, closing the door behind her. It felt so odd, and it hit me: This was my first time at her house since Eloise had died. As much as I loved Adalyn and her family, I felt shaken because it wasn't the same. Nothing was. Nothing ever would be again.

Iris and I got back into the Jeep, and I realized that having Iris there comforted me. More weirdness: I felt closer to this girl I had just met than I did to Adalyn. Iris and I were united by a nightmare, by a person who kidnapped girls and killed them. How could Adalyn ever understand that?

Adalyn had found what she was missing. It had been so simple.

I remembered what Iris had said when we first encountered Adalyn, about where cats liked to hide. I realized then what had stood out to me. It was probably a small thing, or nothing at all.

"You found Esmeralda under the house," I said.

"Yes," Iris said.

"But before, you said cats like to hide under *buildings*," I said. "You didn't say houses."

"Right," Iris said. "Under factories, stores, warehouses . . ." She trailed off.

"And you said alleys, not yards," I pressed.

"Yes, they like to hide behind dumpsters," Iris said. "Even more so if they're strays, because they might need to forage for food." She paused. "It makes it easier to save them—catch them. Because they congregate there, hoping for scraps."

Matt caught the wisp of a clue, the same one I had heard.

"You live in a city," Matt said.

Iris's brow furrowed as if she was trying to grab the thinnest thread of memory.

"Maybe," she said. "Maybe you're right."

"New London," Matt said, naming the nearest city to us, about ten miles away. "Let's start there."

We headed east.

eleven

As we drove on back roads toward New London, I saw Iris staring out the window. What was going on in her mind? Were there any sparks of recognition? We approached Ocean Beach, a little amusement park on the edge of town. I could see the roller coaster and the Tilt-A-Whirl. Eloise used to love taking the railroad around the edge of the marsh, watching great blue herons fish the shallows. Iris gazed at the rides as we passed, but I saw no reaction, making me think she hadn't been here before.

"Do you actually remember a city?" I asked her. "A particular one?"

"It's more like a feeling," she said.

A feeling. I thought about my own life, the little things that mattered to me, that told me who I was and where I was from.

Black Hall, my home. Sand between my toes as I dove into Long Island Sound. The sweet and salty smell of the marshes. The taste of mocha chocolate chip at Paradise Ice Cream. The periwinkle ankle bracelets Eloise and I had made one summer, first collecting the small gray-blue shells, drilling tiny holes in them, then stringing them together on fishing line. Taylor Swift's *folklore* playing nonstop on my phone. Cookouts in our backyard. Going birding. Taking a boat to Dauntless Island.

Those were the thoughts and emotions that defined my life. I wondered which ones made up Iris's. I wondered how it was possible that she had a feeling about a city and a cat, but nothing specific about her home, her parents, and even Hayley. It seemed so odd to me. But when I glanced at her in the back seat, all I could see was a girl who had lost her memory along with her sister.

When people think "city," they might picture the tall buildings of New York, Boston, Chicago, places like that. New London is a small seaport at the mouth of the Thames River. It doesn't have a skyline like other cities: aside from church spires and a radio tower, the eleven-story Mohican Hotel is the tallest building in town. Gram was a history buff, and when I was little, she'd tell me and Eloise facts about the area that became part of our family story.

I knew that Benedict Arnold burned New London down during the Revolutionary War. I knew that in the early 1800s, it was one of the busiest whaling ports in the world. It always made me so sad to think of the whales killed so their oil could light the lamps of cities everywhere.

And I knew that there were ghosts here. Ledge Light, the square brick lighthouse just outside the harbor, was said to be haunted by Ernie, its former lightkeeper. Ella Quinlan O'Neill was said to haunt Monte Cristo Cottage, the house where she lived with her family, including her Nobel Prize–winning son, playwright Eugene O'Neill. One time Eloise went there on a field trip and swore she saw Ella, dressed in a nightgown, hovering on the stairway.

I shivered as we drove past the cottage because now I felt haunted by Eloise. Had she become a ghost? I wished I could see her. And I wished for something else: that we would find Hayley, so we could save her life and keep her here in our earthly realm, with Iris.

"You okay, Oli?" Matt asked, as if he'd felt the chill of sadness coming off me.

"Yes," I said. "I just want to get to her."

And, really, who did I even mean by "her"? Hayley or Eloise? Iris's sister or mine?

Iris looked from side to side, noticing the pink granite public library, the bank, the tattoo parlor, the comics shop, the huge red-brick train station, the little schoolhouse where Revolutionary War hero Nathan Hale had taught. She was slumped in her seat, as if discouraged by the fact that she didn't recognize anything.

I heard her sigh. "This isn't working," she said.

"Iris, give it a chance," Matt said.

"A chance for what? It's hopeless! We're driving around a place I've never seen before, wasting time while anything could be happening to Hayley!"

As if he'd caught her impatience, Matt sped up, driving a little too fast to go through town. He cut down a steep alley between two buildings that took us closer to the water, onto the service road that ran behind shops and restaurants.

"Wait!" Iris shouted. "Back up!"

Matt jammed on the brakes and put the Jeep into reverse. The tires jounced on the road's cobblestones. Iris grabbed my shoulder with one hand and began pointing wildly with the other. Matt stopped the car and we all stared.

Iris was pointing at a stone-and-concrete wall that formed the basement level of the old buildings on Bank Street. The wall was weathered by centuries of fog and salt air, with some stones tilted and coming loose, and the mortar crumbling.

"What are we looking at?" I asked.

"Ghost signs," Iris said. "Advertisements painted years and years ago. They're so faded they're barely visible. I grew up seeing ones like these."

As I stared, the faint colors materialized on the dusty wall. There *were* faded signs there! Most were advertisements connected to the nautical world: a sailmaker's loft, a ship chandlery, a master carver of figureheads, the Whalers Tavern, the Barquentine Pub.

But there was also a life-sized depiction of three girls dressed in long white gowns—the paint was so faded, the girls looked like teenaged apparitions. All three of them had ethereally beautiful faces, with wide eyes and mysterious smiles. Their arms were linked, and they had flowers in their long hair. In spidery print above them were the words *Sibylline Sisters: Oracles*. And the date: *1944*.

"The girls are the same," Iris said, staring. She opened the Jeep door and got out. She stood in front of the ghost sign of the girls.

"The same as what?" Matt asked as he and I climbed out to stand beside her.

"As the ones on the panels."

"What panels?" I asked.

"The goddesses," she replied.

"This is too bizarre," Matt said, giving me a look as if he thought Iris might be losing her mind. "Goddesses?"

"There were panels painted with classical-looking girls," Iris explained. "Young women. They were wearing long white dresses. Pleated gowns, exactly like these." She pointed to the ghost sign. "Remember, Oli? I told you about them?"

"You mentioned paintings," I said.

"Yes," she said, impatiently. "But they were painted on panels— tall pieces of board, taller than I am."

"Where are these panels?" Matt asked.

"In the place where he kept us."

"Kept you?" I asked, my heart pounding. "You remember now?"

She nodded. "Sort of. I'm starting to . . . Up all those flights of stairs. Up in the attic."

"Attic of what?" Matt asked.

Iris gave him a desperate look. "If I knew, do you think we'd be standing here? I'd be running as fast as I could to save Hayley."

"That's where Hayley is now?" I asked.

"Unless they moved her," she said.

"When you say 'they' . . ." Matt said. "Who do you mean?"

Iris didn't answer at first. During her silence, I noticed that Matt was busy texting. Then Iris pointed at the spectral figures again. "These girls on this ghost sign are *exactly* the same as the ones on the panels," she said. "And the girl in the bed was dressed almost the same way, in a long white nightgown."

Wait.

"What girl in the bed?" I asked.

"She had a bed, we had mattresses on the floor."

"Who was the girl?" I asked Iris, but she shook her head, unable to recall more.

I glanced back at the ghost sign and read the words on it. "Who were the Sibylline sisters?" I wondered out loud.

"No idea, and I can't get enough service here to Google it," Matt said, looking up from his phone.

As I gazed at the wall, I saw that there were several doors leading into the row of buildings. I pointed that out to Matt and Iris.

"This section of waterfront is only a few blocks long," Matt said. "Why don't we park, knock on some of those doors, and ask about the sign? Someone who lives or works here might know what the sign means."

I looked at Iris, but she was standing there completely frozen and pale. It must have been a shock to see those ghost signs, the images she remembered from the attic. I didn't want to leave the only spot Iris had seemed to recognize, but it felt important that the three of us stay together.

"Okay," I said. "Let's go park." We got back into the Jeep and Matt started driving again.

Suddenly Iris grabbed the back of my seat.

"Get us out of here!" she screamed.

"Why? What is it?" I asked.

"That!" she said, pointing at a dusty blue van parked in a garage. It looked as if it hadn't been driven in ages; it didn't even have a front license plate.

"What about it?" Matt asked, startled.

"That blue van," she said.

"Like the one in your nightmare?" I asked. "Were you taken in a blue van?"

She looked terrified. "I think so," she said. "Or did I just dream it?" She looked at Matt again. "We can't stay here!" she insisted.

I wasn't sure if this blue van in particular was dangerous, but I wanted to help calm Iris down. I saw how distraught she was.

"We shouldn't go knocking on doors yet," I said to Matt. "Iris needs a break. Let's leave and we'll come back later."

"Where should we go?" Matt asked.

"Somewhere no one will see us, okay?" Iris asked, her voice trembling. "They're following us. I feel it. They're here."

"Okay, Iris. We'll go somewhere safe and hidden," I said, even as my heart was racing. *Were* we being followed?

"I'll take us to Osprey Hill," Matt said.

We smiled at each other. In spite of the stress, all I could think of in that moment was that Matt remembered a place that meant so much to me—because we had been there together.

Twelve

Osprey Hill was across the Thames River, in a tiny little fishing village overlooking the spot where Long Island Sound, Block Island Sound, and the Atlantic Ocean converge. At the top of the hill was the town warehouse, where my grandfather had worked long ago. The warehouse held buoys and mushroom anchors for moorings, lengths of anchor chain thicker than a bicycle tire, old stop signs, orange cones for traffic control—which was a laugh, because the town of Pequod was so small and sleepy, the only busy times were weekends when seafood-craving tourists descended.

I had loved the village since childhood. But last year it had taken on magical status: I'd brought Matt here. Right before school started up again. We had gotten chocolate chip cookies from the Butterfly Café and drove to Osprey Hill to feel the salt breeze and look out to sea. We had parked up here in his Jeep, and I had loved the song playing over the Bluetooth: "Lost in the 16th," by Margot François. The lyrics were about change, but the feeling it gave me was about love.

Now, Matt drove up the narrow gravel driveway and parked behind the warehouse. The three of us got out and walked to a grove of cedars. Matt had the binoculars he kept in his glove compartment, to use for birding. From here, we were hidden, but we could see the harbor, the lighthouse, and all the way out to Fishers Island. We could also see all the roads down below, winding through the village.

Matt raised the binoculars and scanned the area.

"What are you looking for?" I asked.

"Iris seemed pretty freaked out back in New London," Matt whispered to me. "Do you think anyone could really have spotted her there? Is someone following us?"

"I don't know," I said. "She sounded convinced. That blue van scared her."

"But, a blue van?" Matt asked. "You know how many of those there are around? Just think of all the blue minivans you see at after-school pickup. And that we've even gotten rides in."

I glanced at Iris to see how she was doing, and she looked even paler. I noticed that she was looking at the inside of her left arm. She held it out toward me, and I saw a dark but yellowing bruise in the crook of her left elbow. I hadn't noticed it before.

"What's that?" I asked.

"I just remembered," she said. "He did a blood test and told me and Hayley we both have AB negative."

I felt a jolt. Eloise and I had that same blood type, too. I had it on my license. AB negative is the rarest of the eight main blood types. Only 1 percent of people in the entire world has it.

"Who is *he*?" Matt asked.

"The person who kidnapped us. Who kept us there," Iris said. She stared at the inside of her arm. She closed her eyes and shivered. "He stared right at me and told me that if I was lucky, I would be chosen."

"Chosen for what?" Matt asked.

"To be a hero to the goddess."

"Goddess?" I repeated. "Like those women in the paintings?"

"I think he meant the girl," Iris said. "The one in the bed."

I was certain that Iris remembering who that girl was could be the key to everything.

"What was the girl like?" I asked.

"She was nice. Kind of shy, but friendly."

"Can you remember her name?"

"Almost—I almost have it. Something about a storm. . . . I know for sure she dressed in white," she said. "A white nightgown. It looked old-fashioned."

"Anything else about her?" I asked.

"She had a bandage on her forearm."

"Like a cast? Or a brace for a sprain?" I asked.

"No, she'd been embroidering something onto her sleeve, the needle had pricked her. Pretty deep, and it had gotten infected. The guy was really freaked out about that. He gave her a shot of antibiotics and kept checking the bandage."

"What was she embroidering?" Matt asked.

"Just one word: *Sibyl*." She looked up at me with wild eyes. "It's coming back! I remember her name!"

"Tell me," I said.

And she did.

thirteen

"Gale, like a storm blowing off the sea," Iris said. "She guarded me and Hayley in the attic." She let out a breath. "He hardly ever called her by name, as if he didn't want us to know too much."

"What did she call him?" Matt asked.

"I don't remember ever hearing her call him anything."

"Okay," I said quickly, not wanting to break the stream of whatever memories were trickling back. "Just keep going. You said she guarded you."

Iris closed her eyes, and I didn't know if it was because she was trying to bring Gale's face to mind, or to block it out.

"She did what he told her, but sometimes he did what she told him. Like I told you, she had her own bed, a nice one. And my sister and I had mattresses on the floor."

"She slept in the same room as you?" I asked.

Iris frowned. "Some nights. Not always. And it wasn't sleep. It was . . . She kept dying. Then coming back to life."

"*What?*" I asked. A chill went through me.

"That's too creepy to be real, right?" Iris asked. "I must have dreamed that."

I held back from saying yes. It was way too creepy.

"Tell us more about her," Matt said. "The things that are real, not dreams."

"I couldn't tell if she was a girl he'd kidnapped, like us, but who got on his good side. Or whether she was in on it from the start, because they were definitely a team," Iris said. "Whenever she spoke to us, she would whisper, as if she didn't want him to hear."

"Was he always there?" Matt asked.

"No, and that's another strange thing. It seemed as if he was spying on us, even when he wasn't in the room . . ." Iris trailed off. "He slept in the building."

"Building? Not a house?" I asked.

But she didn't answer.

"What kinds of things would Gale say?" Matt asked. "When she whispered?"

"I remember once she said, 'I'm sorry for everything. It's my fault you're here.'"

"Did she explain that?" I asked.

Iris seemed drifty for a few moments. "No. She told me to stay positive, that he'd eventually let us go. She said that the other girl's death had been an accident, it wouldn't happen to us."

"What other girl?" I asked, the top of my scalp tingling. *Eloise?*

Iris kept talking, as if she hadn't heard my question. "I tried to have as positive an attitude as possible—for Hayley's sake. I was trying to keep my sister's spirits up, so we could stay strong and escape when we got the chance."

"I can imagine," I said.

"Sometimes I felt bad for her—for Gale."

"Why?" I asked.

"Her eyes looked sad. She looked tired all the time. Obviously because she didn't sleep well, she . . ."

My stomach clenched, because I had the feeling Iris was about to say "died" again. It was too upsetting to consider. But instead, she went in another direction.

"She hardly ever spoke," Iris said. "She didn't smile a lot, and seemed to be kind of curled in on herself. You know? Her shoulders were always hunched over, as if something inside really hurt."

"Like she'd been injured?"

Iris shook her head. "No. More like her heart ached."

That rang a bell with me. Since losing Eloise, there were times I couldn't stand up straight. My heart had been bruised the day my sister went missing; when I found out she was dead, it completely shredded. Even now, if I heard her name, my shoulders instinctively curved forward, my whole body making a protective little cave around my broken heart.

"It sounds as if she's mourning someone," I said.

"I don't know," Iris said. "She was always exhausted, and sometimes she got sick. I'd hear her throwing up in the bathroom. I said to her one time, 'You're sick because of what he's doing to us. Keeping us here.'"

"What did she say to that?"

"Nothing. But I could tell that what I said really bothered her. She got

104

even more hunched than ever and left the room. I almost felt bad for her. But, see, she could come and go. She had control—we had none."

I tried to imagine Gale's role in what had happened to Iris and Hayley—and to Eloise, because I was convinced that my sister had to be "the other girl" that Gale had referred to.

"And what was the room like?" I asked. "Can you remember?"

"It was in an attic," she said. "But, like an extra-high attic or something. I was out of it when we got there, but the drug was starting to wear off when he jostled me out of the van. We had to go up a bunch of flights. Four, I think. You could tell it was a very old place—the rafters were splintered, and the nails were that rustic, iron kind that you see in museums about New England history." She glanced at me. "And Oli, there *were* dead birds."

"Like in your dream."

"Yes. Mostly owls. Dead, stuffed, with their wings out as if they were flying—suspended from the ceiling. Hanging up there, dangling over our heads."

"With dolls' eyes," I said, remembering what she had said.

I pictured being at the birding station. I loved birds so much, and I tried to imagine the kind of person who would kill them, take them to a taxidermist, and hang them from the ceiling.

"There were windows," Iris continued. "But they were so old and dirty, we couldn't see out. A big chimney stood in the center of the room. Or maybe just a brick enclosure. He went inside it sometimes, through a splintery old door that was set into the brick. Also, there were those strange painted panels, leaning against the walls."

"Like in the ghost signs?" Matt asked.

"Yes. Those same three classical-looking girls," Iris said. "The Sibylline sisters in those draped white gowns, with flowers in their hair, carved marble columns behind them." She paused, frowning.

"What?" I asked.

"Obviously Gale's nightgown was modeled on their dresses." She shrugged and went on. "Once, the guy was standing in front of the panels, and I heard him say 'hella-spon-teen.' Or something like that. Then something that sounded almost like 'arithmetic,' but not quite. 'Aritherin'? A foreign language, I thought. And he said the words in an almost reverential way, as if they meant something very important to him."

"Who is a 'hella-spon-teen'?" I asked, pulling out my phone and typing it phonetically into the search window.

Nothing with that spelling came up, but it autocorrected to *Hellespontine*. When I looked that up, it said she was an ancient Greek sibyl along with two others, *Phrygian* and *Erythraean*.

"Wait, could 'arithmetic' have been 'Erythraean'?" I asked. "Sounds similar."

"Yes, that's it!" Iris said.

I passed her my phone, to show her the painting of the three sibyls that had popped up in the search. Their long white dress were ethereal and delicate, but they had sharp intelligence in their eyes that left no doubt they were women to be reckoned with. Iris peered at them, nodding her head. "These are similar to the ones in the attic," she said. "Not by the same artist, but definitely the same subjects. Sibyls . . . what are they?"

I took my phone back and skimmed the screen. "According to this article, they're women who are oracles," I said, and suddenly it seemed obvious. "The Sibylline sisters!"

"The ghost sign girls!" Matt said.

"They can tell the future?" Iris asked. "Isn't that what oracles do?"

"Yes, according to this article," I said, looking at my phone.

"Do you think the guy who took you drew the paintings? Or did Gale?" Matt asked.

"No, the panels were really old," Iris said. "They looked almost like stage sets, as if they'd been in a theater at some point . . ." She trailed off, and I noticed her voice and energy draining away.

I looked at the time on my phone. It was three in the afternoon. Hard to believe that only a day and a half had passed since I had found her in the ground.

I saw her yawn widely and touch her head.

"You're doing great, Iris," I said. "I can't believe how much is coming back."

"I have this bizarre feeling," she said in a strained whisper, pressing against her temples with her fingertips. "Almost as if I'd been in a hospital, or a clinic. With a band put around my head. Or electrodes or something—attached with that sticky stuff. Like, testing my brain." She yawned again. "I'm really tired and I can't think any-more. I feel as if I'm going to fall asleep."

"Of course," I said worriedly. "You didn't sleep well last night."

She nodded. "I just need a nap—I'll curl up like a cat and be ready to go when I wake up."

"You sure?" I asked.

"Yes. Sleep fixes everything," she said.

Inside the maintenance shed were some lifesaving packets, kept aboard the patrol boats. I got one packet and tried to tear it open. The wrapping was too thick, so Matt handed me his Swiss Army knife, and I cut it open. I shook out the thin red blanket that was inside and spread it on the ground under a tree. There were also bottles of water and power bars inside the packet, and we shared them.

Iris nibbled on a power bar, then lay down on the blanket. Within a few minutes she had fallen asleep, and I covered her with another blanket from a second lifesaving pack. I glanced over at Matt and saw him texting. But when our eyes met, he put his phone into his pocket. We walked to the other side of the shed so we could talk and not wake Iris up. We sat really close together, leaning against a pile of lobster pots.

"I haven't known what to say to you for a long time now," he said. "Ever since Eloise disappeared."

"People don't know what to say," I said. "And when they do, I don't want to hear it."

"I'm not exactly 'people,'" he said.

"I know."

The way he was gazing into my eyes made me feel like crying. I'd been on my own with everything until now—Eloise's death, finding Iris in the woods, not knowing what was going to happen next.

Matt's blue eyes reminded me of summer skies. His expression was so warm it pulled me even closer to him, so I was almost leaning against his shoulder. I thought back to one night last September, when we'd started a tennis match. We had played on the old courts at Hubbard's Point, without lights, until well after the sun had gone down. We played through dusk, into the dark, till we couldn't see anything. We were just friends, that's all we were, but it was as if our rackets were magnetized to the ball, or that we were to each other.

I felt that way now.

"Life is hard without her," Matt said.

"For you, too?" I asked, tilting my head to look at him.

"Yeah. She's your sister, and you two did everything together. But your happiness spread to all of us—to me. When I think of you without her . . ."

I waited for him to finish that sentence, but it seemed he couldn't. He cleared his throat and looked away.

"Sometimes I wonder what it's like for you," he said. "Without her here?"

I closed my eyes. These were not the normal questions people, even close friends, asked. People wanted to know how she died, who found her, what they did to her, whether we got a ransom note. They wanted to know the kinds of details you would read about in a mystery novel, or see on a true crime show. This question was different enough that I felt like answering.

"Lots of times I feel her with me," I said. "In certain places."

"Like where?"

"On Dauntless Island. In the Braided Woods. Or at home, sitting on the couch." I touched the back of my wrist, then the back of my neck. "I'll feel something right here, not quite a tickle, more like the lightest breeze moving across my skin. I know it's weird, but I'm sure it's her. I'm not just imagining things."

"I don't think it's weird," Matt said. "I'd be surprised if you didn't feel her nearby. How can she really leave?"

"Because she's dead," I whispered, and hot tears scalded my eyes. In New London, thinking of ghosts, I had known that Eloise was now among them. The sea breeze swirled around us, smelling of salt air, seaweed, and lobsters. The scents of our childhood, my sister's and mine.

"I think she's here right now," Matt said. "Because she knows you need her." He was leaning so close to me, our foreheads almost touching. I felt lightheaded—was he going to kiss me? I thought back to our almost-kiss at Ocean House last summer.

I had wanted to kiss Matt for so long, but my emotions were crashing through me, as if I were a human earthquake. It was all too much; I couldn't help it, I did that hunching thing with my shoulders and my heart. I looked down at his hands.

Matt wore a Turk's head bracelet—we'd all learned how to make them in sailing class a few summers ago. It was a three-strand braid of narrow white cord, woven into a mysterious knot that seemed to have no beginning and no end. Once you made the bracelet and put it on, you secured the strands until they were pretty tight, but loose enough to not cut off circulation. You didn't take it off. You swam with it on, showered with it on, slept with it on.

But Matt saw me looking at it. He tugged on it, working it free, loosening the bracelet enough so he could slide it over his hand. Then he reached for my left hand and slipped it onto my wrist.

"You need this," he said.

"I do?" I asked.

"Yeah," he said. He held my hand, laced his fingers with mine. "It's a talisman. To make sure everything works out."

"Finding Hayley, you mean?" I asked, looking into his blue eyes.

"That and other things," he said softly, squeezing my hand. "You know about the bracelet, right? It's also called a sailor's knot."

Sailor's knot. I felt a shiver run through my body, but in a good way this time. Mariners out on a ship for months at a time used to make sailor's knots for the ones they loved. Then, when they left land and returned to sea again, the bracelet was a romantic reminder that the sailor's love was strong, and absence was only temporary.

"Thank you," I said.

"You don't have to thank me," Matt said. "It's just how it is."

"How it is . . ." I said quietly.

"You know what I mean, right?" he asked.

"I think so," I said. My heart was pounding. His eyes held a secret message. Was I reading it right? Did he feel the same way about me as I felt about him?

"I've wanted to give you the bracelet," he said. "But I never pictured doing it like this." He glanced back toward where Iris was sleeping.

Iris. I wanted this moment to last forever, but we couldn't get off track. I knew, better than anyone, that this situation was life-or-death. I reluctantly pulled my hand away.

"What is our plan?" I asked. It was hard to switch my thoughts from him putting the bracelet on my wrist to plotting our next move.

"We have to call the cops, Oli. No matter what Iris says."

It was amazing how quickly Matt and I went from that incredible moment, in our own little world, into a different mode. I still felt the magic of the bracelet on my wrist, but now we had a job to do—a mission.

"That's what I thought at first," I said. "But Iris convinced me that it would be too dangerous. They swore they'd kill Hayley. She won't even let us take her to a clinic."

Matt took that in. "Let's try to convince her when she wakes up, okay? And meanwhile I'll call Fitch again. If he doesn't pick up, we're driving over to see him. Iris doesn't seem okay to me. It could be an emergency."

"I agree," I said.

I took a breath as Matt pulled out his phone. I touched the bracelet again, and in spite of everything, I felt my entire face beaming in a smile I couldn't begin to hide.

"Good," Matt said. His smile was as big as mine. I loved the space between his front teeth. It was so Matt. His blue eyes locked with mine as he called our friend.

fourteen

Fitch answered, and Matt put him on speaker so I could hear.

"Can you come meet me and Oli and our friend?" Matt asked Fitch. "We're at Osprey Hill."

"I can't right now," Fitch replied, sounding distracted. "I'm in the middle of something and have to finish it."

"We can come pick you up?" Matt offered.

"Normally I'd say yes," Fitch said, "but it's not a good time to come over here."

"Okay," Matt said.

"You know, 'stuff,'" Fitch said, sounding dejected.

I knew there could be lots of reasons why it wasn't "a good time." Was his mother back from her latest trip? Was he trying to spend time with her? Or was it about Abigail?

"Sounds like something is getting to you," Matt said to Fitch. "What's going on?"

"It's no big deal," Fitch said. "Anyway, is your friend okay?"

"That's why I'm calling," Matt said. "We're worried about her. Why don't we pick you up? Get you out of there. And we'd feel better if you saw her."

"Why don't you take her to the ER?" Fitch asked.

"Long story," Matt said. "But that's not going to work."

"You've got me interested," Fitch said. "Sure, come get me. Just give me half an hour to finish up here. That would be excellent."

"Okay, see you soon," Matt said.

Matt and I started walking back toward Iris to wake her up, but she was hurrying toward us from around the maintenance shed. She was wide awake. Her eyes looked so much brighter, and I realized that she had been right, rest was just what she had needed.

"I remember everything!" she said. "Well, almost everything. It came back to me in my sleep. I think it's thanks to Adalyn and her cat."

"What do you mean?" Matt asked.

"I live in the Cat Castle," Iris explained.

"The what?" I asked.

"That's what it's called," Iris explained impatiently. "My parents run a cat sanctuary—they rescue strays from boatyards, city streets. We live in Newport, Rhode Island. Near the waterfront, the docks, and old warehouses."

Newport. A small city, just about an hour away.

"Tell us more," I said excitedly. "Anything might help us know who took you, and why."

"Oh, I know exactly," she said. And she began to talk.

fifteen

"My last name is Bigelow," Iris said. "Iris Cassandra Bigelow. I'm sixteen, Hayley is fourteen, and we come from a family of eighty-five siblings, but we're the only human ones."

"What?" Matt asked.

Iris laughed. "We always joked about it. My parents love animals, especially cats. We live in this old brick warehouse near the waterfront. Half of the building is our home, the other half is the Cat Castle—a refuge for stray cats."

I tried to picture it, and came up with a magical image of sisters and cats and an old brick castle. The three of us—Matt, Iris, and I—stood at the top of the hill, looking out over the harbor, feeling the wind in our hair. It seemed enchanted, a moment out of time.

Iris continued, "Hayley and I grew up with the cats. We learned how to coax shy and terrified feral kittens out of their hiding places. We gave them treats and spent hours petting and talking to them. The oldest ones made us sad—often their owners had died, leaving the cats without anyone to care for them. We would set out heating pads for them and give them extra love." She paused. "We knew that cats grieve like people."

I swallowed hard.

Iris told us that the Cat Castle became known as the place to adopt the friendliest, sweetest, most cuddly cats anywhere. People came from miles around. The Bigelows carefully vetted potential adoptees, making sure they would take good care of the cats and requiring them to agree never to declaw the cats—that was inhumane.

"My parents made the Castle a kind of destination," Iris explained. "It even got written up online. There are lots of cool features in it, like a library—tons of books in one room. My parents pick them up at tag sales and even the Book Barn, near here. The library has chairs and a fireplace, and the cats are allowed to roam free. People come for the cats, but we also let them choose a book to take home."

"That sounds amazing, like a fairy tale," I said.

"It is," she said.

"We have to get you home," I told Iris, reaching for my phone. "Do you remember your parents' number? You can use my phone to call them right now . . ."

"Shhh," Iris said, as if speaking to an agitated child. "You know that's not possible, Oli."

"But—"

"The first thing my parents would do is call the police, and then you know what would happen to Hayley," Iris said. Her lower lip wobbled, and her eyes glittered with tears.

"Maybe you could just text them, to let them know you're alive?" I said. "They must be so worried."

Iris shook her head. "I can't contact them until I know Hayley is okay. Please don't ask again, Oli. If you start me thinking about my parents, I won't be able to do this—to find Hayley and save her."

"Okay," I said quietly.

"Do you get it?" she asked, looking from me to Matt.

Matt nodded. "I do," he said.

"I do, too," I said. "Keep going. What happened the day you were taken?"

"So," Iris said, and she took a deep breath. "You have to understand that as close as Hayley and I are, we are also very different. Her idea of a big Friday night is taking a bubble bath and bringing a basket full of kittens into her room to snuggle up and watch movies."

"And you?" I asked.

"I like going out," Iris said. "Meeting new people. I think it's because I had so much responsibility with the cats. I've been taking care of creatures my whole life, and I want to spread my wings a little. Have adventures."

"There's nothing wrong with that," I said, understanding what it was like to have a lot of responsibility. Sometimes, too much.

"Maybe there is something wrong with it," she said, looking down. "Considering what happened."

I saw her tense up, and I did, too, scared of what was coming.

"Two weeks ago, my parents went away for their anniversary," she said. "They were going to Block Island, and leaving me and Hayley alone. My aunt and uncle live nearby, and they'd check in on us. I was thrilled that my parents would be gone."

"What were you planning?" I asked.

"Just . . . being free. They said they were closing the Castle for the weekend so we didn't have to deal with strangers. But that was what I was looking forward to—seeing people."

"What do you mean?" Matt asked.

"I'd been dating this guy, Andy. Well, nothing serious, but we'd sort of started hanging out, and I thought . . ." She trailed off for a few seconds. "But then I found out he was seeing a girl from another school."

"Ouch," I said.

"Yeah, exactly. So I was like, we're done. As soon as I changed toward him, he was suddenly texting me all the time, interested again, but there was no way I could trust him after that. I was really down about the whole thing. So I figured, it was a weekend, I'd keep the Castle open, stay busy, and hopefully meet some nice people. Distract myself from thinking about him."

"Even though your parents didn't want you to keep the Castle open," I said.

"Yep," she said. "They hung the CLOSED sign on the door, but as soon they left, I gave Hayley a wicked look. 'While the parents are away,' I said, and I turned the sign back to OPEN. Hayley was so mad at me. She hates when I break the rules. It really bothers her."

"But you opened, anyway?" Matt asked.

Iris nodded. "We headed into the cattery to make sure everyone had enough food and water, and to check on the cats who had had medical procedures and were wearing cones. Almost all of them were napping, either in patches of sunlight or under shelves or in little houses, or in the library."

"And someone showed up?" I asked.

"Yes. He did," Iris said.

She explained how her dad had built a cool feature—an outdoor play yard surrounded by a chain-link fence. The cats could enter it from the Castle, and the yard, full of real grass, was fenced on the other three sides and even above so they couldn't escape. The Bigelows required everyone who adopted a cat to sign a document agreeing to keep the cats inside—to protect them from predators, animals that hunted along the docks, in the dumpsters. To keep them from being hit by cars. To save them from being picked up by terrible people who would harm them.

That afternoon, Hayley and Iris went into the fenced yard to check on the ten or so cats lounging in the sun.

"Right away," Iris said, "I spotted a guy about my age crouched down outside the fence. He was playing with two gray tiger kittens, dangling a string between the slats in the fence. He was really cute, in a brainy sort of way."

"The string," I said. "That was part of what you first remembered. How could you tell he was brainy?"

She thought about it. "He was wearing a Brown University T-shirt, and these glasses that kept slipping down his nose—he reminded me of a boy at my school who's in AP Calculus."

"What did he do?" I asked.

"He just stayed there, playing with the kittens. Hayley got nervous right away. She whispered to me, 'He's weird.' But I didn't think so. And I thought of Andy, and how glad I was that there was a cute boy here . . . He asked me my name."

"And you told him."

"I did." She swallowed hard. "And then he said something that made me suspicious. I should have walked away from him, but I ignored the warning sign. I just kept thinking of Andy, how hurt I was."

"What warning sign?" Matt asked.

"He knew my last name."

"Couldn't he have figured that out because of the Cat Castle? If it was online? He'd heard about your family?" I asked.

"Yeah, and that's what I figured. Hayley was mad at me for talking to him, so she stormed into the Castle. Left me alone in the yard. There was a fence between me and the guy. I saw him watch her go. But we were just talking and he seemed cool."

I felt nervous, waiting for whatever she would say next.

"He said he had driven over from Connecticut, that it was really great to meet us. He said he was an animal person. He said he loved cats. I guess I felt flattered because he just stayed there, talking for the longest time, acting as if he liked me. He kept reaching through the fence to play with this little yellow kitten, and I started to think . . ."

"That you'd let him in," I said.

Iris nodded. "Yes."

"And did you?" I asked, feeling almost sick, knowing that she could have stopped it right there.

She nodded. "I told him to go around the front of the building, but he pointed at a door in the fence. We only use it to get to the dumpster in the alley. But he asked if he could just come in that way."

"So you unlocked the fence door," I said.

"As soon as he came in . . ." She paused. "He said, 'I know you have a security camera in front. Do you have them here, too?' Looking around, he asked, 'So you can watch the kitties from inside?' I knew the question was bizarre, but I answered him, anyway. I told him no, we didn't."

My stomach clenched—I wished she had lied to him. It might have scared him away if he thought he was on video.

"I knew right away I'd made the biggest mistake. His face changed completely. His eyes turned black—that might sound crazy, but they did. He went from being so friendly to looking like a monster. He told me to get Hayley. I said no. He pulled out a hypodermic needle, held it to my neck. 'If you don't get her, she'll find your dead body out here. And when she finds it, I'll do the same to her.'"

I felt horror wondering how close her experience was to what had happened to Eloise.

"He kept talking," Iris went on. He said, 'You're perfect. Two perfect sisters, exactly what I need. AB negative—did you know there's a registry? You're both in the database. Now, be good and get Hayley.'"

"And you did?" I asked.

Now it was as if Iris was in a trance. She recounted the rest, and I was numb, listening.

"'Get your sister,' he said. 'We're going to do it quickly and calmly. There are rules. Rule number one: You can't scream. Rule number two: You can't call the police. NO POLICE. If I see or hear police, you die, she dies, and so do your parents. Everything you do from now on will make a difference, Iris. The difference will be whether you and Hayley stay alive. It's up to you. You're the big sister. Her life is in your hands.'

"'What would you do to her?' I asked, terrified by his words and by the look in his eyes.

"'The same thing I did to Eloise Parrish. You probably heard about her. The girl who's missing, down in Connecticut? It's all over the news.'

"I'd read about Eloise online—there were reels and TikToks of Eloise with her friends; her sister, Oli; and the grandmother they lived with.

"'What did you do to Eloise?' I asked.

"'You don't want to find out,' he said, still holding the needle to my neck.

"So I did what he asked. I called Hayley to come out. He immediately grabbed us both and shoved us into his blue van. He was so strong, it was scary. Hayley and I jumped on him—we fought him, knocked him down. He hit the floor hard, and while he was down there, we tried to open the van doors—but we couldn't unlock them. There were childproof locks. Something a kidnapper would use to keep victims from escaping.

"When he got back up, he said he wouldn't forget that we'd attacked him. He said we'd pay for it. He put zip ties on our wrists and ankles, wrapped scarves around our eyes. *Hayley and I both kept screaming, trying to escape, but no one heard us. We had made him angry. I heard him jab Hayley's arm with the needle first. Then he did the same to me. It hurt, and that was the last thing I remembered until the van stopped—something partly woke me up—the sound of the brakes, I guess. And being dragged out, lifted up, made me less groggy. I felt myself being carried up all those stairs. I wound up next to Hayley in a room with panels painted with three classical-looking girls in white gowns, with dead birds hovering overhead. I didn't know then, but eventually I learned it was an attic.*"

When Iris finished talking, I realized my hands were fists. My nails had dug into my palms. Tears were running down my cheeks. I bowed my head, thinking of Eloise. I felt Matt touch my shoulder. I squeezed my eyes tight, wanting to press the images out of my head. I stood there on the hill in Pequod, overwhelmed by grief and anger.

"Do you remember anything after that?" Matt asked Iris. "What happened in the attic? How you ended up in the woods?"

Iris shook her head. "Not yet. It's still fuzzy. But I think it will all come back soon." She drew in a big breath. "Let's go."

"To Newport?" I asked her, opening my eyes. "Home?"

Iris shook her head. "I want to go straight back to the ghost signs and do what we said we'd do before—knock on those doors until we find someone who knows what they mean. Those sibyls are the answer to where Hayley is."

"We can pick up Fitch on the way," Matt said.

"We don't have time," Iris said. "Please, let's go to the ghost signs now. I appreciate how much you're helping me, Matt, but I have to do this my way. It's my sister. I got her into this, and I need to get her out right away, before he does something worse."

"What about the blue van we saw?" I asked. "You sure you want to go back there?"

"If it gets me closer to Hayley, I'll do anything," she said.

So we worked out a plan: Matt would drop us in downtown New London, and he would head to Black Hall to pick up Fitch. Then he'd return to New London to meet me and Iris near the ghost signs.

There was a lot to be said for following the rules. When life is so unpredictable, and you start losing the things—and people—you love most, obeying the rules provides a certain stability and safety factor.

Ever since finding Iris, the rules had been saying I should call Detective Tyrone, take Iris to the ER. But this time I was one hundred percent following my gut. Hearing what the kidnapper had said about the police, knowing that he was capable of carrying through with violence, convinced me that Iris was right. The police hadn't found any clues about what had happened to Eloise, and already Iris, Matt, and I were unspooling Iris's story—which would lead us to her sister, and to answers about mine.

As Matt drove us back to New London, I felt my strength and confidence building. Instead of just sitting around being sad, feeling helpless, waiting for the authorities to solve these crimes, we were on our own trail to find the truth.

We pulled onto the service road and stopped in front of the Sibylline sisters' ghost sign. Matt and I gazed at each other. He looked at my hand, as if he wanted to touch it. And he did, just lightly.

"I'll hurry," he said. "It'll take me about half an hour to drive from here to Black Hall and back."

"Great," I said, getting out of the car. "See you then."

He took off, and Iris and I began walking. She glanced at the dusty blue van as we passed it. Her posture stiffened, but she didn't say anything this time. There was no turning back.

The cobblestones were uneven—they had probably been there for over a hundred years—and I nearly twisted my ankle. There were a few back doors in the crumbling wall. I tried to open some, but they were nailed shut, as if they hadn't been used in a long time. A walkway angled up the slight hill from dockside toward the street, and we took it.

Most of the old maritime establishments had given way to more modern businesses. Instead of sailmakers and chandleries, we found a florist, a jewelry shop, a coffee bar, and a bookstore. The only name I recognized from one of the ghost signs was the Barquentine Pub, "established in 1850" in small print below it.

Iris and I entered the pub. Along the walls were port-and-starboard ship lanterns, glowing red and green. There was a wooden plaque adorned with sailors' knots—bowline, sheepshank, monkey's fist, square knot, clove hitch, and Turk's head—like the bracelet Matt had given me. The wall was also covered with black-and-white photos of other venerable seaside buildings, including a beach pavilion in Black Hall, a row of shingled cottages, and the Miramar—an old Victorian hotel in Silver Bay. That hotel had always seemed so romantic to me, the corridors and cupola filled with a hundred years' worth of stories.

The pub was empty, but then again, it was between lunch and dinner. Iris hovered near the front window—she was keeping watch, which let me know that in spite of what she had said, she was still worried about the blue van.

"Hello!" I called out, walking farther into the restaurant. "Anybody here?"

A door in the back swung open, and a girl in a waitress uniform stepped through. She was about sixteen, with long black hair in two braids. I didn't know her—she definitely didn't go to Black Hall High.

"May I help you?" she asked.

"Yes," I said. "But it's kind of a weird question."

She gave a half smile. "My favorite kind."

"It has to do with the fading signs behind this building," I said.

"Those signs have been there for nearly a hundred years," she said proudly. "This restaurant's been in my family for generations, and my parents run it now. The town council always wants the businesses here to paint that wall, make it look new, but we'll never do that. It's part of the waterfront's heritage. I'm Sirena, by the way."

"I'm Oli," I said. "That's Iris." I gestured toward the front of the pub where Iris still stood looking out the window.

"So, what's your weird question?" Sirena asked.

"It's about the painting of the three women," Iris called from up front. "The *Sibylline Sisters: Oracles, 1944.*"

Sirena laughed. "Of course. People always come in here to ask about that sign. Then they stay for a chowder or a plate of calamari. You want to order, by the way?"

"Uh, we don't have time," I said, because I could see Iris getting impatient and agitated. "We'd just like to find out whatever you can tell us about that sign."

Sirena nodded. "I know all about it because of my friend, Minerva Morelock. In Greek mythology, sibyls—oracles—were mediums. They made predictions and gave advice."

"We don't need a definition of oracles," I said, knowing I sounded a little short but not caring too much. "We need to know who the women in the painting were."

"They were three sisters," Sirena said. "Just like the sign says."

"Were they really oracles?" Iris asked.

"Yep," Sirena said, seeming to revel in telling the story. "Sailors are very superstitious. This is a maritime town—ships coming and going, from all around the world. Navy, fishermen, smugglers.

Sailors could be gone from their families for months at a time. And they wanted to know things: Would they return alive, would their wives wait for them, would they have success and come home rich?"

"What does that have to do with the three sisters?" I asked.

"Well, according to Minerva, the three sisters were able to tell fortunes," Sirena said. "In fact, we've capitalized on the fortune-telling legend. We've learned how to read the tarot—Minerva's actually good at it—and sometimes my parents hire mediums to come into the pub with their crystal balls. Brings in customers like you wouldn't believe!"

I wondered who this "Minerva" was, but I didn't want to interrupt Sirena until she was finished talking.

"So, the sisters had second sight—an ability to see into the future," Sirena went on. "They traveled up and down the East Coast, appearing on stages, in theaters, even in taverns like this, drawing huge crowds who would pay a lot of money to learn their futures."

"And the sisters came here?" I asked. "To this pub? Did they perform in New London?" I looked around; the tavern seemed small, hardly large enough to hold a crowd.

"Well," Sirena said. "That's what Minerva says. She has a great-aunt who's, like, a hundred, and she's somehow related to the Sibylline sisters. Apparently the sisters lived upstairs in this building for a while, but then they moved somewhere else. There was some kind of family tragedy."

"Tragedy?" I asked.

"Yeah," Sirena said, and I noticed her flinch. "Poor Minerva. She carries the weight of it. Even though it didn't happen to her personally, she feels the old trauma."

That pierced my heart—I thought about losing my parents, and Eloise. I knew what it was to carry the weight of family trauma.

"Have you ever seen other paintings of the sisters?" I asked, desperate to learn more.

"Apparently some exist," Sirena said. "But Minerva would know more about that."

"We need to meet Minerva," I said. "Right away."

"Yes," Iris said, trembling so hard her voice shook. "Where is she?"

"That's easy," Sirena said. "Her shop is right next door. Mermaid's Pearls. You can't miss it."

sixteen

We thanked Sirena and hurried into Mermaid's Pearls, the jewelry store next to the pub. It was narrow and long. No one was at the front counter, but we noticed a girl sitting on a tall stool at a workbench in back. She had wavy red hair and wore a shimmery blue-green sundress, the color of a mermaid's tail.

"Excuse me, are you Minerva?" I called.

"I sure am! Hello, mermaids!" she said, beaming and beckoning us toward her workstation.

"I'm Oli, she's Iris. Do you own the store?" I asked, thinking she looked too young for that. She was not much older than Iris and me.

"My great-aunt is the owner," she said. "But I've been an apprentice here forever. Can I help you?"

"Do you make the jewelry?" Iris asked.

"Yes," she said. "A lot of it."

I looked in the glass case and couldn't help but be dazzled by the rings and charms in there. Each one was a miniature canvas for enamel paintings set in fields of diamonds: a white owl, a pearlescent cat with wings, a silvery mermaid, and one that really caught my eye—a tiny white witch flying through fog, just the suggestion of mist on the face of a gold charm barely larger than a dime. The sight of it made me shiver.

"You like that one?" Minerva asked, leaning over next to me.

"It's beautiful," I said, frowning because even though I said *beautiful*, that's not what I felt. My mind was swirling. The witch made me think of something evil that I couldn't quite define.

"Thank you," Minerva said. "She's my favorite. When you live by the waterfront here, you see lots of sea witches."

I glanced up, thinking she had to be kidding, but when I looked into her eyes, in spite of a friendly glint, she seemed dead serious.

"We're actually looking for sibyls, not witches," I said.

"The Sibylline oracles?" Minerva asked. "From the sign out back? A lot of people come in here with questions about it."

"That's what Sirena said," Iris said.

"Ah, I wondered how you knew my name." Minerva nodded. "Is this for a school project? Or are you just into art, history, the waterfront?"

"We need to find out about the sibyls. Especially about the other paintings of them," I said, avoiding the question directly. "Sirena said the sibyls were distant relatives of yours."

"They sure are," Minerva said. "Three badass sisters who also happened to be oracles. It fires my imagination to think of being related to them. They're actually the inspiration for the sea witch design. I immortalize them in precious metals and enamel. I make talismans. And they inspire me to throw the tarot, and to work on my powers . . ."

I heard Minerva's words, but instead of looking at her, I was staring into her showcase. I felt mesmerized, as if I was under a spell—a lost memory making my legs feel liquid, like I might sink to the floor. Eloise was here, I felt her with me. What was she trying to tell me? *Family trauma*, I heard my sister say, and I silently thanked her.

"Sirena mentioned a tragedy," I said, looking back at Minerva. "She said you carry its weight."

Minerva didn't speak for a long moment. She regarded me with cool eyes, as if deciding whether to tell me or not. "Weight. That's an interesting word. I suppose it's apt. A burden. See, the sisters passed down a gene. It affects some of the women in my family." She took a deep breath. "Some of my relatives call it 'a curse.'"

"I'm sorry," I said.

"Don't be. I choose to give it a positive power. The gene adds to how special the Sibylline sisters were. I think of it as a spell, a kind of scientific magic. In fact, I think it's the key to their clairvoyance. Possibly to mine. Definitely to my great-aunt's."

Do science and magic go together? I wondered.

"It sounds evil," Iris said. "And there *is* evil in the world. I know it."

"I don't think of it that way," Minerva said. "I choose to concentrate on the beauty, their talents, the way the sisters shone their light into the world. I don't like to think of that darkness."

I glanced at my phone to see what time it was. Forty minutes had passed, and Matt would be coming back soon.

"Minerva," Iris said. Her voice was shaking, and I could see the emotion on her face. "I've seen other paintings of the sibyls. Panels. In an attic."

Minerva's eyes widened. "How do you know about those?"

Iris gasped. "So you've seen them, too? This is so important, Minerva—it's actually life-and-death."

"Life-and-death?" Minerva asked, frowning.

"*Murder*," Iris said. "It already happened once. To Oli's sister."

I heard the words, but once again, I was drawn to the image of that white witch. And suddenly, all the fog lifted, the swirls of worry and urgency, the quest to find Hayley. I thought of the gold dust sprinkled amid the dry leaves and dirt that had covered Iris's face. I reached into my pocket, and my hand closed around the charm I had found at my sister's and Iris's burial spot.

The tiny enameled gold disc with—not a white witch, but a ghost girl—so delicately painted on it.

And I knew, at that moment, that the charm I'd found in the Braided Woods had been made right here, by the girl standing in front of me. By Minerva.

seventeen

I had to stay calm, not freak out, not give Minerva any clue that I knew her charms were somehow connected to the girls' disappearances, to my sister's murder.

"*Murder?*" Minerva asked, echoing Iris.

"Yes!" Iris said. "A girl was murdered. And my sister could be next. She and I were kidnapped by some boy. He left me for dead in the woods, and he still has my sister."

Minerva looked completely shocked.

"And the panels," Iris went on. "With the oracles on them. They're in the attic where my sister's being held."

"This is too weird," Minerva said, holding her head in her hands. "I have to think about this." She began to pace.

"Well, think fast," Iris said. "I have to find Hayley!"

"And can you tell us everything you know, about the panels or the oracles?" I asked Minerva, striving to keep my voice even.

"It all goes back to the Sibylline sisters," Minerva said. "When the gene began to affect them, they needed treatment. So they moved into a boardinghouse, kind of like a health spa. A center of magic."

"More spells?" I asked, my hand closed tight around the charm.

"Yes, in a way," Minerva said. "Magic combined with medicine, at least according to my great-aunt. Because she was there for it."

"Do the spells involve gold dust?" I asked sharply. "Or charms? Like the ones you make? *Talismans?*"

"What are you talking about?" Minerva asked, taking a step toward me.

"Where is the boardinghouse?" Iris asked, not noticing the drama brewing between me and Minerva.

"Not far from here. Silver Bay," Minerva said to Iris while continuing to stare at me. "It's very noticeable. Victorian, with gingerbread around the porch and windows, and a big cupola on top. Our family actually owns it."

My heart skipped—that sounded like the Miramar, the old hotel in the photo on the pub wall. The Miramar was right on the Silver Bay waterfront, four stories high, so I was sure there had to be an attic. If that was the boardinghouse where the sisters had stayed, maybe it was also where the panels were located—and where Hayley was now.

I glanced outside. As soon as Matt and Fitch arrived, I'd ask Matt to drive us straight to the Miramar. I grabbed Iris's wrist, ready to pull her out of the store, onto the street.

But Iris dug her heels in and turned toward Minerva.

"Do you know someone named Gale?" Iris asked.

"No, not that I can think of," Minerva said.

"Whose blue van is that out back?" Iris asked.

"It belongs to our family foundation. My cousin drives it mostly. Why do you ask?"

Family foundation. The words sent a shiver down my back, but why? Something was connecting for me, but I couldn't reach it. *Sisters, needing treatment . . .*

Minerva stepped forward and touched my shoulder.

"Something shifted with you," she said to me. "What is it? Did I say something to upset you?"

I didn't reply. I just pulled my hand out of my pocket, opened my fist to show her the charm. She stared at it, bending close. She lifted it gently from my palm.

"Not that one," she whispered, unable to take her eyes off it. "Please, not that one . . ."

Before I could ask her what she meant, I heard a horn outside—it was Matt's Jeep. Iris and I ran to the door, stepped onto the street. I couldn't wait to get to the Miramar. My questions for Minerva about the charm could wait.

I saw Matt at the wheel, Fitch in the passenger seat. I grabbed the back handle as Fitch jumped out and accidently bumped the door, closing it behind him. He had on his black-rimmed glasses, and he wore a Yale cap.

"Hi, Oli," he said. Then he glanced at Iris and he looked startled, like he'd seen a ghost.

That's when I noticed that Iris was backing away. She looked terrified.

"Iris?" Fitch said.

"Guess Matt told you her name," I said.

"That's not how he knows it," Iris said. "That's him! He's the one who has Hayley and tried to kill me!"

eighteen

Time froze, and so did we. I stared at Iris.

"It's him! I know those glasses, I recognize his voice!" she said, her voice rising. "He's the one who kidnapped us!" She was almost babbling, in shock, trying to convince me.

So much happened during the next few moments:

Fitch lunged toward Iris and grabbed her by both arms.

Iris struggled away from him.

I shoved Fitch as hard as I could, kicked him in the shins, and screamed for Matt.

Matt did nothing—it was as if he didn't hear me. The Jeep doors were closed—but he was right *there*, in the driver's seat. I saw him staring down at his phone, completely ignoring my cry for help. Was he pretending he didn't hear it?

Fitch had lost his balance when I'd pushed him, and my kick had tripped him right off the curb. I pulled Iris away and the two of us ran as fast as we could down the alley toward the river. I knew it would take Fitch only a few seconds before he and—unbelievably—Matt came after us.

When we rounded the corner onto the service road, I looked wildly for a place to hide. A row of large rocks lay atop a seawall that slanted down to the water—but it was too wide open and visible. There was the spot tucked off the road where the blue van was parked.

I heard tires on the cobblestones. Maybe it was a stranger's car, or maybe it was Matt's Jeep, but it would round the corner in just a few seconds, and my strongest survival instincts kicked in. There was that row of ancient wooden doors in the brick wall, next to one of the ghost signs. I had tried a few earlier and they were nailed shut. They all looked as if they hadn't been opened in years. I rattled the rusty knob on one. No luck, it was locked, but the lock felt loose, and the door was splintery.

This wasn't my property. I knew I was doing something wrong, but I rammed the door with my shoulder once, twice. It hurt, but I did it again, and this time the door creaked open. I grabbed Iris's hand, pulled her into the dark space, and shut the door behind us. It smelled musty, as if it had been closed off for years. I realized we were in a damp and chilly cellar.

The only light came through cracks in the door, and there were cobwebs everywhere. They clung to my face and arms; I felt a spider in my hair. An animal scuttled across the floor, claws scrabbling on the cement. I held my screams inside and stood right against the door, my eye pressed to the slit in the old wood.

How was it possible that Fitch had taken Iris? And Eloise? *My friend Fitch?*

The terror I was feeling was not only because of that. *Matt* had been tricking me. Matt was involved in taking and hurting girls— hurting Eloise.

Killing Eloise.

Now the sound of the tires was louder. I heard the vehicle bumping over the cobblestones, getting closer. I peered out, and I saw Matt's Jeep drive past very slowly. The brakes squealed, the Jeep stopped, and I heard one door open. Male voices spoke quietly to each other.

"They ran down here," Fitch was saying.

"Well, I don't see them," came that voice, Matt's voice, that had always lifted my heart, made me tingle, and now made my eyes burn with tears.

"We have to find them," Fitch said. "Iris was acting irrational. That's a sure sign of a head injury."

"Definitely," Matt said. "Let's split up and look for them."

I was still staring out the narrow crack. I couldn't see clearly, but there was a glitter of water in the harbor, the shadow of a passing ship, and, then, Matt. He walked one way down the service road, stopped right in front of the ghost sign depicting the Sibylline sisters. Then he turned and walked back in the other direction—as if he was pacing.

"Oli," he called out. "Can you hear me? Oli, please talk to me—this doesn't make any sense. I need to find you!"

Of course I didn't answer. But my heart hurt at the sound of his voice, and I was filled with longing for how it used to be—or how I had thought it was, just a few minutes ago.

"He's right there," Iris whispered in my ear.

"I know. Shhh," I whispered back.

I didn't want to believe it. Matt? *My* Matt? And *Fitch*? Sweet, smart Fitch?

I looked at Iris. I wanted to doubt that she could have recognized Fitch on the street just now. But his reaction upon seeing her—the way he had grabbed for her—made it obvious that she was right. He had been her captor.

But even without all that, I knew. In that instant, all the clues I'd been trying to put together came to the surface. Minerva's mention of the family foundation: the Agassiz Foundation. The one Fitch was a member of. Fitch, the cousin who drove the blue van.

"Oli," Matt called again. "Oli!" Then, more as if he was talking to himself instead of me, "Where did you go?"

I heard him walking on the cobblestones. He headed one way, then the other. But now I wondered if he wasn't pacing: Maybe he was a hunter stalking his prey.

I had never felt like prey being hunted, before. Especially not by Matt.

After a few minutes, the sound of his footsteps receded. He had left the service road. For now.

"I think he's gone," Iris whispered. "Should we go out?"

"We can't chance that," I said, my throat aching with the tears I was holding inside.

Iris nodded. "Fitch and Matt . . . they must be working together," she whispered.

I didn't want to hear it. My head and my heart were not in sync. I'd been feeling so happy, for the first time since Eloise died. Matt had brought me out of that terrible place. But now I felt despair. I thought of all the times in the last hours that I'd seen Matt on his phone—probably texting Fitch. The bracelet he had given me felt like a snake around my wrist. I tried to rip it off, but he had pulled the knot too tight.

The math of it all was adding up to pure horror. If Iris recognized Fitch as her kidnapper, and if he had tried to capture her again just minutes ago, and if Matt was driving him—with him even now, trying to get us—then the sum of it all meant that Matt might have helped take Eloise. I felt as if I was going to be sick.

My phone vibrated—it was Matt calling. I just stared at the screen. I wanted so badly to answer, to hear his voice tell me I'd made a mistake, misinterpreted what I'd seen, and that I could trust him after all. But I kept replaying the scene on the street, Fitch grabbing for Iris, Matt doing nothing. I waited to see if he left a voicemail, but he didn't. He texted.

Oli, where are you?

My fingers twitched, wanting to reply. Should I do it, see his response? Finally, I decided I had to try.

What are you doing? I texted.

Looking for you! Where are you?

Where's Fitch? I asked.

He's looking for you, too. Why are you acting like this? Matt wrote.

He's bad, Matt.

WHAT? he asked.

143

Fitch's the one who took Iris and Hayley, I wrote. Are you in it with him?

Oli, that's INSANE!!! Matt said.

I started typing a reply, but then another text came in—but it wasn't from Matt.

It was from Fitch.

Oli, don't listen to Iris. She's delusional. That can happen with a head injury, with brain trauma.

I didn't reply, then Fitch texted again:

You could be in danger with her. She's lying to you, and we don't know what she's capable of. From what Matt tells me, her sister is being held somewhere—or is she? Is there really a sister? Matt and I are waiting for you. Come find us. Please. We'll get Iris the help she needs.

A few seconds later, Matt texted again:

Fitch explained everything to me, how Iris is totally unhinged. Come out and find us—I'm so worried about you.

I wanted to believe him. More than anything, I wanted that.

The basement was pitch-dark. Iris was standing against the wall. I gazed at her through the darkness. I had to ask myself: How well did I know her? I had met her just yesterday. What if Fitch was right, and she was unwell? I knew that trauma could cause changes in personality and behavior.

Had she made everything up? Or what if *she* was evil—the person behind what had happened to my sister?

I felt a quick rush of relief and told myself, *Matt's not involved, he's on my side.*

But then I remembered finding Iris in the grave, the same one where my sister's body had been found. I could still see Iris's panic, the terror in her eyes. I had pulled her out of that fissure in the rock. I had seen the cut on her head, the scrapes on her arms and legs, the mud and leaves caked onto her skin.

And I knew for sure: Iris wasn't making anything up.

She had not climbed into that grave herself. Someone else had buried her there. And held her prisoner.

Fitch. She had recognized him. He had tried to kill her just as he had killed Eloise.

And maybe Matt had helped him.

"Let's try to find the stairs," I whispered to Iris. We inched away from the sliver of light slanting through the crack in the door. Even though I was afraid of what I might touch, of what bugs or mice might be hiding in the dark cellar, I felt my way along the walls. My fingers traced brick and stone. If we could find the stairs, we could climb up to street level—and escape the building when we were sure Matt and Fitch were gone.

I stumbled and fell, banging my knee against something sharp. It was the corner of a box, and when I felt around, I realized it was one of several. I pulled the lid off one, and even though the darkness was almost total, there was just enough light from the broken door to illuminate pots of enamel.

Suddenly, I knew where we were—directly below Minerva's jewelry shop. And I had the feeling the ghosts of sea witches and sibyls were encircling us.

"Over here, Oli," Iris whispered. "The stairs."

I went toward the sound of her voice, then hesitated. I remembered Minerva's face when I showed her the charm I'd found at the grave. I could hear her whisper: *Not that one . . . please, not that one.* She hadn't denied knowing what it was, or that she had made it. Would she hurt us? Was she involved?

I felt trapped between two hunters, both of them after us. Which one was worse?

I decided Iris and I had a better chance against Minerva. My heart was pounding as we climbed one story up the stairs. We opened the door at the top and stepped into the back of the bright store.

Minerva was sitting at the counter, and I saw her jump when she heard the door hinges creak. Her brow was furrowed, and she narrowed her lips, as if unsure of what to say to us. Then, finally, "You ran out so fast." She held out her hand, and I saw the charm. "You left this behind."

Iris walked toward her. I hung back. My eyes were on the plate glass window in front, monitoring for the Jeep. It wasn't there. Matt and Fitch must have been driving around, looking for us.

Minerva's expression turned to alarm when she had the chance to get a good look at us. "Yikes, you're covered with spiderwebs."

She reached beneath the bench and handed us each a white muslin towel.

Iris and I wiped off the dust and cobwebs; I hoped I'd brushed away the spider I'd felt, too.

"What were you doing down there?" Minerva asked, holding the charm out toward me again.

"I'll tell you if you tell me about that," I said, without taking it.

"I'm just surprised you have it. I gave it to someone and . . . well, I wouldn't have expected it to wind up with you or anyone else. It's kind of precious, at least to me. How did you get it?"

I wanted to blurt it all out, tell her that I had found it next to the crevice where my sister and Iris had been discarded like trash. From the way Minerva stood so tensely, eyes burning into mine, I knew she was waiting for an explanation. But I was jostled by Iris as she ran past us to the shop's front window. She peered out, scanning the street where we had encountered Matt and Fitch in the Jeep, where Fitch had tried to grab her.

I stood frozen next to Minerva.

"Aren't you going to tell me?" Minerva asked. "I made this piece. Don't you think I deserve to know?"

"Here they come again," Iris said, shrinking away from the glass.

"Who? What's going on?" Minerva asked. She walked to the window, stood staring at the street.

"Don't let them know we're here," Iris said in a begging tone.

I crouched behind the counter. From there I had a clear view as Matt's Jeep slowly passed by. I could see him at the wheel, Fitch beside him. Fitch's glasses glinted in the afternoon light.

"Oh," Minerva said. "That's my cousin Fitch." She waved, and from my hiding place—peering over the counter—I saw Fitch wave back. He said something to Matt, and the Jeep halted. Fitch opened the door and got out. I knew he was going to enter the shop, and I had only a few seconds to convince her.

"Minerva," I said. "Please let us hide. Don't tell Fitch we're here. I'll explain."

"Wait," Minerva said, eyes wide. "Did Fitch give you the charm?"

"I think he dropped it," I said. "And I found it."

"Oh my God," Minerva said. "You don't have to explain, things are actually making sense. I'll tell you why after I get rid of him." She pointed at a closet, and both Iris and I scrambled inside. It was full— a mop and a bucket and shelves of jewelry-making supplies. I eased Iris behind a tall stack of boxes and held my breath, afraid we might jostle a box or jar or make a noise. The door didn't close tightly, so we had air. We could hear everything.

"Hey, cuz," Fitch said as he entered the store.

"Well, if it isn't the wannabe doctor," Minerva said. "What are you cooking up in your lab these days?"

"Not much," he said. "Listen, have you seen . . ."

"You mean the cure is out of reach? No Nobel Prize for you this year?" she asked with a sharp edge in her tone.

"Minerva, I've apologized for hurting you that time," he said.

"I should have told someone," she said. "My parents, your parents. I could have called the cops on you, Fitch."

"I told you I was sorry!"

"Are you doing it to other people?" she asked.

"Of course not! It was a mistake, I told you. Just leave it, will you? This is important. I'm looking for two girls who probably came in here," he said, and I heard him describe me and Iris.

"Nope," she said. "Haven't seen them."

"They were standing right out front twenty minutes ago," he said.

"I told you, no one like that has come in today. What do you want them for?" she asked.

"One is very sick, on the edge of a breakdown. The other is my friend's girlfriend."

At the word *girlfriend*, I couldn't help it, but my heart jumped. Did Matt think of me that way? How could I still feel excited when I knew Matt might be behind my sister's death? I felt guilty and ridiculous for it, so I shut that feeling right down.

"Well, I'll keep my eyes open for them," Minerva said.

"Okay," Fitch said. "Text me if you see them."

"I will," she said. Then, "How's your sister?"

"She's not doing well," Fitch said. "More episodes."

"Well, give her my love," Minerva said. "My little cousin Abby-Gale."

I exchanged a look with Iris. Gale. Abby-Gale. Abigail.

And now more things began to click for me. Fitch's sister, Abigail, who had had a seizure and had to leave school. The illness that had affected the Sibylline sisters, the disease that ran in the family. Related elements, falling into place.

"Listen, I need some dust, and the keys," Fitch said.

"The keys, fine," Minerva said. I heard her open a drawer and the jingle of keys as she handed them to him.

"Now the magic dust," he said.

"Go away, Fitch," Minerva said. "It's valuable, and I need it for my work."

He laughed. "You're here only because Daphne is subsidizing you. You're her little favorite. If you won't give it to me, I'll just take it."

I heard his footsteps getting closer. He opened the closet door, and light poured in.

nineteen

Iris and I shrank farther into the shadow of the boxes. I could see Fitch reach up to the highest shelf, grab a jar. As he did, gold dust sprinkled down on us. It tickled my nose, and I nearly exploded, holding a sneeze inside.

He closed the closet door behind him.

"You know, cuz," he said. "Your attitude is really disturbing."

"My attitude?" Minerva asked.

"You know I need this for my work. My research. It's integral to finding the cure."

"Gold dust, Fitch?" Minerva asked. "Have you been reading the old tome? Daphne's magic spells? I thought you were the scientist of the family. How would your mother feel to know you've forsaken medicine for soothsaying?"

"Shut up, Minerva. Leave my mother out of it," Fitch said, and I heard anger building in his voice.

"Doctor Constance Martin," Minerva said. "You could have made her proud."

"I *do* make her proud," he said.

"Right. By telling people you're going to find a cure. But Fitch, you're really just trying to reverse the curse. Good old Sibylline magic. Here you are, stealing the dust I sweep off my workbench.

The ore, the spent tailings, the leftover grindings of all that precious gold . . . for what? For a new spell? Next you'll be wanting wool of bat and eye of newt."

Fitch muttered something, and I heard the shop door slam behind him. I strained to hear, finally letting myself sneeze as the Jeep revved and drove away.

"He's gone," Minerva said, letting us out of the closet.

"Why did you say I didn't have to explain about Fitch, that you get it?" I asked her.

"Because he's obsessed, in a way that hurts people," she said. "He's brilliant, but he's got problems. He's so focused on this 'cure,' but it's just as much about proving himself to his mother."

I knew that part, about his mother, but until I'd learned all these unfolding truths, it had just made me feel sorry for Fitch—a kid worried about his sister, whose mom left them alone too much.

Minerva took a deep breath. "I love my Aunt Constance, but she's so preoccupied. In a way it's understandable, dealing with the gene that only affects the women of our family. Daphne—our great-aunt—says it's like the Sword of Damocles."

There were songs about the Sword of Damocles. My parents had a record where someone sang about the sword about to fall. But it was the Greek parable that affected me most: a deadly weapon hanging over your head. You might escape it forever, or it could crash down at any moment. Like an evil monster hovering above, biding his time, deciding whether to take you or not.

"So all of you have the gene, but not everyone gets the disease?" I asked.

"Yes," Minerva said. "And we don't know who it will hit—whose gene will mutate into the full-blown disease. That's the thing about Abigail. She's had the antibodies for a long time, but the disease didn't manifest till she was almost a teenager."

"It's progressed?" Iris asked.

Minerva nodded. "Every night she's at risk of dying," she said.

That stabbed my heart. I ached to think of anyone losing their sister. But what part did kidnapping girls play in Fitch's search for a cure?

"Why did Fitch apologize for hurting you?" Iris asked. "What did he do?"

Minerva's face twisted with remembered pain. "An experiment. I'd like to forget about it," she said.

"But you lived to tell," Iris said.

"Of course I lived, it wasn't life-threatening. What do you mean?" Minerva asked.

"Fitch kidnapped my sister and me," Iris said sharply. "Gale—Abigail—was with him. They shoved us into a van and took us somewhere."

"Took you," Minerva said, looking into the distance as if at a bad memory. "Earlier, you asked me about the blue van."

"And you said it belonged to a family foundation," I said. The detective in me knew even before she spoke what she would say.

"Yes, the Agassiz Foundation," Minerva said, and I nodded.

"Fitch loves to talk about that foundation," I said. "He makes it sound so important."

"The van is registered to the foundation," Minerva said.

"It's his kidnap van," I said, watching the color in Minerva's face drain away.

"What did he do to you and your sister?" Minerva asked Iris.

"I remember everything now," Iris said, looking determined. "He took us to the attic that had those panels—the ones of the Sibylline sisters. He told us we were doing something good for humanity. We were going to save the goddess. Then he took blood samples to make sure we were AB negative, like his sister."

"Like all the girls in our family who carry the gene," Minerva said. "It's my blood type, too."

Mine too, I thought. If Fitch's research required girls with AB negative blood, was I on his list? Why couldn't he have taken me instead of Eloise? I wished he had, so she could still be alive. I would have fought him off, hurt him before he could kill me or my sister.

"He put a band around my head, tightened it," Iris said. "He hooked me up to a machine and said it would just take a minute, it was just to measure brain waves. But it looked as if it came out of a horror movie—it was so old-fashioned and weird-looking."

Minerva nodded. "I know that equipment. Remember when I said the Sibylline sisters were moved to the health spa?"

"The Miramar?" I asked.

"Yes. All kinds of doctors came there, trying to help the sisters. The girls were famous, and beloved, and everyone wanted to save them. They were in their early twenties . . . it was nearly eighty years ago. You can imagine how old the equipment is," Minerva said. "Fitch used it on you?"

"Yeah," Iris said.

"Me too," Minerva said. "That was what I was referring to, when I said he hurt me. I thought he was joking when he first put the band around my head. But he flipped the switch, and it shocked me."

"Us too," Iris said. "He told us he was putting us to sleep, that we'd wake up refreshed. Then he gave us sedatives or something. He'd run the test, but it would hurt—it felt like a shock. And then the last time, I didn't wake up for a while. It must have looked like I died. I only regained consciousness when Fitch was burying me in the woods. I realized what was happening and played dead, because I knew it could be my chance to escape."

"Oh my God," Minerva said. "Iris! Fitch buried you? He tried to kill you?"

Iris looked down, as if trying to gather her thoughts. "I don't know if he meant to," she said. "I think it was an accident, because he cried. I could hear him when he was burying me. And I felt his tears on my face. He sprinkled something on me—it tickled my face. He kept saying he was sorry."

"How sorry could he have been?" I asked harshly. "Considering he was shoving you into a hole in the ground?"

"Come on, Oli," Iris said. "It was just an impression."

"And considering he did the same thing to my sister," I said, feeling almost rageful at Iris for describing Fitch in such an understanding way.

"What are you talking about?" Minerva asked.

"I found Iris buried alive," I said. "In the same place my sister was found."

"The same place?" Minerva asked, stunned.

"Yes," I said.

"You're saying Fitch put your sister there?" she asked.

"He must have," I said.

"Is your sister okay?" Minerva asked me.

"No, he killed her," I said. "He murdered Eloise." Grief welled up inside me, washing over the rage, merging with it, creating one gigantic tidal wave of terribleness, of loss, of the worst feelings in the world.

Minerva held one of my hands, and Iris held the other. Even though I hate crying in front of people, nothing could have stopped the sobs from ripping out of my chest, the tears from flooding down my cheeks. Iris and Minerva were new in my life, but it felt as if I had known them longer than anyone else, anyone but Eloise.

When I was finished crying, Minerva used one of those soft white towels to dry the tears from my eyes. Iris brought me a glass of water from the sink next to the workbench. I sipped it until I could breathe normally again.

"We have work to do," Minerva said.

"Like what?" I asked.

"First, Iris—you said Fitch sprinkled something on you, when he thought you were dead."

"Yes, what was it?" Iris asked.

"You know, don't you?" Minerva asked me.

"Gold dust," I said. "Like the kind he took from you?"

"Yes," she said, looking more worried than before. "He might think he's doing medicine, as far as the brain wave tests go, but he's also practicing alchemy. He's taking a page from the tome."

"What tome?" I asked.

"Daphne's magic book," Minerva said. "It's the Sibylline version of *Malleus Maleficarum*—the *Hammer of Witches*."

"Witchcraft?" I asked, thinking of the little charm, the tiny witch flying through the fog.

"Not exactly," Minerva said. "It's more like a family treatise about goodness, healing, seeing the future to improve lives, to bring love, to cause happiness. We're an old New England clan. Daphne traced our lineage all the way back to Alse Young—the first girl executed for witchcraft in America. She was a botanist from Windsor, right here in Connecticut, blamed for a flu outbreak."

"You're related to Asle?" I asked, with some awe. Minerva nodded. We'd learned about the Connecticut Witch Trials in school; they had started in 1647, held in Hartford, just up the river from where Eloise and I lived in Black Hall.

"Some said the Sibylline sisters contracted the disease as retribution for Alse cursing the state with flu," Minerva said. "Others were accused of fortune telling—just like the Sibyllines—and people called them witches. It all weaves together, and I think Fitch might have bought into it more than he'd want anyone to think."

I remembered more about what I'd learned. The Connecticut Witch Trials of the 1600s were evil and devastating, totally wrong and unfair, and directed mostly at women. Awesome women who threatened the status quo—including Lydia Gilbert, who was accused of bewitching Thomas Allyn's gun. So when on October 3, 1651, Thomas killed a man, it was deemed not his fault, but Lydia's— for having cast a spell the gun. And she was executed for it.

Just within the last few years, our Connecticut state lawmakers had officially absolved twelve of the seventeenth-century witch hunt victims, eleven of whom had been executed. It had only taken them 370 years.

"But Alse was innocent," I said.

"Totally innocent," Minerva said. "Like all those accused witches, she did have powers—but we all do! Emotion is power. Love is power. My creating charms to celebrate our family legends—power. Those tears that just shook you to the core, Oli—they are power. Iris, your desire to save Hayley—that is power."

I nodded. Minerva was absolutely right.

"But we have to move fast," Minerva said.

"And get to the Miramar?" Iris asked. "Are we even sure that's where he has Hayley? Does it have an attic? Full of dead birds and panels painted with the girls in long white dresses? The sibyls?"

"It does have an attic just like that," Minerva said. "But the Miramar is a strange place. Too many corridors and back staircases and secret passages. I don't even know how to *get* to that attic."

"Maybe we need to slow down and figure out a strategy," I said.

"There's no time, Oli," Minerva said.

"What do you mean?" I asked.

"The gold dust," she said. "I hadn't put it together before, but now that I know he sprinkled it on you, Iris, after he thought you were dead . . ."

My pulse raced, and the blood in my veins felt cold.

"It's written in the *Hammer of Witches*," Minerva said, "that the dust of silver and gold is for anointing the dead. So if he needs more . . ."

"It means he's going to kill Hayley," Iris said.

Minerva grabbed her car keys, and the three of us ran out to the street.

twenty

We tore down the back way to a small parking area. The blue van was gone, so I assumed Matt and Fitch had split up and were probably each driving around, looking for us. Minerva had a lime-green MINI Cooper; I squished into the passenger seat and ducked down, and Iris lay flat on the back seat. We stayed out of sight until we were out of town.

As we drove into Silver Bay, I saw the big Victorian hotel looming over the cove.

"*Miramar* is French for 'by the Sea,'" Minerva said. "This hotel started off as a resort and a health spa. A magnet for wealthy people from New York and Boston."

I gazed at the ramshackle old wreck and tried to imagine that it had been grand in its day.

"After two of the sisters died, our family sort of lost hope," Minerva continued. "We kept the building, but we let it get run-down. It's basically just a boardinghouse now."

"Who lives there?" I asked. My mind was racing. I needed to know everything I could about the hotel if we were to go inside to get Hayley. I kept looking over my shoulder, nervous that Fitch or Matt would pull up behind us at any minute.

"Hardly anyone," Minerva said. "As the tenants die, the rooms are not re-rented." She paused, and her eyes flashed with anger. "But one of my favorite people in the world lives there. And she's the reason I'm upset the family's not taking care of the property. She deserves better."

"Who?" I asked.

"You'll see," Minerva said.

We reached the stately, faded-yellow hotel. It had balconies trimmed with ornate white gingerbread, and front stairs adorned with fancy carved railings that made it look like a wedding cake. But the paint was peeling, the trim cracked and broken, and a few black shutters dangled, banging in the wind. It was four stories high, and at the top was a turret.

An elderly lady in a white dress stood on the front porch. She looked as old as the Miramar itself. Thankfully, there was no sign of Matt's Jeep or Fitch's blue van. We must have beaten them there, so we had some time.

"This is the place," Iris said as Minerva drove alongside the hotel.

"I thought you didn't see it," I said.

"I feel it, Oli," she said. "Like . . . a force. I know Hayley is in there."

I reached back and squeezed her hand. I completely believed her, because I understood the pull of sisters, something unseen and unspoken. A force—just as she had said.

Minerva circled the hotel, and I made a note of all the entrances and exits. There were six doors: one at the top of the wide stairs, two in back, and one that I guessed led to a kitchen, considering the dumpster right outside besieged by screeching gulls. The other two doors opened onto the side porch. There was also a driveway that slanted downward toward garage doors.

"Does Fitch live here?" I asked.

"Not officially," Minerva said. "But he's constructed this whole persona as a researcher who needs his own space to work on the cure. That's why he uses the attic. He calls it his 'lab.' Everyone just indulges him. It's easier that way."

I craned my neck to peer anxiously at the top floor. If the huge place was mostly vacant and the family didn't care, it explained why no one had intervened with Fitch taking the girls up to the hidden attic.

My older sister–ness kicked in, and I began to plan. Even though Matt and Fitch weren't here yet, I didn't know who else might be stationed inside, to guard Hayley. I figured that Abigail could be in the attic with her.

"What floors are the occupied rooms on?" I asked Minerva.

"Scattered through the hotel," Minerva said. "Lower floors, though—the elevator is always broken, and the older tenants find the stairs too difficult."

Minerva parked on a side street, and the three of us jumped out of the car.

"Ready?" Iris said. "Let's go inside."

She was so revved up, it was easy to forget the fact she had been buried alive less than thirty-six hours ago. But it was obvious the physical and emotional trauma had taken a toll. She was so pale, her head wound stood out like Halloween makeup, a black slash. She had dark circles under her eyes. She was clenching her hands to hide the fact they were shaking. I knew it would take super-human strength for her to return to the attic, the site of where she'd nearly died.

"I'm ready," I said, hiding the fact that I was scared. Not just for my own safety, but because I was afraid I would fail. Fail Hayley and fail the spirit of my sister.

"Iris, can you lead us up to Hayley?" I asked.

"I can try. But we were blindfolded and barely conscious when we got here," Iris reminded me. "And when Fitch took me out to bury me, I was totally unconscious. So I didn't see anything."

"How about you, Minerva?" I asked. "Fitch did that test on you in the attic, right?"

"Yes, but like I said, the inside is a maze," Minerva explained. "Staircases everywhere, but they don't go straight up, floor-by-floor—they kind of zigzag through the hotel. Walk up to one floor, then down a hallway, then up to another. We could wind up at a dead end or trapped inside a utility closet or something."

"I don't get it," I said. "Why would a hotel be built that way?"

"A combination of things," Minerva said. "Don't forget, it used to be a place where people came to get well. Some of them were famous, like stage actors from New York, so the owners came up with a design to protect their privacy. So the attic, where treatments were given, was very hard to find."

"What else? You said a combination of things . . ."

"Magic and intrigue," she said. "The Sibylline sisters were part of the Miramar's allure. Nothing could be straightforward or simple. Guests wanted to feel they'd checked in to an enchanted hotel. So the owners filled the interior with magical elements, like mirrors everywhere, stars painted on the ceilings, twisty hallways that don't always lead where you expect them to."

Iris sighed, frustrated. "I don't care. We'll head in there and we'll find our way somehow."

Minerva shook her head. "I know I said we should rush over here, but you were right, Oli. We shouldn't just storm in until we know exactly where to go. Do you want to get trapped again, Iris? What we really need is a map."

"What are you talking about?" Iris demanded.

"There's an old brochure that I'm pretty sure maps out the interior so guests could choose their rooms back in the day," Minerva explained. "I think my great-aunt has it. Come on."

Iris and I followed Minerva to the front of the hotel, where the very old woman was standing on the wide porch. She was extremely thin, with long, flowing white hair, her face scored with soft wrinkles. Her ankle-length dress was white, printed with faded yellow flowers. She leaned on a cane, watching us carefully. After a few seconds, she sat in one of the rocking chairs.

"Who is that?" Iris whispered to me. "What if she's part of Fitch's scheme?"

"I have no idea," I whispered back. "Let's talk to her. Find out what she knows."

Iris and I walked slowly toward the woman, but Minerva ran over to her and threw her arms around her in a huge hug.

When they pulled apart, Minerva turned to us with a glowing smile.

"This is my great-aunt Daphne," she said.

I felt shocked and amazed—we were actually meeting one of the Sibylline sisters. She lived right here.

"Good afternoon," the woman said, offering her hand. "I'm Daphne Agassiz."

"Hello," I said, feeling another shock at her last name. I shook her hand and noticed that in spite of her apparent frailty, she had a strong grip. I introduced myself and Iris.

"What brings you to the Miramar?" Daphne asked. "Are you here to take the waters?"

"Take the waters?" I asked.

"Yes. You know that this is a place of wellness. Surrounded by the bay, with salt air and fog coming off the ocean, and the chance to swim and heal," she said.

"That's not why we're here," Minerva said. "Aunt Daphne—"

"Sit with me, girls. I'm the only one of my sisters left now . . . Minerva, you know it gets lonely, having no one to talk to."

"Aunt Daphne, we would love that, but I need something first. The brochure," Minerva said.

"What brochure?" Daphne asked.

"That old one from the Miramar. You know, with the map of the interior, so guests could choose their rooms."

"Darling, I don't have it anymore. I donated most of the old mementos to the Silver Bay Historical Society," Daphne said, then frowned. "Or was it the library? Hmm. I spread them around, not wanting to leave any local establishment out. It could even be at the Elbridge Museum."

I saw Iris's shoulders slump, but Minerva seemed galvanized. "The Silver Bay Historical Society is just a few blocks away," she said. "That's the first place you mentioned, Aunt Daphne—are you pretty sure it's there?"

"Oh dear, at my age, I've learned that nothing is sure."

"Well, it's worth a try," Minerva said. "If I hurry, I can get there before it closes. Hold tight, I'll be right back."

"What do you need the brochure for?" Daphne asked, but Minerva was already racing toward her car.

Daphne sighed. "The young ones are always in such a hurry," she said. "They haven't learned yet that life is long."

"Not for everyone," I said.

Daphne looked at me with a glint in her eyes. "Death comes for all of us, but in its own time. Or is there something specific you'd like to tell me?"

I glanced over my shoulder at Iris, thinking she would tell Daphne about what Fitch had done. But she was silent, and I saw her backing away. Was this all too much for her?

"Your last name is Agassiz," I said, turning back to Daphne. "Are you connected to the Agassiz Foundation?"

She nodded. "My family started it years ago. My father, to be precise. He sought a cure for a terrible disease. He knew that this variety of parasomnia affected girls with a rare blood type."

"Type AB negative?" I asked. I'd never heard of parasomnia, but it must have been the condition that ran in the family.

"Yes, how do you know?" she asked.

"I know it's the disease that took your two sisters. I'm so sorry," I said.

"It did," she said. "I had the same blood type, but somehow I lived. It never seemed fair."

She closed her eyes and looked pale, as if my words had brought all her grief flooding back. I couldn't help taking her hand. She tilted her head, reading my expression. "You understand," she said. "You've lost someone you love."

"Yes," I said. "My sister. And I think she died right here. At the Miramar."

"Please, no!" Daphne said.

I knew she could see the sorrow in my eyes. We shared that emotion; it came from the unbearable fact of losing a sister. She still gripped my hand.

"Do you know what your great-nephew does upstairs?" I asked.

"Fitch?" she asked, and gave a half laugh. "He's a sad case. He pretends to be a scientist. Some people present themselves one way, when they are really another." Daphne paused and shook her head. "You're never too young to learn that truth of human nature."

"Do you ever go up to the attic, to see him?"

"Heavens, no."

"He never takes you up there? Does he do tests on you?"

"What kind of tests?" she asked, clearly puzzled.

"To work on his cure, for the family disease?"

She snorted. "What silliness. How can a boy with no medical or advanced scientific training work on a cure? He's probably just playing with that obsolete equipment from the old days. He does worry about his sister, I will give him that much credit."

"She's up there with him, right?" I asked. "And the other girls he brings here?"

"Dear, I don't know what you're talking about. What girls? I find him tiresome. He has appropriated the Agassiz Foundation for his own reasons—to make himself seem like a big shot. He struts about, but I'll tell you this, Oli: Scratch the surface of a self-proclaimed genius and you'll find either a pathetic soul or a megalomaniac."

The latter, I thought. I saw her staring at my wrist.

"Who gave you this?" she asked, tapping the Turk's head Matt had given me just hours earlier, when everything had been so different.

"A boy I thought I liked," I said.

"It's a sailor's knot," Daphne said. "A romantic gift."

I had actually believed that. But that was before I knew, before I heard Matt's voice whispering for me while he and Fitch scoured the waterfront looking for us.

"It's a sign of strong feelings—going all the way back to the days when sailors left for months, even years at a time," Daphne went on. "The gift of a sailor's knot was a promise, a sign of love. My father gave one to my mother. Their love—for each other and for us—was stronger than anything on earth."

"They sound wonderful," I said, thinking sadly how I'd been imagining that for me and Matt.

When I shook myself out of that momentary reverie, I saw that Daphne was staring over my shoulder, where Iris had been standing. She was frowning so intensely, I turned to follow her gaze. There was no sign of Iris. "Your friend—she was there just a minute ago," she said. "But someone beckoned her inside."

"Who did?" I asked, upset that I'd been distracted and hadn't noticed.

"The boy," she said. "Not Fitch—one of his friends."

"What's his name?" I asked. I could hear the ocean roaring in my ears, only it was really my blood, my heart pounding as I waited to hear her say "Matt."

"I don't know," she said. "He didn't introduce me."

Matt, I thought. The friend was Matt. I didn't wait to hear anything else. I needed to catch up to Iris and Matt.

"Oli, come back when you can. I enjoyed our visit," I heard Daphne call as I ran across the wide porch, into the Miramar's open door.

But they weren't the last words I heard.

"Hello, Oli," he said, that familiar voice ringing in my ears as I felt the sting on my neck, as I felt the cold rush through my veins, freezing me, turning me into ice that cracked and splintered and sent me collapsing to the floor.

Twenty-one

That was the moment I died.

I'd always wondered how death would feel. To be awake and alive one moment, and then to die. Would everything stop all at once? Would it be like stepping from sunlight into darkness? Would it be like falling asleep?

I used to think, yes, it would be like sleep. Like drifting into a dream that would go on forever. Never waking up again, but still having a presence. Being able to see the world as I used to know it, to keep watch over the people I loved, the way I felt Eloise did for me after she died.

And I thought I would see the people I'd lost—my parents and my sister. I thought they would be waiting for me. They would be there to walk me from one life into the next. We would hug and they would hold me, and I would tell them how much I had missed them. I was sure of that.

But this death was different.

It was more like stepping into the fog. If you've ever spent time by the ocean, you know the kind—thick, gray billows of mist that sweep in from the sea, blanket the beach and docks and town, so heavy you can't see through it. But then it starts to roll out, just a little at first, letting some light in, allowing you to see the contours of houses, and people, and trees, and the tall masts of boats. In and out goes the fog.

And that's how it was for me. Everything was obliterated—I was lost in a cloudy muddle—but then I began to see the things around me. Slowly at first, just a shadow here, a shape there. At first I heard only a buzzing, like static in my ears, but then sounds became more distinct. I could hear voices, one in particular calling my name.

Eloise, I thought, because who else would it be?

"Wake up!" a girl—not my sister—said.

I could barely hear her. The voice drifted in and out of my mind. Or maybe it was me, coming and going like waves on the beach. Would I stay, or would I wash away, out to sea?

"Are you there?" the girl asked. "Did he give you too much?"

"Am I dead?" I tried to ask, but my mouth wouldn't move, and the words caught in my throat.

"I don't know!" the girl's voice said, so she must have heard me.

When Gram, Eloise, and I would go the cemetery and straighten up my parents' graves, my grandmother would call it "a thin place." She said that at times, in certain locations, the wall between the living and the dead was so fragile, we could pass in and out, almost without knowing it, to be with one another. Eloise and I would always exchange looks. It sounded weirdly funny, but also comforting—to think our parents could be right there with us.

I felt as if just then, hearing that strange girl's voice, I was in a thin place.

That meant that Eloise was near—she had to be.

I called her name.

"Oli," my sister said back. "Oli Oli Oli Oli."

"I love you, I missed you," I said.

"I missed you."

"But we're together now."

"Only for a minute in this way," she said.

"What way?"

"Well, that you're dead like me. But not for long . . ."

"I'm on the other side?" I asked. "Of the wall? In the thin place?"

"Yes. And it will stay thin, Oli. I'll be with you through what you are about to face. But you'll go back to being alive, and I'll still be dead. Believe that, Oli. Let me give every bit of what I know, what I've learned. Listen hard. You'll hear me, Oli. I love you . . . I have to go now . . ."

I couldn't bear losing my sister again, so I drifted deeper into a dream of night, and when I came back into the reality of day, Eloise was gone. I felt small hands on my shoulders, shaking me hard, and I heard the strange girl's voice again: "Open your eyes! You have to, come on!"

She was holding my wrist, pushing the rope bracelet out of the way, fingertips searching for my pulse. "I've got you, hold on to my voice, wake up, you can do it!"

The mental haze began to clear, and I saw a familiar face peering down at me. Just seeing her made me choke up because I saw the resemblance to Iris. They had the same dark hair and brown eyes.

"Hayley," I said, my voice croaking. Finally I'd gotten to her, though not in the exact way I'd planned.

"How do you know my name?" she asked, sounding shocked.

"Iris told me."

"You know my sister?" she asked, tears in her eyes.

I nodded.

"He killed her," Hayley said. "A few days ago. He's going to do the same to us."

Right. She still believed Iris was dead. "No, he didn't," I tried to raise my head, look around for Iris. Hadn't Hayley seen her, hadn't Fitch brought her in here? Where was she?

"Do you know where we are?" Hayley asked.

"The attic?" I asked, and my throat was so dry, my voice was barely a squawk. "Hayley, we got to you in time."

"'We'?" Hayley asked.

"Yes," I said, craning my neck. I didn't see Iris. That gave me a jolt. Daphne had said "the boy" had taken her inside the hotel. Maybe Iris was lying down across the room, still knocked out. Maybe Matt and Fitch were hiding, watching us.

"Who are you?" Hayley asked.

"My name is Olivia. Oli," I said.

"How did he catch you?" Hayley asked. Her voice shook. She looked as if every good thing she had ever known or felt had left her forever.

I was flat on my back, on a thin mattress. I struggled to prop myself up on my elbows. I reached in my pocket for my phone, but it was gone. Someone had taken it.

I had a lot to tell Hayley, but first I had to establish a few crucial details. She had said "he." But which one?

"Where is he now?" I asked.

"He went downstairs," Hayley said.

"When will he be back? And what's his name?" I asked, my heart pounding.

"He comes and goes," she said, not answering my second question. "There's no set time. It kind of depends on her." Hayley pointed across the attic to a four-posted canopied bed where someone was sleeping. From here, I couldn't tell who it was, but I had a pretty good guess.

I forced myself to stand up. It was hard, because of the strong sedatives Fitch had given me.

My determination to get us out of there made my muscles move. Hayley supported me so I wouldn't topple over. My head felt fuzzy, but it was clearing up.

"Where's Iris?" I asked, looking around.

Hayley's expression became a combination of anger and wild grief. "I told you—he killed her. Right here in this attic—I watched him murder my sister."

"No, Hayley," I said. "She's alive."

Hayley's eyes widened. "Don't torture me! You're still out of it, dreaming, I know what I saw! She wasn't moving, he carried her out of here. I screamed and grabbed at him, but he shook me off and just kept going. I think he took her somewhere outside to bury her."

"She survived," I said. "He only thought she was dead. Hayley, I found her. I pulled her out of the ground. And she's here. We came to the Miramar together."

"But she's *not* here," Hayley said, her eyes wild. "Why are you saying she is? Don't lie to me!"

I felt madly confused. If Iris wasn't in the attic, where was she? Had Fitch and Matt done something terrible to her? The shock of it all felt like a bucket of ice water, and it had the effect of washing the rest of the cobwebs out of my brain.

"Look, Hayley," I said. "You can believe me or not, but we're getting out of this attic."

I knew that Minerva had driven to get the map of the Miramar. When she returned and found both me and Iris gone, she and Daphne would take steps to find us. Rescue us from Fitch and Matt. Now was the time to call the police. But why was it taking her so long? What if the brochure wasn't at the Historical Society after all? Maybe she had to go to the other places Daphne had mentioned.

Was that a look of hope on Hayley's face? Or doubt? Most likely both.

"Do you promise my sister is alive?" Hayley asked.

"I do," I said.

"Tell me everything about her," Hayley said, her brown eyes wide. "What did she say, how did she look, did she talk about me?"

"She talked about you all the time. From the minute I found her, you were all she could think about. Every single thing she did was devoted to getting you out of here," I said. "And she told me everything. About the Cat Castle. How you like to stay home and she likes to go out . . ."

"I can't believe it," Hayley said. "For the last two days, I was sure that I'd never . . ."

"I know, you thought you'd never see her again. But you will," I said, even though the fact of Iris's absence made me worry if that was true. "I have to know something. How many are there?"

"How many?"

"Yes," I said. "Fitch and who else?"

"Fitch? Is that his name?" I nodded. "He's the only one who comes in here. But . . ." Hayley frowned as if trying to bring something to mind. "I think there might be someone else. Because 'Fitch,' if that's who he is . . ."

"I promise you, that's who he is," I said grimly. I wondered if Fitch had kept his name secret as a way to protect his identity. Or did he have enough of a conscience to keep a part of himself separate from what he was doing?

"Anyway, he always seems to know more than he should," Hayley went on. He stays overnight in one of the guest rooms, so he's usually close by. There are cameras, but it's got to be more than that."

"Like what?"

"He can't be watching the monitor every minute, can he?" she asked, looking up at the ceiling.

I couldn't stop myself from looking up, too. There were two stuffed raptors—a snowy owl and a kestrel. "I wouldn't think so."

"It feels as if someone else is spying on us. Because there's never any time between."

"Time between what?" I asked.

"Between whatever happens in here and him arriving. Once, when he first brought us here, Iris and I rummaged through the drawers where he keeps his medical stuff, trying to find a weapon to attack him. There was no way he could have known that from downstairs, but just a couple minutes later he came through the door."

"Couldn't he have been watching the camera feed?" I asked.

She shrugged. "The cameras can't cover the whole attic. There are blind spots."

I was shaking. I remembered Iris telling me and Matt that someone had been spying on them in the attic. Matt had asked her questions about her imprisonment, seeming to care so much. But now I wondered—had *he* been the spy? Had his concern been fake, just to throw us off?

"Did you ever hear Fitch say the name Matt?" I asked Hayley, afraid to hear the answer.

"Yes," Hayley said. "It surprised me, since he never told me his own name. Why, how do you know that?"

"I just do," I said, my heart falling. "Go on."

"Fitch told us he was in a nature club, that he had friends who would help him if we ever gave him trouble. Their names were

Matt and Chris, he said. They were always there for him."

So it was definite—Matt was part of this. My heart felt like a stone. I closed my eyes and turned away. I couldn't stand hearing anything more.

I felt incredibly thirsty. Drinking water would flush the rest of the sedatives out of my system sooner. I paced the perimeter of the attic and found the bathroom—about the size of a closet. I cupped my hands, filled them with water from the faucet, and drank.

There was a mirror above the sink; I stared into my own eyes and saw a different girl than I'd been before.

My sister had been murdered by our friend.

And the boy I loved was evil.

I would never be the same again.

Twenty-Two

I stepped out of the bathroom. I had to stop thinking about Matt. Stop worrying about how I could have read him so wrong.

I had to look around, plan a way to escape.

The light from sconces on the wall was very dim, but I could make out the splintered wooden rafters, the old rusty nails, the crumbling chimney bricks, and all the dead birds hanging from the ceiling that Iris had described to me.

There were a couple of windows, so opaque from salt spray I could hardly see out. It was starting to get dark. I pressed my forehead against a windowpane. Streetlights and harbor lights, four stories below, glowed through the murky glass. Shouldn't Minerva have brought help by now?

Then it hit me: She had led us here, Iris and me. What if Minerva was working with Fitch and Matt? She had the gene—it was to her advantage for her cousin to keep going with his research, to find a cure. I felt despair, to think I might have been so wrong—not only about Matt, but about Minerva, too.

Then I felt a jolt of hope. If "the boy"—Fitch or Matt or even Chris—hadn't grabbed Iris, could she have run away? But if that was the case, why hadn't she sent someone save us? Was she still scared to call the police? My mind was spinning in circles, an out of control merry-go-round.

I gazed at that filthy window, at the lights shining up from the street, and thought of life going on down there. All the cars, all the people out to enjoy the June night. And how no one passing by had any idea that Hayley and I were being held prisoner in the attic of the Miramar Hotel.

Iris had spoken of a brick chimney, and there it was, right in the middle of the attic. It must have served fireplaces on the lower floors, but all it did up here was block us from seeing directly across the space—there were no hearths to light, to warm the vast attic. As I rounded the brick column, there—leaning against the attic's far wall—were the panels of the three sibyls: the same sisters depicted on the ghost sign down by the harbor.

I stopped and stared.

"The reason we're here," Hayley said, following my gaze.

"You know about the Sibylline sisters?" I asked.

"Yes, two of the three died of the family disease—the ones who had the same blood type as Iris and me. Fitch thinks genetics holds the key to finding a cure. To healing his sister," Hayley said. She gestured toward the person asleep on the canopied bed across the room.

I'd known it had to be her. I walked over to the bed and stared down at Abigail Martin. I hadn't seen her in a while, since she'd stopped going to school. Fast asleep, she was wearing a long white nightgown, like the dresses worn by the girls in the panels. Her skin looked dry and pasty, as if she had a fever. I felt her forehead with the palm of my hand; it was hot. She didn't wake up at my touch.

Standing beside her, I saw thin wires attached to the bed frame.

"What are those wires for?" I asked Hayley.

"He has a machine that monitors her sleep," Hayley said. "It tells him when there are changes, and it's supposed to jolt her awake. That doesn't always work. When it doesn't, he comes running."

"Why?" I asked, not getting it.

"Because she dies in her sleep, sometimes," Hayley said.

That's what Iris had told me, but I still couldn't believe I had heard right.

"She stops breathing," Hayley says.

"And she literally *dies*?" I asked.

Hayley nodded. "It's like sleep kills her," she said. "If Fitch wasn't paying attention, she might not be able to wake up. When she gets like that, I've yelled, shaken her, but she just lies there, not breathing."

"But she eventually does breathe, obviously," I said, gesturing at the sleeping Abigail.

"So far," Hayley said. "The episodes don't happen every night, but when they do, it's so scary. I worry about her so much."

"Is that the condition that Fitch is trying to cure?" I asked.

Hayley nodded.

"But what are we doing here? What do her 'episodes' have to do with us? With you and Iris? With Eloise?" I asked.

Hayley glanced surreptitiously up at the ceiling, where earlier she had indicated that there were cameras. Then she gently took my arm and led me back toward the corner, next to one of the windows. We stood there, our backs to the room.

"We have to be careful," Hayley said. "You know he has cameras on us."

I nodded. "The birds see all," I said.

"The birds?"

"Yes, it's perfect for birders like Fitch and Matt."

"Well, he keeps track of what's going on up here. And he always knows when Abby-Gale—Abigail—goes into an episode."

"Why does he need a camera or a spy? Doesn't the monitor, whatever those wires lead to, tell him that?" I asked.

"It's supposed to buzz when she hasn't moved in too long. Once it was close, she almost didn't come out of it, but he got to her in time." She paused. "He's very attuned to her."

"I know their mother travels all the time," I said. "She's not exactly present in their lives. But seeing all this," I said, gesturing around. "How does she not have a clue about what her son is doing? Or does she?"

"I've heard Fitch and Abigail talking," Hayley said. "They say the family has tried all the conventional treatments, but nothing has worked. Not just for Abigail, but for all the women who have the gene."

"What is the gene, anyway?" I asked.

"I don't know," Hayley said. "They just say 'the gene.' And they talk about AB negative. The only ones who get sick have that blood type. He doesn't have enough subjects to do his research on, so that's why he took me and Iris, and the other girl, too. Because we have it."

Other girl. My sister.

"Anyway, I know his mother is a doctor," Hayley said. "I think he's raided her office, to get the knockout med."

"Doctors have to keep track of that stuff," I said, thinking of how careful Gram's physicians were about prescribing her medications, especially ones to relax her or help her sleep. "Maybe his mom gives it to him."

"I really doubt she knows anything," Hayley said. "She never shows up here. Fitch gets angry because he feels she's given up on Abigail."

"How could someone give up on their daughter?" I asked.

"Because it's such a hopeless situation," Hayley said. "It's really bad, Oli. She honestly does die. It tears him up."

"Well, I don't feel sorry for him," I said harshly. "He's a criminal. Hayley, for him to do what he's doing, he has to be a psychopath."

She didn't respond. I knew she was thinking of Iris, of what he had done to her.

"He killed my sister," I said.

"What?" she asked, shocked.

"Before he took you and Iris, he took my sister. You said the 'other girl'—that was my sister. She knew him, she trusted him. They were friends. It wouldn't have taken much for him to convince her to go somewhere with him. She loved birds." I looked up at the stuffed owls and hawks hanging overhead. "She had planned to go owling with another friend the day she disappeared. I think Fitch used that somehow to trick her . . ." My mind was racing, wondering exactly how he had done it.

"I'm so sorry, Oli. He tricked us, too—he pretended to love cats," she said. "What was your sister's name?"

"Eloise. She was your age. She was wonderful—so smart, funny, the greatest sister ever. My best friend." I felt my face turning red, but I wouldn't cry. I needed my anger right now, not my sorrow. I needed rage to stay fierce and get us away from here. "I'm going to make sure he never hurts anyone again," I said. "I am going to see him punished. We're going to do it together, Hayley."

"Good," she said, and she flashed a big smile. She stood straighter and looked strong.

I saw her glance down at Abigail—still fast asleep, out cold.

"In a way, it's hard not to blame her," Hayley said. "He says we have to be a hero to the goddess. He means Abigail—this is all for her. He doesn't care who suffers as long as he gets his answers. So she can live. He thinks if he can induce seizures in us, he can figure out a way to stop them in her."

I stared down at the sleeping girl. I remembered that her seizures, and their serious underlying cause, were the reason she had left school. It was obvious that Fitch loved Abigail very much, in order to do what he was doing. I understood sibling love as well as—better than—most people. I would have said it was impossible to love anyone more than I did Eloise. But would I sacrifice other people's lives for her? Because it seemed pretty clear he was doing just that, to find a cure for his sister.

"They're terrible," Hayley said, shivering. "Her seizures. I hate when she has them. It's almost as if she's possessed—by a spirit, an awful force that wants to destroy her. A demon."

"It's not a demon," I said. "Fitch's whole thing is science and medicine. That's how he's going about it. He thinks it's the only way to get credit, make his mother love him. All our friends know it—we just didn't realized that he was hurting people to do it." But then I thought of what Minerva had said about the alchemy of gold dust, the magic of the *Hammer of Witches*, and wondered if Fitch was really as scientific as he made himself out to be.

As if Abigail knew we were talking about her, she moaned in her sleep and turned over in her bed. Now that I had promised Hayley we were going to escape, all I had to do was come up with a plan to accomplish the impossible. But I was exhausted. I tried my best to fight through it.

I told myself I wouldn't fall asleep in that attic, wouldn't give in to exhaustion and lie down on one of the mattresses lined up against one wall, but I couldn't help it. With all the adrenaline I'd been running on all day, my limbs felt as if they were filled with sand. I yawned, and Hayley saw.

"Lie down," she said. "Get some rest."

"I have to stay alert, to be ready for him," I said.

"You can't be ready for anything if you're falling asleep on your feet. Don't worry—I'll stay awake."

"Promise you'll wake me up if he comes back?" I asked.

"Yes," she said.

So I walked over to a mattress and flopped onto it. My eyelids fluttered, and just before I drifted off into sleep, thoughts of gold dust, magic, and the *Hammer of Witches* flashed through my mind. I saw Hayley sitting cross-legged on the floor beside me, gazing at me, keeping watch over me, the way I wished more than anything that I could have kept watch over Eloise. Shades of gold flashed behind my eyelids, and I tumbled into a deep sleep.

twenty-three

Dreams came quickly, and they were full of Matt.

We were on Dauntless Island, and the sun was high overhead. We swam, and climbed out of the sea onto a raft, covered with salt, only the salt was made from diamond fragments. Our hair sparkled, and Matt ran his hand across my shoulders, and his fingertips shimmered.

But then it got dark—not the way night falls slowly in real life, with a sunset and twilight, but all at once, as if someone had pulled a black curtain over the sun. There were stars, though, and it wasn't diamond dust on our skin but embers falling from burning stars. I was terrified—not just for myself, but for Matt. I thought hard about how we could escape, and my fervor turned the raft into a submarine, and we drifted underwater.

"How will we breathe?" I asked, realizing I had gotten ahead of myself: By creating one solution, I had caused another serious problem.

"We're like whales," he said. "We took a big breath of air, and it will last until we need another one."

"Don't we need it now?" I asked.

"No, we have each other," he said. "I'm saving you, and you're saving me."

He kissed me then, and I felt a shiver of warmth, of air, of life, and in that weird way of sleep haze, I had the clear thought: *I just had my first kiss, but it's not real, it's just in your mind, it's only a dream.*

When we pulled apart, we knew we needed to get to the surface. Matt started to swim up, and when he was above me, he glanced back to make sure I was on my way up. But my arms and legs couldn't move. I stared at the rope bracelet he had given me, wanting it to save me. Matt swam back down and began to gently unravel it. He held one end of the nylon line and tugged it, pulling me up toward the sky.

I had a moment of fear: What if he was leading me to danger?

That's when I woke up, in a panic. I heard a low pulsing sound filling the attic. I felt my heart racing like the tide, but then I thought about how calm I had been with Matt, how unafraid. How much I had loved his kiss. And then I realized I was silently sobbing because how was it possible that I could trust him so much in my dreams while remembering, now that I was waking up, that he was on Fitch's side? I wrapped my hand around the Turk's head bracelet on my other wrist and felt despair, wondering what it really meant, when I had thought it meant he had feelings for me like I had for him.

"Oli!" Hayley whispered, shaking me to make sure I was fully awake. The low buzz was louder.

"What?" I asked.

"Shhh," she said. "It's happening."

"What?" I asked.

"That's the alarm. Abigail is having one of her spells," Hayley whispered. She grabbed my hand. I shook off the last vestiges of sleep, then eased myself off the mattress. I followed Hayley, tiptoeing across the attic.

Abigail was lying on her beautiful bed—an actual bed, not a mattress on the floor. It had angels carved into the wood. Tall posts rose almost to the ceiling, and they were draped with a white canopy of fine, delicate lace. It looked as if it had been created for a princess— or a goddess.

Hayley and I inched closer.

"Watch," Hayley whispered.

Abigail was lying stiff and rigid, as if she was a doll whose limbs couldn't move or bend. Her hands formed tight fists. Her jaw was clenched, tongue jutting out between her upper and lower teeth.

Her face was pink, then turned bright red, almost as if her blood was coming to a boil. Her fists seemed to swell to twice their size, and her arms shot straight up. Her eyes were wide open, their usual gentle expression flashing with aggression. She looked ready to attack. Her red skin darkened to purple, then shifted to dull blue, and her eyes rolled back into her head so only the whites were visible.

"She's not breathing," I said, lurching forward, grabbing her. "Abigail, wake up!" I shouted.

"It won't help," Hayley said. "She won't wake up until the spell is over—until he stops it."

I barely heard. I just kept shaking Abigail as hard as I could. This scared me so much, and I wanted to save her. Her eyes were pure white in the sockets, her non-stare like a lifeless doll, like a girl in a horror movie.

"She's dying!" I cried out. Or was she already dead? Iris and Hayley had said she died in her sleep. Now I was witnessing it.

Just then the attic door burst open and Fitch came running in. He shoved me away from Abigail so hard I fell flat on my back.

"Give her the rescue medicine!" Hayley yelled at him.

He didn't reply. He roughly turned Abigail onto her side, checked her mouth, allowing saliva to drain onto the pillow. When he did, Abigail began to raise her stiff arm. Her legs were rigid, toes pointing downward.

Fitch didn't speak or try to get through to her. He reached into his pocket and withdrew a hypodermic syringe. He pulled off the cap with his teeth and quickly gave Abigail a shot in the top of her arm. Almost instantly she relaxed. Her body went slack, and her eyelids fluttered.

Neither Fitch nor Abigail spoke a word. But she was awake now, and she gazed up at her brother. He went around the corner and came back with a blood pressure cuff and thermometer. He took her vital signs, then sat on the edge of her bed and typed notes onto the keypad of a tablet. Her eyes were open. She smiled at him.

"Thank you," she said.

He just kept typing.

"That was a bad one," Abigail said. "I felt . . . someone was pulling me under."

191

Fitch took a few more notes, then got up to walk away. I followed him while Hayley stayed sitting by Abigail.

I didn't want Abigail to hear, so I spoke to Fitch a low voice. "What's wrong with her?" I asked him.

"Don't tell me you don't know," he said.

"Of course I don't," I said. "How could I? You should know that, you drugged me and brought me up here. All I know is that she has seizures. But that . . . seemed like something else."

"Kids at school make fun of her," Fitch said, and I could see the effort it was taking him to sound calm. "They have, ever since they saw her have that seizure. Even if you're not part of that clique, Oli, you still never defended her."

"Fitch, I never saw anyone bully Abigail. I know she's had health problems, but that's nothing to make fun of. No one should have done that."

"Everyone knows she's different, and they say it straight to her face. She's heard it all, and it devastates her. Can you imagine how that makes me feel, to see my sister crying because of bullies like them?" he asked. "And people like you just let it happen. You're just as bad."

"Me?" I asked, shocked that he would think that. "I thought you knew me! I thought we were friends."

"No one knows anyone," he said bitterly.

Maybe that was true.

"You're right about one thing, Fitch. Standing by and watching bullying happen is horrible. But I would have stepped in if I had seen anyone doing that," I said, anger building inside me. "And what about you? Kidnapping girls. *Killing my sister!*" I couldn't hold myself back and went crashing into him, banging at his chest with my fists. He held me off at arm's length.

"Oli, that was an accident," he said. "I didn't mean for her to die."

"But she did!"

"Things went wrong," he said. "She was fine, and then . . . she wasn't. I tried to revive her. It was one of the worst days of my life— I'd lost control of the research, and Eloise paid the price."

"Don't say her name," I said. "You don't deserve to."

"You're right," he said. His words were humble, full of regret, but behind his glasses I saw a fiery glint in his eyes. His expression didn't match his tone. I felt as if he was acting a part, trying to convince me that he was sorry for what had happened. But the look in his eyes gave it all away.

"How did you get her to go with you?" I asked, my heart pounding.

"She wanted to," he said. "Sort of. It was pretty convenient, actually. She was waiting for the late bus that morning after we went birding. I offered her a ride to school."

"What happened after she got into your car?" I asked.

"Don't ask, Oli. You don't want to hear it."

"I do," I said, steeling myself. I needed to hear everything my sister had gone through.

"I told Eloise that Gale was sick, couldn't go to school that day.

And that I had to stop by to make sure she had her medicine, and I asked if she'd stop by with me—that it would cheer Gale up to have a visitor."

I thought of my sister and her big heart, and how she would definitely have wanted to help.

"So we came here, to the Miramar. Eloise was curious about why my sister was here instead of home, so I gave part of the story—how there was medical equipment here, that it was our family's private clinic. She came right up the stairs, without any trouble. She *wanted* to," he said.

"Only because you were lying to her," I said.

"No," he said. "I wasn't. I told her the truth—that my sister was sick. And I told that detective the same thing. That I'd been a little late getting to school that day because I had to take care of Gale, and that I came straight home after school for her, too. No one even questioned it. My sister's condition is in her records. She needed me."

"She needed you to kidnap my sister?" I asked harshly.

"Gale had no part in that." He smiled at me. "I wish you had been at the bus stop, too, Oli. I was going to grab you both."

"I would have saved Eloise if I had been there," I said.

"You would have tried," he said. "But I would have stopped you." He held up the hypodermic needle, and I felt my stomach churn. "This is how I stopped Eloise, too, once she realized I wasn't going to let her go. That she was going to have stay here in the attic."

She must have been so scared, I thought. I imagined her fear and panic, and I squeezed my hands so tight, I felt my nails dig into my palms.

"Did she try to get away?" I asked.

"Of course," he said. "I knew she would. So I increased her medication. I am sorry for that part, Oli. I didn't mean to give her too much." He shook his head sadly. "She seemed to fall asleep. I went to school after that but when I came back later that night, she was . . ."

"She was dead," I whispered, unwilling to hear his fake apology. "And then you buried her. We didn't know where she was for two days. You knew how close she and I were. Didn't you care how that felt, waiting with no idea of whether she was okay or not? Didn't you care about her, Fitch? She was your friend."

"I cared," he said. "But there was no alternative. She was my friend, but Gale is my sister. My entire reason for living right now is to find a cure for Gale. If I got caught, my work would stop."

I filed that one away: He was giving me fair warning that he couldn't let me and Hayley go—because he would get caught.

"I had to be very careful," he went on. "Studying science is helpful in so many ways. I made sure to wear gloves, I took steps to keep from leaving any DNA when I buried her."

"In the Braided Woods," I said quietly, thinking of how sick it had been of him, to choose a place she and I had loved so much.

Fitch nodded. "It was quiet there," he said softly.

"If killing Eloise was an accident," I snapped, "what about Iris?"

"Same thing," Fitch said. "I made a mistake. I misjudged. Look,

I've had enough of these accusations. You're in a medical trial, think of it that way. This might not be a state-of-the-art research facility, but the work I'm doing will cure a disease. It's more important than anything else."

"Fitch," Abigail said from the bed. "Just stop it. Stop making excuses."

He blinked at her, almost as if he'd been slapped.

"I can't listen to Oli," Fitch said to his sister. "She doesn't understand. You do, though. That's all that matters to me."

"You're upsetting me now," Abigail said. "Please go back downstairs, Fitch. I can't rest when you're like this."

The fight seemed to drain out of Fitch. "Whatever," he said. He gestured toward the tall panels painted with the ethereal Sibylline sisters. "You want to be like them, Gale? The two who died? Only one survived. I need you to survive, and you will."

Abigail didn't reply. She looked away from him. Fitch glared at me and Hayley in an accusatory way—as if blaming us for upsetting his sister. He locked the hypodermic in a metal cabinet, left the attic, and closed the door behind him. I heard the key click in the lock. I hurried over to turn the knob, to see if we were really locked in, and we were.

The Miramar was the kind of building my grandmother would call a firetrap. Architecturally beautiful, but built entirely of wood, with all those twisty and hard-to-navigate hallways, at the edge of the bay where a sea breeze could catch a spark and send the hotel up in flames. If there was a fire, we'd never get out.

I walked around the attic again. I paused at each window. I wished I could see out more clearly, but the glass was so salt-caked it was impossible. I tried to peer down to the street. We were four stories up; we could jump, but we'd break bones, might not even survive the plunge. I banged on the windows with both fists.

"We've done that," Hayley said. "No one comes."

"Then let's break the glass!" I said, glancing around for something to use. I grabbed a heavy book from the top of a chest.

"Go ahead and try," Abigail said. "It's hurricane glass."

I lowered the book. I knew what she was talking about. We live close to Long Island Sound, and when hurricanes come roaring north during the summer and fall, they can bring massive destruction that wrecks property. A category 5 hurricane can tear hundred-year-old trees up by the roots, lift outdoor furniture and fling it into the air, send massive waves and acres of beach sand across roads and into houses, rip shutters off walls and break windows, and splinter seemingly solid wooden structures as if they were made of matchsticks.

So it didn't really surprise me that there would be hurricane windows in the Miramar.

But for Fitch, the benefit of having such thick, strong, impenetrable windows was not only to keep storms out, but to keep girls in.

"Oli, I'm sorry he brought you here," Abigail said, sitting up in bed.

"So am I." I stood next to her, feeling churned up inside. "Abigail, you came to Eloise's memorial at school. You looked straight at me and said how sorry you were that she died."

"I meant it," Abigail said quietly. "I was sorry. I *am* sorry."

"When we couldn't find her," I continued, "when we didn't know what had happened to her, your brother was in the search party. So was Matt. They helped put up flyers. Passed them out at school. And the whole time you knew. You knew she was never coming home. You knew she was already dead."

"I didn't want my brother to get caught," Abigail said. "As much as you love Eloise, that's how I feel about Fitch."

"There's no comparison," I said. "My sister was wonderful, loving, innocent. Your brother is a murderer."

"No," she said vehemently. "He was telling the truth. What happened to Eloise was an accident. He never would have hurt her on purpose. He didn't mean for her to die. He panicked, that's why he buried her, so no would connect it to us, to what he's trying to do for me . . ."

"What about Iris?" I asked.

Confusion crossed Abigail's face. "He let her go," she said. "That's why she wasn't here anymore. We woke up and she was gone. Right, Hayley?"

"That's what he told you," Hayley said. "But, Abigail, did you seriously believe him? He thought she died—and so did I."

"Abigail, he was sure he'd killed Iris," I said. "He took her into the Braided Woods, and he buried her there."

"No!" Abigail said. "I don't believe you!"

"In the exact same grave where he put Eloise," I said.

Abigail shook her head, covered her eyes with the heels of her hands. "He didn't," she whispered. "He promised he wouldn't do anything bad to her. To *any* of you. Not on purpose."

I stared at Abigail. In what warped world could she imagine that kidnapping girls and keeping them locked up here wasn't doing anything bad?

"Tell me how Eloise's 'accident' happened," I said, not believing that it was anything but on purpose.

"Too much electricity, too much medication," she said.

That sounded terrible, and I found myself looking at the wires leading to her bed, the ones attached to an alarm. Had he done that to Eloise?

"Did you see it happen?" I asked.

She bowed her head.

"You did, didn't you?" I asked. And the next words tore out with a part of my heart. "Was Matt part of it?"

"Matt Grinnell," Abigail said. "I know you like him. Eloise told me."

"Did Matt hurt my sister?" I asked.

When she raised her eyes, I saw fire in them. She spoke as if I hadn't just asked the hardest question in the world.

"You're not going to make me say bad things about Fitch," she said. "I know he's not perfect. He's making mistakes. But he's doing this for a good reason. To save me and people like me. You could have the gene, too. All of you could. Your blood type is AB negative, too, right?"

Hayley and I nodded.

"So," she said. "You see? In a way, he's trying to help you, too."

My emotions were wild. I despised Abigail for protecting Fitch, but I also felt sorry for her. I knew that if I wanted to get any real information out of her, I would have to calm down. I would have to stop my brain from crackling with static, from thinking about Matt and how he was involved in this nightmare. I would have to find as much kindness toward Abigail as I could, and try to understand her.

That's what Eloise would do, I told myself. My smart, clever, kind sister, subversively feisty, intractably fierce, patient only when she had to be, but when she was, no one could shake her. That's why she was such a great birder—she could sit still behind the hedge and wait forever.

"Abigail," I said in the gentlest voice I could manage. "Tell me, if it's not too painful, about what you have." Should I call it a disease, an illness, a condition? I wasn't sure, and I didn't want to offend her. "The thing Fitch is trying to cure."

It seemed my tone of voice had worked, because I saw the tension go out of her jaw, saw her shoulders lower and her fists unclench.

"Do you really want to hear about it?" she asked.

"More than anything," I said, and that wasn't a lie.

twenty-four

"I've had this condition since I was born," Abigail said. "But the symptoms didn't start showing up until I was twelve."

And then she described to me and Hayley what it had been like.

It started on the same day she got her first period. Her mother was always so preoccupied with her patients and lecture schedule, she hadn't really told Abigail what to expect. Abigail knew in a general way, from her friends, that periods were no joke. But when she woke up that morning and found blood on her sheets, she was shocked. On top of that, her belly began to cramp, so bad she had to double over.

For a doctor, her mother could be oddly squeamish. It was as if she focused so hard on her patients, on their medical messiness, she wanted only health and order at home. So Abigail told her mother she was sick with a stomachache and she said Abigail didn't have to go to school. Fitch seemed weirdly alert—he asked Abigail all kinds of questions. What kind of stomachache? Exactly where did it hurt? Did she feel sick, like she might vomit? Did she have a headache? All she knew was that she wanted to be alone. She was embarrassed and didn't tell anyone the real reason she was staying home. They finally left, for work and school.

Abigail went into her mom's bathroom and took a pad from a shelf in the closet. The whole ordeal made her feel exhausted. She went back to her room to change her bed. She pulled off the bottom sheet and put it in the washing machine. She threw in bleach and extra detergent. Then she went back to bed and immediately fell asleep.

"I remember there were thunderstorms," Abigail said to us. "And even though I was asleep, I could hear the rain hitting the window, so hard I thought the glass might break. And the thunder sounded violent, as if it was attacking the house." She closed her eyes. "It was the strangest feeling—as if I were in a trance, more than asleep, waiting for something to happen. Something awful. The worst thing."

The trance gave way to dreams. She had the sense of walking down a path between tall trees, into a tunnel made of interlocking branches overhead. It started out warm and beautiful—no more thunderstorm—with sunlight dappling through the leaves. It seemed familiar, and she knew it was the Braided Woods.

The weather changed. It was winter. The trees were bare, their branches coated with ice. The ground was deep with snow. The forest disappeared, and she was in the Arctic. Everything was white, and the glare blinded her. The world was frozen, including Abigail.

"I was a statue," she told us. "Carved of ice. I couldn't move. My eyes were wide open but I couldn't blink. Animals surrounded me—polar bears, arctic foxes, and snowy owls. I wasn't sure if they were protecting me or were going to eat me. But I knew something was going to happen."

She got colder and colder. She couldn't take a breath. Her eyes were wide open. She saw three columns in the distance. They approached her, getting closer and closer. She saw that they were the women in the panels at the Miramar, the hotel her family owned. They wore long white dresses. Two of them were dead, and that's when Abigail knew she was one of them.

"One of them?" I asked.

"A gene carrier," she said. "I knew I had the family disorder."

Later that day, Abigail learned that Fitch hadn't gone to school after all. He had left the house, pretended to head to Black Hall Middle School, then circled back and let himself into the house. He had sensed that this was about to happen. Even though Abigail was only twelve, and he was only thirteen, he had been studying the family disorder since he first learned about it, when he was nine and Abigail was eight. Their mother had warned Abigail, gently, to be on guard against strange sleep patterns. That if she found herself unable to breathe, she should wake her up.

Fitch had said: "If she can't breathe, she's dead."

"Well," their mother had said. "Death isn't instantaneous, dear. There is a warning. And when Abigail feels it, she should call us. Besides, this won't be a concern for many years."

"Until when?" Fitch had asked.

"The condition won't manifest until puberty, if at all," their mother had replied. "So let's not worry about it, shall we?"

That day, when Abigail got her first period and the condition manifested right on time, Fitch was prepared. He had been studying medical texts and family histories ever since their mother's warning.

By then he knew more than anyone, even their mother.

While Abigail stood on the tundra in her dream, a frozen statue surrounded by the Sibylline sisters, Fitch was shaking her and calling her name.

Abigail heard his voice. She felt him throttling her. But she was still a statue, she was still made of ice, she was still dead. The Sibylline sisters were telling her to come with them, they would take her to the peaceful place. She wouldn't have to suffer. She wouldn't have to live a lifetime of the nightmare. They whispered their names to her: Athena, Daphne, and Circe.

"Don't listen to them," Fitch screamed. "Stay here, stay with me! Breathe!"

He began pounding her chest so hard she could almost hear her ribs crack. She felt the rhythm—one-two-three-four. He breathed into her mouth, artificial respiration, like she'd been taught in junior lifesaving at the beach.

And then she woke up. She gasped, drinking air as if she'd been dying of thirst and it was cool spring water. Her breastbone and ribs felt as if they were broken instead of just bruised. She was no longer in the frozen north, but in her bed at home in Black Hall, Connecticut.

"Why did you do that?" she asked, crying and hurt, staring through tears at her brother.

"Because I thought you were dead," Fitch said. "I was just about to call 911." He gave her a half smile. "But I'm glad I didn't."

"Why?"

"This is our chance," he said. "I don't want outsiders studying you."

"Studying me? What are you talking about? Why would they do that?"

"Because you're special. You're rare. This was your first episode, right? You never had that happen before?" he asked.

"No, never," she said.

"Good," he said. "Because this work is going to be all mine."

"Work?" she asked.

"Gale, I have been waiting for this. I know it might sound terrible, but I have been hoping you had the disease. It runs in the women in our family, and if someone has to get it, I'm glad it's you—not Minerva or even Mom."

"Well, thanks, Fitch!" she said, furious.

"Hear me out," he said. "I believe this condition comes with gifts. You know how the legend is that the Sibylline sisters were clairvoyant?"

"Yes. You're telling me I'm going to have second sight? That I'll be able to tell fortunes every time I have one of those . . ." She tried

205

to think of what to call the awful, freezing, airless feeling that had come over her.

"Seizures," he said. "That's what you had. And no, not fortune telling the way you see in movies. More like heightened sensitivity."

Abigail shivered. She wouldn't wish her experience on anyone—how could her brother call it a gift? She had a friend in school, Jeannie, who had epilepsy. Jeannie had seizures, where she would feel an aura just before they came on. She took medicine that kept them under control.

"Do I have epilepsy?" she asked.

"No," he said. "It's something else."

"What?" she asked.

"Never mind for now—I think I know, from things Daphne has said, but I'll establish a definite diagnosis going forward. Meanwhile, don't tell Mom what happened. About the seizure. Just for now."

Abigail shrugged. Not telling their mother would be nothing new. Their mom was always so distracted, and she didn't approve of complaining. Abigail knew that Fitch cared more about her than their mother did.

He was secretive in his own ways, always studying. At thirteen, he had the reading ability of someone with a doctorate. Birding was his only outdoor activity, and sometimes he came home with dead birds to dissect. Then he would embalm them so he could hang them from the ceiling. Abigail told him that was creepy and gross, but he said it was science, and that science was his life.

Eventually, she told her mother, who then sent her to Dr. César, a specialized neurologist in Boston. But Fitch decided he could take better care of her and learn more about the condition. So they let their mother think Abigail was still taking the train to Boston to see Dr. César, but instead Fitch would bring her here, to the Miramar. Their mother never paid too much attention to medical bills—she had an accountant for that—and never even noticed that she wasn't getting charged for the doctor visits.

Now, in the attic of the Miramar, I listened as Abigail spoke. If her episodes had started when she was twelve, she had been suffering them for almost four years.

"I'm so sorry you've been going through this," I said to Abigail. "Not just the seizures, but being your brother's guinea pig. Did he ever answer your question?"

"Which one?" Abigail asked.

"About the condition. What is it?"

"Parasomnia," Abigail said.

Parasomnia—the word Daphne had mentioned. I turned the word over in my mind. Insomnia, parachute, parasol. "What does it mean?" she asked.

"It means *beyond sleep*. Or *apart from sleep*," Abigail said.

"But you are asleep when the episodes come," Hayley said. "We've seen you."

"It might look like regular sleep," Abigail said. "But you can't see what's going on inside. It's anything but regular."

"What do you know about parasomnia?" Hayley asked Abigail. "What does Fitch tell you?"

"He hardly tells me anything," Abigail said. "He wants to keep all his knowledge to himself. But I've read about it on my own, of course. Parasomnia isn't exactly a disease. It's a disorder—it's called a 'disorder of arousal.' Meaning I can't be aroused from sleep, I can't wake up. It happens during really deep sleep. But only part of the brain is asleep. The other part is awake."

"Is that the part that feels as if it's in a trance?" I asked.

"Yes. In many cases, the disorder is not rare. But mine is an extreme form. Instead of having convulsions and thrashing, like some people do, I turn into stone. My muscles tighten, and I don't move. Not even my lungs, not even my heart."

"So you actually *could* die each time you have one," Hayley said.

"Yes," Abigail said.

"What do blood types have to do with it?" I asked.

"We're not really sure. Maybe nothing. But all our family members who have developed full-blown parasomnia had AB negative. Like me. Like all of us."

"Like Eloise," I said.

We were all silent for a few minutes. Thoughts raced through my mind. Whatever Fitch was doing to find a cure for Abigail had killed my sister. And was he even trying to help Abigail? Or just use her?

She had said she believed he had personally killed the birds hanging from the ceiling. I looked up, at all the dead and dusty gulls and owls and songbirds swinging from the old rafters, and wondered how he had felt taking their lives. What kind of monster was he?

"You mentioned the Sibylline sisters' names," I said.

"Yes," Abigail said. "Athena, Daphne, and Circe."

"Daphne," I said. "I met her, downstairs."

"Yes, that's her," Abigail said. "My great-aunt. The only one of the sisters to survive. And *really* survive—she's a hundred."

"Is she in on this?" Hayley asked. "Does she know about Fitch, what he's doing with AB girls?"

"She's not," I said, and I felt sure of it.

"I agree," Abigail said. "She knows I have the disorder, and she's so sympathetic. I can tell she's skeptical about Fitch—he acts nice to her, but she sees through him. She's an oracle, after all."

But did Daphne know what was happening up here? It seemed she didn't. And what about Minerva? Was she on her way back with the brochure? What would she think if Iris and I weren't outside waiting? I could only hope that she would ask Daphne if she had seen us, and Daphne would tell her that we were inside.

But maybe they were all on Fitch's side; maybe they didn't want us to get away.

At one point I would have hoped that Matt's and my connection was strong enough for him to come bursting through the door to rescue us, like a hero in a fairy tale, but I knew that was just a fantasy. One that had been smashed to bits.

Be a hero to the goddess, Fitch had said. No: Hayley and I were going to be heroes to ourselves. If only we could figure out how to escape this unescapable prison. It was up to me, and I was going to make sure we did.

Twenty-five

It was dark. I had been pacing around the attic, tapping on walls, looking for cracks, for any sliver of light that would show me a weakness in the wood that I might be able to break through. A few slants of dull, yellow light came through the salt-coated windows. Outside the wind had picked up. A storm was brewing or had already arrived, blowing off the sea. It felt weird to not be able to see the weather, but my body registered it, as if I were a human barometer. The whistle of the wind made the voice sound distant, made me jump.

"Hello, Oli," I heard.

At first I wasn't sure who it was.

Before I could turn, he reached for my hand. For one second the warm touch lifted my spirit. But then he leaned closer, and I saw his face, and I felt as if I were grasping a snake—cold-blooded and scaly, with flat, black eyes behind thick lenses.

It was Fitch.

He tried to pull me away from the window, but I resisted. The harder he tugged, the more I leaned back, bracing myself with my feet and strong legs, trying to get away from him.

"You have a choice, Oli," Fitch said. "Do what I say, or I'll give you another shot, like the one when you first got here. This time the drug will be stronger. You might not wake up." As he spoke, he let go of my hand and reached into the pocket of his white coat. He held up the hypodermic needle again, but this time it was loaded.

I glanced around the attic. Hayley and Abigail were watching.

"It won't last long," Abigail told me. "He'll take his tests, measure the results and write them down, and you'll be done in time for breakfast."

Breakfast? Was she serious? Who cared about that? Besides, I planned to get us out of here long before sunrise.

Hayley said "fight." Not out loud, but with her eyes. Her expression was ferocious. I could tell by the tension in her shoulders that she was about to launch herself at Fitch so we could take him down together. Fitch saw it, too.

"Don't even think about it, Hayley," he said. "There's enough here for you, too. Oli, the ball is in your court. Comply, or put yourself and Hayley in danger. I'm sure you realize that I know how to hurt her."

He'd said the magic words, probably the only thing that could get to me, that he would hurt Hayley. So slowly, I stood up. There might be no worse feeling in the world than "complying"—to use his word—with your captor, the person you know to the depths of your being is your enemy. The boy who killed your sister. Believe it or not, that terrible feeling of following him to whatever he planned to do overcame the fear of what it would be.

So I trailed Fitch around the attic's central chimney, through a door in the brick. We were in a small room, and that's when I realized it wasn't a chimney at all but just a hollow column—possibly meant to support the Miramar when it was first built, but now used for another purpose.

The space had no windows. When Fitch flipped on bright lights, I could see that it was furnished like a doctor's exam room. There was a padded table, a stainless steel cart with an array of medical instruments, a container for sterilizing them, and a machine with wires and dials.

Had he stolen all this stuff from his mother?

"You think you're a real doctor, don't you?" I said. "You're not, Fitch. You're just in a school club where you pretend to be one."

"Tell yourself that," he said.

"You're a rich kid," I said. "Must be nice to be able to use your allowance to buy your little toys here. Or did you just raid your mother's office?"

"On the table, Oli," he said, unperturbed by my questions. "I'm sure you want to get this over with."

He picked up a stethoscope. That seemed harmless enough, and it made me roll my eyes—a little kid pretending to be a doctor. I reluctantly sat on the edge of the padded table while he took my pulse and listened to my heart. I cringed at his touch. He made notations on a tablet, and I was pretty sure it was the same one he used when we birded together at the banding station.

"You have a fast heartbeat," he said. "But that's natural. I'm sure you're scared, aren't you?"

I didn't reply.

"You're terrified, aren't you, Oli?"

I had the definite feeling he wanted me to say yes, that terrifying me was half the point—wasn't that what psychopaths liked? In movies, at least. So even though, yes, fear had begun to build, I stayed silent. I wouldn't give him the satisfaction.

Then he took my blood pressure.

"A little low," he said. "You might be anemic. That would be interesting. One of my theories is that low BP can contribute to parasomnia."

"But I don't have parasomnia," I said.

"Well, then, you're a perfect candidate for my control group," he said. "AB negative blood type without the attendant symptoms of a nocturnal seizure sufferer."

"How did you find out we're all AB negative?" I asked, thinking of Eloise, Iris, and Hayley.

"Because you're all such good citizens," he said.

"What do you mean?"

"You participate in blood drives. You know, the ones we have at school every fall. They test and type your blood, Oli."

"But that's confidential!" I said.

"I was one of the student volunteers," he said. "Along with Chris and Matt, don't you remember? We were the ones who gave you juice and cookies after you and Eloise finished. Because I'm president of Future Doctors, I had more responsibility."

And my heart sank. Now I recalled Fitch sitting at a table off to the side with a laptop, marking down which students had shown up. He must have found a way to look at the results of the technician's tests, figure out which of us would be candidates for his experiments.

"But Iris and Hayley don't even go to Black Hall High," I said.

"Right. They were a little more challenging. See, my mom works all over the place, including Rhode Island. She has access to so many databases . . ."

"She was their doctor?" I asked.

"No, but she consults at the hospital where their pediatrician has privileges," he said. "And it's not hard to hack into my mom's records. I've been doing it forever." He grinned. "It's fun."

"What a great son you are," I said.

"She uses the same password for everything." He smiled. "Email, Instagram, magazine subscriptions, her patient records. It's the name of the Greek god of medicine. Asclepius. Sometimes with a question mark at the end, if the site requires special characters. What about you, Oli? Don't you use the same password, to make it easier to remember?"

I didn't answer.

"Well, I do," he said. "Mine is a little more creative than hers. *Sibylline*, and their initials. *ADC*. Athena, Daphne, and Circe. The three sisters. Because that's what this is all about. Those ancient girls are my inspiration to find a cure for this terrible disorder."

Why would he tell me his password? It seemed so weird. What if

I decided to log into his email or social media once I got my phone back? If I ever got my phone back.

He turned and began to set the dials on the big machine. When he walked around again, I saw that he was holding two yellow plastic circles, one in each hand, with wires leading back to the controls.

"What are those?" I asked.

"Electrodes," he said. "To measure brain activity. Ideally, you would be asleep when I run the test. That said, I would like to give you a sedative. Not an injection, Oli. Just a little pill that will put you into a dream state. Do you consent?"

"You're actually asking me?" I asked.

"Yes," he said, giving me that wide smile again.

"Then no. I don't consent."

He laughed. "I knew you would say that. You're predictable. Well, guess what? I don't want you asleep the first time. Having you awake will establish a baseline. There will be time for dream tests. The next time, and the one after that."

Let him think there would be a next time. Whatever it took, I was going to get out of here before that could happen.

"Lie back, Oli," he said, giving me a tap on the shoulder.

I thought about kicking him, shoving him and running, but his words about hurting Hayley rang in my ears. If I was going to attack him, I would need the element of surprise. Just then, alone with him in a bricked-up room, my options were limited.

So I lay back, and the next part was bizarre. Here was this boy from my high school class acting like a mad doctor. It was as if he was playing the lead role in a school play about Dr. Frankenstein. And I was his subject.

He dabbed some gel on my temples. He didn't even push my hair back; I instinctively reached up, and it felt gooey—just like the sticky stuff Iris had mentioned had been put on her head.

"Keep your hands by your sides," he ordered.

Then he attached the electrodes. That was painless. He walked over to the machine and examined the dials. He put on ridiculous-looking goggles—orange-tinted, with a strap that went around his head. They had built-in headphones. They also had a mic, like the kind performers wear onstage.

He began talking into the mic.

"Subject is Olivia Parrish. Sixteen years of age. Pulse one hundred, blood pressure one hundred over seventy. Sister of previous subject Eloise Parrish. Both have, well in the case of Eloise, *had*, blood type AB negative."

The word *had* felt purposeful, and I noticed how he was staring at me with a spark in his eyes, as if he wanted to upset me again. I refused to react.

Mentioning Eloise had the opposite effect than what he intended. It gave me strength. It made me summon her spirit, her goodness. Instead of making me grieve her loss, and what he had put her through, it inspired me. I looked over his shoulder and conjured her beautiful face. Her intelligence, her humor, her kind heart.

Fitch flipped a switch on the machine, and I heard a crackle, like electricity. I felt a slight sensation in my left temple, then my right. It wasn't painful, but it was unsettling. I closed my eyes and willed the time to pass. Minutes ticked by, with pressure alternating from one side to the other, left-right-left-right, the feeling intensifying to the point it felt more like a jolt, as if he was shocking me.

That's when I really got scared. Would this affect my brain? Could it change me, damage me for good? I kept thinking of Eloise, and I knew she didn't want this for me. I reached up to yank the electrodes off.

"Don't do it, Oli," Fitch said sharply. "We're almost finished. If you interfere now, I will give you that drug and restrain you and start over. Now lie still and let me measure your respiration. Breathe normally. That's it."

I tried to control my breath, but I couldn't. I was too churned up. I could see that Fitch was absorbed in the dials on the machine, taking notes about whatever data they were revealing. That's when he hit one more switch, and a current ran through me, as if I'd been struck by lightning, and my body shook—a huge shiver that went from my head to my toes. I heard myself whimpering, saying the name Matt out loud.

When it passed, I saw that he was grinning.

"Matt, haha," he said. "You really wanted him to be your boy-friend, didn't you?"

I clamped my jaw shut, unwilling to say a word. It hurt too much to think about what I had wanted once-upon-a-time, like yesterday.

"That's not going to happen. You realize that, right?" Fitch asked.

I bit the inside of my cheek to keep from screaming at him.

"Oh, I upset you? Well, sorry. But it's healthier to face facts," he said. "That's a reality."

Fitch liked seeing me that way, hurting badly. I believed in that instant that everything he was doing had less to do with research and more to do with harming people—physically and emotionally. He was like that person who pulls the wings off flies just to see them suffer.

"It wasn't an accident, was it?" I asked.

"What, Oli?"

"Eloise dying. You said it was an accident. Abigail says so, too, that you didn't mean to do it."

He didn't respond right away. There was a large black book on a shelf beside the table. He bent over it and began to turn the pages, stopping at one to read. I saw his lips moving, as if he was chanting something. Then he opened a cupboard and took out a saltshaker. He sprinkled something into the palm of his hand, then blew it away. I watched, but didn't ask what he was doing.

"Abigail is my sister," he said. "She loves me, just like you loved Eloise. Of course she would say that. She sees the best in me."

"But she's wrong, isn't she?" I asked.

He smiled that frightening smile.

"You murdered my sister on purpose," I said.

He tilted his head.

"Just like you tried to do with Iris," I said.

"I don't like girls who defy me," he said.

"So I'm right?" I asked. "You deliberately killed Eloise. You knew what you were doing?"

"That's not what I said, Oli. Listen. Open your ears. I said I don't like girls who defy me. I might get upset when they do, and that might cause me to make mistakes. I would never purposely hurt anyone, much less kill them."

"If that's true," I asked, trembling, "why did you just tell me your password? Isn't it because you're already planning to not let me go?"

"It bothers me that you're so determined to see the worst in me," Fitch said. "Because I'm good, Oli. The whole point is that I care. It's why I do what I do." Still holding the saltshaker, he tilted it up above so that sparkles rained down on me.

"What is that?" I asked, flinching.

"It's gold dust," he said. "Fresh from Minerva's jewelry bench. It's a symbol of how precious I think you all are."

"Like the charm you left when you dumped Iris in the grave?" I asked.

"Yes, solid gold," he said, looking deeply into my eyes. "That's what you all are to me. I don't take any of you for granted."

"What about the feather?" I asked. "The gray-blue feather? Did you leave that, too?"

He tilted his head and looked surprised. "You noticed," he said.

"Like the feather you left with Eloise?"

He nodded. "Yes, I collected Eloise's that morning when we birded in the Braided Woods. I took it from the warbler that you and Matt were holding. It seemed symbolic to me. Flight . . . from one state of being to another. Eloise, transforming from a regular girl to a hero to the goddess." He paused. "I wanted that for Iris, too."

I forced myself to keep my breathing steady, to not scream.

"What is that book?" I asked, but I already knew. He gave me a skewed smile and held the book close to my face, so I could see. The cover was black leather, cracked with age, and embossed with words in a language I couldn't read.

Daphne's magic book, Minerva had said. *The Sibylline version of* Malleus Maleficarum—*the* Hammer of Witches.

I tried to remain expressionless as I stared straight into Fitch's eyes and remembered what else Minerva had said: *It's written in the* Hammer of Witches *that the dust of silver and gold is for anointing the dead . . .*

That's okay, I told myself. I'm not dead yet.

Twenty-six

When I went back into the main attic room and lay down on my mattress, my defiance began to fade. Fitch's tests had left me with a headache and the awfulness of knowing the truth about Matt: that what I'd felt between us had been nothing but a lie. Those two things made me feel so devastated, I nearly stopped believing in myself, in my ability to escape.

Hayley tended to me while Abigail sat across the room, watching. There was a microwave and a cupboard full of canned food; Hayley zapped some instant ramen. I didn't feel hungry, but she pushed the mug into my hands.

"You need to keep up your strength," she said. "Don't let him win."

"Hayley, look at us," I said. "He's already winning."

"This doesn't sound like you," she said. "You're an upbeat, we-can-do-this, we're-outta-here person."

"That's nice, but you hardly know me," I said.

"Sometimes you just know—you know the most important things about a person right away."

Her words should have made me feel good, but they were a kick in the stomach. I had thought I'd known Matt. I stared at the rope bracelet on my wrist. If I'd had a knife at that moment, I would have cut it off.

"Are you hearing me?" Hayley asked.

"Yes," I said.

"So come on, Oli. Pull it together. Eat that soup."

I obliged her.

Even though it was just instant, made from powdered chicken broth, I had to admit it tasted delicious. I felt the warmth when I swallowed, and it went all through my body. I ate the whole mugful quickly. It helped me think. To make sure my brain was okay, uninjured by his stupid machine, I kept challenging myself. I tried to mentally run through my life list— all the birds I had seen over my lifetime so far. Starting with the most common—our Connecticut state bird, the American robin—all the way through my most recent, the merlin at Ocean House.

After listing about fifty more, I felt my feistiness returning. I stood up, did a couple of squats, and punched the air.

"She's back!" Hayley said, and that made me laugh. I glanced at Abigail. She was lying down again, reading a book. She seemed not to be listening to us.

"I've been thinking about Fitch watching us," I whispered to Hayley. "Whether there's another person spying or not, we need to find the cameras."

"I think you were right. There are two, in the taxidermy birds. The snowy owl and the kestrel."

I looked at the stuffed raptors again. I couldn't see any wires or other evidence of equipment.

"How can we be sure?" I asked.

"One time after Iris and I first got here, he took those two birds down, and I heard Abigail ask him why. He said they 'weren't working.'" Hayley glanced at Abigail again to make sure she still wasn't paying attention to us.

"I'm pretty sure he wasn't referring to dead birds not working," I said.

"Exactly. I didn't realize it at the time, but guess he thought the cameras were broken. It turned out we'd had a power outage—just for a few minutes, but enough to interrupt the signal and send them offline," Hayley said.

"That's what we have to do," I said. "To get ahead of him. Break the cameras for real."

"Then what?" Hayley asked.

"He'll come to investigate, and because the cameras are broken, he won't see us hiding by the door. We can grab him, knock him down, tie him up," I said. "Whatever it takes to get away, we'll do it. Then we call the police, get Detective Tyrone to come and arrest him."

"Detective Tyrone?"

"Yes, she's in charge of my sister's case. I wanted to call her as soon as I found Iris in the woods, but Iris wouldn't let me," I said.

Hayley nodded. "The boy—Fitch, I still can't get used to knowing his name—threatened us, right from the minute he took us," Hayley said. "Told us that if one of us ever got away and told the police, he'd kill the other."

"Iris took it to heart," I said. "No matter how much Matt or I begged her . . ."

"Matt?" Hayley asked. "You mean, Fitch's friend?"

"Yes," I said, flinching. "I thought he was my friend, too. But never mind, that's over. How do we disable the cameras?"

"We can't reach the birds," Hayley said.

It was true. The attic walls were at least twelve feet high. And we didn't even know for sure in which birds the cameras were hidden. I glanced at Abigail. She seemed to be asleep again, but was she? Or was she really eavesdropping? Would she tell Fitch what we were planning?

Hayley and I had been standing with our heads close together. If Fitch was watching, he might know we were conspiring, so we stepped apart and went to different parts of the room. I walked around the perimeter of the attic. I studied every inch of the walls again and saw how the old wood was splintered in places, how some of the rusty nails protruded.

My grandmother used to say that if we stepped on a rusty nail, we could get lockjaw. That made me oddly paranoid—seriously, how many nails, rusty or not, are lying around on the ground? But for a long time, I never walked barefoot without looking down at my feet. As I circled the attic, I have to admit, I was a little groggy from the tests, but I imagined Fitch slamming into one of these nails and getting lockjaw.

And that's not me—I never wish bad things on anyone. It bothered me that I was having such a terrible fantasy, but I told myself, and I knew it was true, that I had to somehow disable Fitch in order for us to escape. I had vowed to Iris that we would free Hayley.

Thinking of Iris made my stomach flip—where was she? Had Fitch finally succeeded in destroying her? This was a monster who buried girls in the dirt. I wasn't going to let that happen again.

But lockjaw—what was it, anyway? It might keep someone from being able to talk, but it wouldn't exactly take them down enough to keep them from hurting us. So I kept moving, because I wanted to find a weapon to use.

I had to thank my grandmother for giving me the idea that danger could hide in ordinary objects, like a nail hidden in the grass. On my second route around the room, I paused in front of the sibyls. The sisters were lovely—beautiful in their own distinct ways, but with the same sisterly similarity I saw between Iris and Hayley, between me and Eloise.

I studied Athena, Daphne, and Circe. Having met Daphne downstairs, it was easy to tell who she was. In the painting, her hair was dark and neatly curled, instead of flowing long and white the way it was now. I gazed at her peaceful face, her kind eyes, and wished she could tell me what to do, what she knew that might protect us.

And in a way, Daphne did help. Because my gaze went from her face to the window beside her panel, and in the particular way the yellow streetlight was shining through, I saw a small crack. It was in the middle of the glass, shaped like a starburst. I wanted to go closer and examine it, but I was afraid Fitch might be watching.

"What is it?" Hayley asked, picking up on my excitement, walking over to me.

"Don't look now," I said. "But I think there's a tiny crack in the window."

"I'm listening," she said.

"Abigail said it's supposed to be hurricane glass, but if there really is a flaw, the window can be broken," I said.

"Okay," she said. "But even if we broke it, what would we do? Jump? It's how many stories down to the ground?"

"Four," I said.

"So it wouldn't really help us," Hayley said.

"It might," I said. "We could at least signal to someone outside."

"Right," Hayley said. "We could wave a sheet until someone on the street noticed."

I closed my eyes, pretended I was outside. How many times had I passed the Miramar in my life? I could see the sprawling Victorian mansion rising tall on the edge of the harbor. I pictured the old yellow hotel, shabby after being in the salt air and wind for a century and a half, with the white-curlicued gingerbread trim broken off in places, some black shutters hanging by one hinge. And, zigzagging its way up the side was that creaky, rusty-looking stairway to the top.

"There's a fire escape!" I said.

"Seriously?" Hayley asked. She didn't live around here, so of course the hotel wasn't emblazoned in her mind the way it was in mine. The Miramar was a shoreline landmark.

She lurched forward, starting toward the window, but I grabbed her arm. "Remember—he's watching," I said, nodding toward the stuffed raptors.

"Right," she said. "So what do we do?"

"Didn't you say the feed cut out at one point?" I asked.

"Yes," she said. "When the electricity went out."

I nodded, scanning the walls around the stuffed birds. Power had to come from somewhere, either a battery pack or a regular old plug in an outlet. Growing up around boats meant that I had stuck by my father's side when he had to fix the various systems on all the vessels: the diesel engines, the steering cables, the water tanks, and the electrical panels.

I tried not to be too obvious, staring up at the snowy owl and kestrel, but I quickly saw what I'd been searching for. Cords were hidden in the birds' feathers, and discreetly plugged into outlets in the rustic ceiling, painted the same color as the splintery brown wood.

"Okay. You know where the cameras are, right? Don't look now. But all we have to do is unplug them," I said, and of course Hayley looked. Human nature. I almost had to laugh because I was practically giddy with hope and with the knowledge that we had a way out of the attic.

"How do we do it?" Hayley asked.

"That's what we have to figure out," I said. I smiled, as if I thought the solution was right there in my grasp.

But the truth was, I had no idea.

228

Twenty-seven

I paced around, looking for a way up to the electrical cords. On my third circuit of the attic, I stopped to gaze at Abigail. She hadn't had an episode since that first one, but it seemed to have taken so much out of her. She looked pale and thin on her canopied bed, in her long white dress. She seemed to be asleep, but she wasn't.

"Why are you staring at me?" she asked.

"I'm trying to understand you," I said.

"I'm just like you, but I have this disorder."

"Not really. We're nothing alike. I wouldn't do what you're doing. You could help us get away from your brother, but you're not."

"I want to help you," she said. "It's complicated."

"You told me it was an accident," I said. "What Fitch did to my sister. But you know what? I don't believe you."

"Stop," Abigail said, shaking her head hard as if she could dispel the horrible thought.

"I loved her," I said. "As much as you love your brother."

"I know," she whispered. "And she loved you."

"She told you that?"

"Yes," Abigail said, her voice shaking. "She begged him to let her go, so she could return to you."

"But he wouldn't let her," I said. "Because she stood up to him. He said he doesn't like girls who defy him."

"That's what happened with Iris," Hayley said.

"Yes," Abigail said. She glanced at the owl, lowered her voice. "It's why you have to get away. Because I can't stand if he does it again—if he sends any of you to the dirt. It can't happen." She took a deep breath. "I already know, he's going to do it to me, too."

"No, he loves you," I said.

"He won't after this," she said.

"After what?" Hayley asked.

"After I stop being the sweet little sister," Abigail said, and Hayley chuckled.

"Oh boy, watch out," Hayley said.

"Danger zone," Abigail said. "The oldest ones rely on us being exactly the way they want us to be, right, Hayley?"

"One hundred percent," Hayley said. "We have to know our places in the little-sisters box."

I watched Abigail give Hayley a big smile, and Hayley smiled back. I was struck by it all—the bonding of younger sisters, hearing what it was like for them. Had I kept Eloise in a box, expected her to be a certain way?

I realized then that Abigail and Hayley had a sort of friendship. In spite of the circumstances, the horror of it all, they had become close.

But now, Abigail turned away from Hayley. I noticed she was staring hard at the panels.

"I used to wonder what it was like for them," she said, pointing at the Sibylline sisters. "I knew about parasomnia, and how the two younger sisters died in their sleep, but it seemed so far away, so impossible. Like something that could never happen to me." She swallowed hard. "But it *is* happening. I don't know how many more episodes I can live through. They're getting worse. I didn't think I'd survive the last one."

"But you did, Abigail," Hayley said. "And you'll keep going."

"You will," I said. I realized that in spite of her part in this, I really wanted Abigail to be okay.

"Maybe for a while," Abigail said. "But I won't survive my brother."

"Fitch?" I asked, confused.

"I'm going to help you get away," she said. "And he'll kill me when he finds out."

"No, we won't let him hurt you," I said, excitement building inside as I thought of the possibility of really getting out of there.

Abigail shrugged. "I'm going to die, anyway."

"Don't say that," Hayley said. "You're not going to die."

Abigail gave Hayley a skeptical smile.

"How are we going to do this?" I asked.

"I heard you two talking about the window, and the cameras," Abigail said. "Like I said—the glass will be almost impossible to break, but you're right—there's a little crack. If we focus on that one spot, hit it over and over with something sharp, it might be possible."

"But first, the cameras," I said. "We have to get up to the ceiling, to unplug them . . ."

"That's one way," she said. "But they're controlled by an app. He can run it on his phone or a laptop."

"And we don't have either of those," Iris said.

Abigail smiled. "Not his," she said. "But the system is wired into the control panel, and I know where it is."

Twenty-eight

Fitch had found a good place to hide the white metal box that held the router and other Wi-Fi components necessary for running the security cameras. It wouldn't have been the first place most people would look, but it certainly had symbolism. If Abigail hadn't told us, we never would have found it—but once she did, it made perfect sense.

She gestured toward the Sibylline panels.

"It's behind that one with Daphne painted on it," she said.

I was dying to get my hands on the box, but the irony was, the cameras were most likely trained on us now, making it almost impossible to disable the electronics. Fitch would see us, and that would defeat the purpose. Abigail had come up with a plan that would require serious synchronization. The success or failure of our operation depended upon her acting abilities.

So Hayley and I pretended to be absorbed in working on the thousand-piece jigsaw puzzle, and Abigail lay on her bed. I felt tense, waiting for what I knew was coming. And then Abigail got started.

I never thought she could have done it well enough to fool Fitch, but within half an hour, she was faking an episode. If Fitch was monitoring the seizure the way he had last time, we'd have about one minute from the moment Abigail went rigid to the instant Fitch came bursting through the door. During the time it would take for him to run upstairs, no one would be watching the monitor, so that was exactly as long as we had to get into the system.

Abigail moaned and tossed in bed. It seemed so real. Real enough that it was easy for me and Hayley to look at her with concern.

We saw her stiffen up. She was forcing herself to lower her respiration so Fitch would see she wasn't breathing right. A great stillness filled the room. I remembered how scared I'd been to think she had actually died, and it was a tribute to her acting that I felt it again now.

I heard the quick throb of the buzzer attached to her mattress, and I knew that was our sign—it meant that Fitch had been alerted, and he'd be running up to the attic to tend to her.

"Now!" I said sharply.

Hayley and I ran to Daphne's panel. We tilted it forward—it was super-heavy, and our muscles were straining just to support it and keep it from crashing down on top of us. Behind the tall sheet of wood was a small door cut into the wall. While Hayley steadied the panel, I scoped things out. There, inside the cupboard, was the alarm box containing the router and modem.

"The system is password protected," I said, even as I was typing the password Fitch had told me: SibyllineADC. The window on the apparatus began to blink. I knew we were in. As soon as the flashing stopped—theoretically—I would cut the power.

But that didn't happen.

Across the screen appeared the message: *Nice try, Oli!*

And that didn't surprise me one bit—I had expected Fitch to have been one step ahead of me, or to think he was, and I had to stop myself from laughing out loud. This chess move was playing straight into what I had hoped would happen.

Then the attic door opened slowly, and Fitch walked in, with that cruel grin on his face. "I knew you'd try to hack into something of mine—I actually 'forgot' my laptop in the exam room so you'd try that, but you didn't look in there. Did you honestly think I was careless enough to allow that password to access my security system?"

"Not careless, Fitch. Stupid is the word," I said, deliberately wanting to rile him and get him off guard.

"I'm not stupid," he said, fury in his voice. "And I'll make you pay for saying that."

I tried not to look at Hayley. Disabling the Wi-Fi had actually been plan B, but we hadn't let Abigail in on plan A. As much as she wanted to help us, hurting her brother might have been too much for her to handle, and she might have stopped us. Fitch hadn't left any obvious weapons around, but after conspiring—heads together as we'd worked on the puzzle—Hayley had found the perfect thing.

As Fitch stood there glaring, I distracted him by walking toward Abigail. Hayley crouched down to pick up the doorstop—antique iron, shaped like a swan.

"You know what bothers me?" Fitch asked. I thought he was talking to me.

"What?" I asked. But then I realized he was addressing Abigail.

He was staring straight at her. She had given up her act. Sitting on the edge of her bed, one arm slung around one of the posts, she was watching everything unfold.

"You betrayed me," he said to Abigail, ignoring me. "They would never have found the camera control box if you hadn't told them about it. After all I've done, sacrificed, to work on this cure. To help you. My sister. And this is what I get from you."

"Fitch . . ." Abigail began.

"I was testing you as much as I was Oli," he said, sounding genuinely heartbroken. "I thought you loved me."

"I do," Abigail said, her voice cracking. "But not the way you are now, Fitch. Finding a cure, helping me, was so important. You were devoted to the work, even when Mom and Dad broke up, and when Mom stopped caring."

"I'm *still* devoted to the work," he said.

"But for the wrong reasons," Abigail said. "Not to save me, not even for your personal glory. I've seen you, Fitch. I wanted to believe that everything you were doing was for good. But Fitch . . . you cause pain. And I'm worried"—her voice dropped—"that you like it."

"It's part of the research," he said. But instead of looking upset at being accused, he looked pleased.

Out of the corner of my eye, I saw Hayley inching forward, gripping the doorstop in her hand behind her back. Fitch's phone buzzed, and he took it from his pocket and read a text. His smile grew wider. My stomach flipped, anxious for Hayley to make her move. I saw her raise the doorstop above her head, ready to smash it down on Fitch and give us a chance to get away.

"We have company," Fitch said, half-turning toward the door just as Hayley began to bring the doorstop down. It hit him with a glancing blow to his shoulder. He shoved her away, as if she was no more than a mosquito, knocking her to the floor, and stepped past her to unlock the door.

And there he stood, the boy I had thought I loved.

"Sorry I'm late," Matt said to Fitch, not even glancing at me.

"Hey, you're here now," Fitch said. "That's what counts."

I took a step forward. I stood between Fitch and Matt, making it impossible for Matt to avoid looking me in the eyes.

"I never would have believed it," I said.

"Hello, Oli," Matt said coldly.

"You're really part of it," I said. "Were you there when he killed Eloise? Did you help bury her? I need to know."

"There's a lot you don't know," Matt said, his eyes narrowed. I barely even recognized him. I saw nothing of the old Matt, the one who had made my heart race, calmed my spirit, eased the sadness I'd felt from losing my sister.

"You were just pretending to help us," I said. I remembered him on his phone—he must have been texting Fitch our location. It was why he immediately suggested meeting up with him. "You drove me and Iris all around. You were just having fun, waiting to deliver us to Fitch."

"The point," Fitch said, interrupting me, "is that you are right where you belong, Oli. You and Hayley. And my disloyal sister."

"Where's Iris now?" I asked him.

"What have you done to her?" Hayley asked.

"Don't worry," Fitch said. "I'll find her."

What did that mean? He didn't have her?

"Anyway, I'll give you time to think about things, but we'll be back very shortly," Fitch said. He gestured at Matt. "Come on, let's go."

Matt nodded. His eyes bored into mine, and for just a split second, he glanced down at the rope bracelet on my wrist: the Turk's head, our sailor's knot. Then he turned away and headed downstairs, with Fitch right behind him.

twenty-nine

After Matt walked out, I felt like a zombie.

No one had any energy left. Hayley sat at the card table, staring at the puzzle, not even trying to fit the jigsaw together. Abigail sat on the edge of her bed, staring straight ahead. Her arms were wrapped around herself, as if trying to hold her whole spirit together. Talk about the Sword of Damocles: It was over our heads, swinging lower.

It sliced away our hope: hope for rescue, for getting out of there. For me, the main hope I'd lost was that I had meant something to Matt, that I had been wrong about him and he was nothing like Fitch. I wasn't going to let a broken heart defeat me. I had until they returned to come up with a new solution.

The old dilemma was still there: We had to knock out the camera feed before we could break the window and head down to the street, and the ceiling was still twelve feet high. The stuffed birds hung down twenty inches or so, but that still left them way too high off the floor for us to reach.

And it wasn't as if Fitch had left a ladder to make things easy for us.

I felt a combination of galvanized, discouraged, determined, and apprehensive. I knew I'd hear footsteps on the stairs before long, and that might be the end of us. I didn't know for sure what Fitch had in mind for us, but I was positive it couldn't be good.

I found myself standing in front of the panels. The Sibylline sisters had left clues for us all along, I realized. They had triggered Iris's memory, told her where to look for Hayley. In a way, they were where it had all started: the first sisters known to have the family malady. I hadn't spent any time with the panels—with the oracle sisters— since Fitch had drugged and hauled me into the attic.

Each of the three panels was a rectangle made of wood—about six feet tall, three feet wide—with the surface painted in oils. From a distance, the sisters looked similar: tall, slender, standing in a classical pose reminiscent of ancient columns, wearing identical pleated white dresses that fell to their ankles.

But up close, the sisters' features were different. Circe and Athena bore a family resemblance—they had the same golden-red hair as Minerva did, and Daphne had her dark hair. I noticed that all three sisters were wearing necklaces—fine gold chains with a charm attached.

When I leaned closer to see what was etched in the gold, I saw, to my shock, that the jewelry was real, not painted onto the wood— the chains were attached to the panels with delicate silver wires, and the charms dangled freely.

I couldn't believe it: The charms were exactly the same as the ones Minerva made at her shop—gold, set with tiny diamonds. And just like the one I had found at the grave site in the Braided Woods. I reached out to hold the disc on Athena's necklace in my hand, and I saw that Athena's exact features had been etched into the delicate circle of gold.

Then I peered at the other two charms. Each one contained a portrait that resembled, exactly, the girl who was wearing it. The craftsmanship was brilliant and uncanny.

"Abigail," I said, beckoning her over. I pointed at the three necklaces.

"Just like the ones my cousin makes!" she said, coming to stand beside me. "They're exactly like Minerva's."

"That's how they look to me, too," I said. "But is there any way to tell how old they are? Were the charms made when the panels were painted?"

"Well, there are some scratches in the gold, so that could mean they're old. But they look exactly like the ones Minerva makes so . . . I don't know."

"Abigail, does Minerva ever come here, to the attic?" I asked.

Abigail looked upset. "He brought her here once. To do a test on her. She didn't like it."

"I know, it hurt, she told me. But I mean, does she come here other times? Does she know what's going on, with what Fitch did to my sister?" I asked.

"I don't think so," Abigail said. "I'm pretty sure that I'm the only one in the family who knows." She looked troubled, filled with shame. "And I've stayed quiet. I haven't told. Oli, thank you for even talking to me. For asking me about these necklaces. You must hate me."

"I know it's complicated for you," I said. "I get that you love Fitch. It must be hard to see him this way. And you're helping us now. So thank you."

She nodded, her expression lightening a little.

I stared at the necklaces again. They seemed such a different addition to the panels—clearly laden with meaning. I wondered if Minerva had attached them. If she had, it meant that she was in on everything. She had driven us here to the Miramar. She had spoken badly about Fitch, but what if that had been a way to put us at ease while she delivered us straight to him? Deep down, I couldn't believe that.

I heard very faint footsteps in the hallway. The sound was different than usual—as if someone was sneaking up the stairs and didn't want to be heard. I was suddenly on high alert—Fitch had said they would be back before long.

I heard the key quietly scratching at the lock, then a long silence, and that was strange, too. I'd noticed Fitch's way was to shove the key in so hard, it was almost violent, as if he was attacking the lock in preparation for getting to us. He'd barge in, come directly over to us, make his presence known in an aggressive way, to assert his domination. I was so lost in the fear of what was about to happen that, when the door opened silently, I had my eyes closed.

"Oli."

He whispered my name, and I turned.

My pulse jumped, and I nearly did, too.

Matt was standing there, barely inside the room, his back to the door. Tall and lanky with that familiar brown hair falling into his blue eyes. His smile wasn't there. That gap-toothed smile that always gave me butterflies was gone, replaced by a worried frown. He looked like himself, not like Fitch's evil accomplice. He put his finger to his lips, in a shushing way, telling me to not make a sound.

There was so much I wanted to say, wanted to shout. My thoughts raced with words of blame and hurt, with one big scream of despair. I wanted to run at him with my fists, hit him as hard as I could, attack him for whatever part he had played in my sister's murder, in our imprisonment, in tricking me into loving him.

But his eyes stopped me. They held a combination of sadness, intensity, and acute warning. There was urgency in his gaze that made me stay totally quiet, stand right where I was. To pay attention to whatever he was trying to tell me.

Without a word, he pointed overhead, at the snowy owl and the American kestrel—the birds that held the cameras. Because the lenses were directed toward the center of the attic, where the bed and mattresses were located, Matt was out of the cameras' lines of sight.

If Fitch was monitoring the attic, he wouldn't be able to see Matt.

I knew I should be afraid. Fitch must have sent Matt. But my old feelings were sweeping in, like the tide flowing in from the sea and rising on the beach.

I tried to fight those emotions, to tell myself to stay strong and keep my heart hard, but again: The expression in Matt's eyes was telling me something else. His gaze was so focused on me, as if he couldn't get enough of seeing me, that I felt a rush of hope.

He beckoned me toward the door.

I shook my head. There was no way I would follow him.

He held out one hand.

His blue eyes had a spark that reminded me of the time we'd gone crabbing in the marsh, when we had to cross a cracked and weathered plank over a muddy creek.

He was doing the same thing here in the attic—reaching out for me to take his hand, to steady me as I balanced my way across. At the creek, I'd been the first to cross. I had turned, reached out for him, pulled him to the opposite bank.

That memory shook me up. Here I was, in the attic, facing this boy I had known forever. He held his hand out. He was either going to trick me, take me to Fitch and whatever nightmare he had in store, or it would be something else.

It was something else.

I stood in front of Matt, so close the toes of our shoes were touching. I took his hand.

We stared into each other's eyes.

So much bad stuff had happened. It had scared me, made me

doubt everything. I felt my whole body ready to burst with pent-up suspicion and anger.

"Were you part of it?" I whispered.

He shook his head. "I had to make him believe I was," he said. "It killed me that you believed it, too."

He put his arms around me.

I was shaking.

He pulled me against his chest.

I could feel his heart pounding, or maybe that was mine.

I realized I was holding my breath, but I couldn't help it.

When I let it out, I felt it escape my body, along with the biggest shiver ever.

"Are you okay?" Matt whispered.

"No," I said, not in a whisper.

"We're going to get through this. We are. We'll do it together."

Together, he said.

"But you're with *him*," I said.

"You don't believe that," he whispered. "You know I'm not."

"I saw you with him. On the waterfront." I shoved him away. "When you pulled up outside Minerva's store, he tried to take us—and you just sat there! You didn't do anything, try to stop him!"

"I didn't know what he was doing!" Matt said. "I feel like an idiot—I didn't even see what he was doing. I was trying to get a song from my phone on the Bluetooth for when you got into the Jeep."

"A song?"

"Yes," he said. "'Lost in the 16th,' by Margot François."

The song we'd listened to once. The song about change, the feeling about love.

He squeezed my hand, and after just a few seconds, I squeezed back.

"Oli, you're still wearing my bracelet," he said, one finger touching the woven rope around my wrist, then lightly tracing my skin, his voice so low I could barely hear. "You wouldn't be wearing it if you didn't know, deep down, that I'm with you. That all I care about is you, getting you out."

I glanced down at the bracelet, and his words, spoken in his gentle, familiar voice, ran through me, and I knew he was right.

He held me even closer. We were pressed against each other, his mouth against my ear so no one else could hear him when he spoke.

"We're going to escape, but we have to move fast," he said.

"With Hayley and Abigail," I said.

"Of course," he said.

"We've lost Iris," I whispered with a ripple of grief.

"No, we haven't. Iris is fine. I'll explain in a minute. But for now, we've got to make a plan to get out."

"How?" I asked.

"Through the window on the left. The one with the fire escape."

"It's hurricane glass, but there's a tiny crack," I said.

"It'll shatter," he said. "But the timing is what counts. We have to do it fast. Fitch doesn't know I'm up here, but he'll figure it out eventually. He thinks I'm getting something out of the van."

"For what?"

He paused. "For some new type of test he's planning for all of you."

That was a punch in my gut. "Why would he tell you that?" I asked. "If you're not part of it?"

"You're going to have to trust me on this," Matt said.

"But how did he even let you in on the fact that he had us up here?" I asked, stubborn and needing to know.

"Minerva helped convince him."

"Minerva?" I asked.

Matt nodded. "You know I was looking everywhere for you at first—with Fitch. At that point, he seemed to be on our side, genuinely wanting to help Iris. I had no idea what his real goal was. You mentioned when we saw you outside Mermaid's Pearls?"

"Yes, when Fitch tried to grab Iris."

"Well, I didn't see that. All I saw was you and Iris running away—I had no idea why. We drove all around, trying to find you. When we didn't, Fitch said he had to get back here to the Miramar. He didn't tell me why, but it seemed important. I dropped him off and was on my way back to the waterfront to look for you when I saw Fitch's cousin parked outside the library."

"Minerva."

"Yes. We'd met once before, at Fitch's house. This time, she seemed scared of me, and I didn't know why. Eventually we figured out what was going on, and she knew I was frantic to find you—for good reasons, not Fitch's. Minerva said she'd dropped you off here.

And we began to put it all together. She can't stand her cousin, Oli. She told me Fitch is sick. Maybe so, but he's also evil."

"He is," I said.

"So Minerva and I came up with a plan. We came back here, separately, and she stayed hidden," Matt said. "I found Fitch standing outside his van, in the parking lot. I started to talk to him—I told him what Minerva had said. But I put it in a different way from what she meant, so he would think I admired him. So he would trust me."

"Admire him for what?"

"Trying to cure his sister, even if it meant kidnapping girls. I played on his ego, on all his science stuff, told him that I believed he was doing important work. And that I really wanted to help him. He likes flattery. It made him susceptible, and he believed me."

"And then what happened?" I asked.

"I messed up, Oli. My timing was off by just a couple minutes. I left Fitch in the parking lot, and I saw you and Iris on the porch, talking to an old lady. I didn't speak out loud, because I knew Fitch was nearby, and I didn't want him to hear. I just wanted to get you both out of there without him trying to stop me."

I thought back to how it had been, how Daphne said a boy had beckoned to Iris.

"I gestured for you both to come inside," Matt said. "I was going to take you out the back way so we could escape. But only Iris saw. I rushed her into a vacant room, to hide her, and by the time I returned to get you, you were gone."

"Fitch got to me first," I said.

"Oli, that was the worst moment of my life," Matt said. "Knowing he had you."

His expression was intense, and in that instant, all doubt slipped away: I knew with everything I had that Matt had gone along with Fitch so he could save me—save us.

"It killed me to fake being on his side," he went on. "I would have bypassed him completely, but Minerva told me this place was a maze. I didn't know if Fitch had you tied up, locked in somewhere. I couldn't take that chance—I needed him to show me where you were."

I stared into Matt's eyes and saw anguish; I could see what it had cost him to play along with Fitch—a boy he had thought was his friend.

"He could be coming back at any minute," I said.

"We have a slight reprieve," Matt said. "I left him outside on the porch, talking to that old lady. His great-aunt or something. She was telling him a story about their ancestors, how the good ones prevailed."

"Daphne," I said, looking over at her painting on the panel. "She's one of the Sibylline sisters."

"I had the strangest feeling," Matt said, "that she knew what was going on. That she knew I was here to help you, and she was keeping him occupied till I could get you and the others out."

"She's a sibyl," I said. "She doesn't know the details of what Fitch has been doing, but I think she has a sense that he's bad. She can see things the rest of us can't."

"Well, let's hope she senses that we need some time," Matt said. "Oli, we have to get those cameras right away."

"They're up so high," I said, studying the ceiling.

"I know," Matt said. He explained how Fitch had told him he'd hidden the cameras in the two raptors—owl and kestrel. How Fitch thought it was funny, so ironic, that people thought of him as a birder, someone who cared about birds.

"Once we knock the cameras out," Matt explained, "Fitch will hear an alarm, even if he's still on the porch."

"How long will that give us?" I asked.

"About two minutes to break the window and climb out," he said.

I figured that would give us another minute to head down the fire escape and hit the street running.

"How are we going to do all that in such a short time?" I asked.

"You and I are going to take out the cameras," he said.

"Okay. I'll tell Hayley and Abigail what's going on, and that they have to be ready to move as soon as we give the signal," I said.

"Walk to them slowly—he has a camera app on his phone, not just a monitor inside, so assume you're being watched. Don't act like it's urgent," he said.

"Right," I said. "We don't want Fitch thinking we have anything like a plan."

He held on tight; letting go of each other was incredibly hard, but I knew time was ticking away, so I forced myself to do it. I strolled over to Hayley and Abigail. Abigail was lying down again, Hayley leaning against the bedpost. Abigail's eyes were closed, but Hayley had seen me and Matt talking, and she looked scared to death.

"What does he want?" Hayley asked.

"He's on our side," I said. "But speak quietly so Fitch doesn't hear. We have to do this quickly . . ."

"Do what?" Hayley asked.

"Matt and I are going to take down the cameras, and then we'll break the window. We'll climb out onto the fire escape and get down to the street."

"Okay," Hayley said, her eyes brighter than they'd been since I'd met her. She looked excited. Having a mission will do that—I felt it myself. Then she glanced down at Abigail, who seemed to have fallen asleep again.

"This has been a lot for her," Hayley said. "Confronting Fitch really got to her. I don't think she can handle all this."

"She has to," I said. "Wake her up."

"Okay," Hayley said.

Matt had edged his way around the attic's perimeter so that he was standing just out of sight of the snowy owl. I meandered over to him. I had no clue about how we were going to get up to the ceiling to get to the surveillance equipment.

"How are we doing this?" I asked.

"Get on my shoulders," Matt said, pulling his Swiss Army knife from his back pocket. He handed it to me. "Then reach up and cut the ropes that attach the birds to the rafters."

I followed his thinking: When the first bird fell, it would yank out of the plug. "Once you hit one, I'll move fast to the second, and we'll do the same thing," he said.

Matt knelt down, and I straddled his shoulders. While he stood up, I held the knife and looked overhead. I reached up my arms as high as they would go, but I wasn't close enough.

"It's too high," I whispered. "But hold on. I'm going to try to stand."

I stuck the knife in my waistband. Matt reached up so I could brace myself against his hands. Using that grip as leverage, I pushed myself up until I was standing. It took teamwork and balance. I could feel the tension in his arms as Matt held them steady. I wobbled, positive I was about to tumble, but then I felt someone pulling me straight up. I felt the softest grip, and I knew it was Eloise.

My sister helped me, I swear she did. I could hear her voice as if she was hovering just above me: *You can do it, Oli. You've got this.*

And I did. Eloise, Matt, and I were doing this together. I rose up, one foot on each of his shoulders, Eloise supporting me on this ladder to the sky, and I grabbed on to the owl's feathery body. I sliced the cord, and as the owl fell to the floor, so did I. I knew I had Eloise to spot me, so I hit the floor standing, just like a gymnast sticking the landing.

Matt removed the camera from beneath the owl and clicked off the volume control. Then he, I, and Eloise repeated the process with the kestrel.

"Now!" Matt called softly to Abigail and Hayley. "The window!"

But they didn't move. Hayley was crouched beside Abigail, with Hayley shaking her shoulders.

"Wake up!" Hayley said. "C'mon, Abigail! Now!" She turned to me, panic in her eyes. "She's having an episode!"

I ran over, and I saw that Abigail had gone rigid, just as she had before. Her eyes were rolled back into her head, and she wasn't breathing. The color in her face had drained out, and she was turning gray. Hayley kept shaking her, but she didn't move.

At the same time, I heard the thud of Matt hitting the window, smashing it with a chair, then the crash of glass falling. A whoosh of fresh salt air filled the attic.

"Hurry!" Matt shouted.

"Yes, come on!" Iris yelled. She was standing outside on the fire escape, waving madly.

Iris! I understood then: Matt had hidden her in that empty room, but once she found out that he and Minerva had a plan, and that he was on our side, she joined forces with them to rescue us.

"Abigail's having a seizure!" I said. "We can't leave her!"

"If we don't get out now," Matt said, grabbing my shoulders, "we won't be able to help her at all."

Iris jumped in through the broken window, ran to us. Hayley screamed out with shocked joy. "You're here!"

"We'll have the best reunion in the world once we're down on the street," Iris told her sister after one incredibly tight hug. "Now, get out—I came up the fire escape to make sure it's safe, but it's only hanging by one bracket per floor, and they're rusty. Be careful, okay? One at a time."

"I can't leave Abigail," Hayley said.

"Hayley, this is it. I'm your big sister, you're going to do what I tell you. Move *now*. I'm not letting you stay here for one more minute," Iris said.

Hayley nodded, glanced once at Abigail. Iris pulled her away, and the Bigelow sisters clung to each other. Iris saw Hayley safely onto the top rung, waited for her to descend a few steps, then stepped out behind her.

I stood by Abigail, looked at Matt.

"We have to carry her," I said. "I don't know what Fitch will do to her if we don't."

Matt didn't ask questions. He just reached down and grabbed hold of Abigail. He tried to put her over his shoulder, in a fireman's carry like we'd learned in lifesaving, but her body was too stiff from the parasomnia. He lowered her onto the mattress.

Neither of us wanted to climb out that window without her, but for now, she was beyond help. I felt a sob rise up in my throat.

"I can't leave her with a murderer," I said. I thought of what Fitch had done to my sister. I didn't care that he had claimed he didn't mean to kill her—the fact was, he had.

"Fitch's focused on you at the moment—not Abigail. In spite of everything, she is his sister. But if he hurts you, I couldn't . . ." Matt sounded too upset to finish. When he saw that I wasn't moving toward the window, he took a deep breath.

"We can do this," I said, looking into his eyes. He nodded.

I lifted Abigail's feet, and Matt slipped his arms under hers from behind. She was still rigid as we carried her to the window. But whether it was the blast of cool air or some inner determination, Abigail came to—without any help from Fitch or his medication. Her eyes looked cloudy, and I didn't think she could make it down the fire escape on her own—Matt obviously thought that, too. Once again, he hoisted her over his shoulder.

Matt went ahead with Abigail, and I followed them. As we made our way down the fire escape, I realized I was holding my breath. My heart was back there in the attic. I was grateful we were getting away, but not all of us. Not Eloise. The one sister who couldn't escape.

I was still thinking of her when my feet hit the ground. I saw Matt's Jeep right there, with Minerva behind the wheel. Iris and Hayley helped Abigail into the back seat, right between them. Matt grabbed my hand and pulled me onto his lap in the front. Minerva glanced at me.

"You made it," she said.

I nodded. "Thanks for being our getaway driver."

She smiled and gave a little salute. "Sorry not to make it back sooner. Daphne's memory about where she sent the map was a little rusty. But I'm here now."

She had been parked at the back entrance, and she pulled around to the front. I gazed at the porch. Fitch wasn't there. I realized he must be running up to the attic—I loved imagining what he'd think when he found us gone.

But Daphne was still in her rocking chair. In her white dress, she reminded me of the girls on the panels, the Sibylline sisters—because she was one of them. She saw me through the window of the Jeep, and, just for a second, our eyes met.

She touched her heart and nodded.

And I nodded back. She was the only surviving Sibylline sister, and I felt that her magic, her sisterly love, had helped all of us to escape today.

"We have to call the police," I said to Matt.

"I already have," Minerva said, holding up her cell phone. "The minute I saw you all coming down the fire escape."

And she had: I heard sirens. They got louder, and a moment later I saw the flashing strobe lights as three squad cars and a black sedan pulled up in front of the Miramar.

It was okay for the police to be called now. Iris and Hayley were together and safe, and Fitch's threats meant nothing anymore. Detective Tyrone climbed out of the black car. She came straight over to me, concern in her eyes.

"Oli, are you all right? What's going on?" she asked.

"We got him," I said, and forgot the fact I never cried in front of anyone. My voice broke, and tears spilled from my eyes.

"What are you talking about?" Detective Tyrone asked.

"We know who did it. We know who killed Eloise, Detective Tyrone. It's Fitch Martin. He's in there right now," I said, pointing at the hotel.

"He took all of them," Minerva said.

"All of them?" Detective Tyrone asked, staring at me.

"Yes," I said. "My sister. Iris and Hayley. And me. But we got away—all of us except Eloise."

Detective Tyrone took a step toward me. She hesitated, then put her arms around me. As I leaned my head against her shoulder and saw all those officers running toward the hotel door, I felt as if it was finally over. We had finally gotten him.

But it turned out I was wrong about that.

thirty

Fitch escaped.

I guess having a maze-ridden hotel with an old, boarded-up but-ler's staircase to the basement helps you make a clean getaway. By the time the police reached the attic, we learned, Fitch had disappeared with his records and as much of the equipment as he could load into a rickety old luggage cart. They found the cart at the base of the hidden stairs. He had left the blue van behind. Instead he had driven away in a family car he'd kept parked in the underground garage.

Detective Tyrone and members of the Silver Bay, Black Hall, and Connecticut State Police departments hovered around Iris, Hayley, Minerva, Daphne, Matt, Abigail, and me in the parking lot of the hotel. They questioned all of us about Fitch and what had happened, and we answered as best we could, given that we were all tired and dazed and, in the case of Daphne, finally learning what had really gone on in the attic.

The police contacted Iris and Hayley's parents. Rhode Island is right next to Connecticut, but in some ways it seems like a world away. There were two separate police forces investigating the miss-ing girls. And because Eloise had been found in October, months before Iris and Hayley were kidnapped in late May, the investigators didn't connect the cases. Only now were they putting it together, that a serial kidnapper—and killer—had been at work, crossing state lines along the way.

Iris and Hayley's parents had returned from their vacation to the nightmare of missing daughters. Their story had been huge on local and even national news, but I had missed it, because I'd been avoiding the news and social media. Now, I berated myself. If I had stayed alert, read about missing Rhode Island girls, I might have linked their disappearance with Eloise's case and told Detective Tyrone. The case could have been solved sooner—saving Iris and Hayley from at least some of the trauma.

Their parents were now on their way from the Cat Castle to pick them up. They would be reunited within the hour.

Darkness was ebbing; morning stars still blazed bright, but one-by-one they began to dim in the dawn light. A line of orange appeared on the eastern horizon, and the sun rose on the third day since I'd found Iris. I heard a distant siren—the ambulance coming to take Abigail to the hospital. The police were trying to track down her and Fitch's mom.

Detective Tyrone told me that every police department in New England had Fitch's description and the license plate of his family car. There were so many places he could be. He was smart, he could hide anywhere, but they would find him. They were tracking his cell phone data. He couldn't get away, she said.

I wanted to believe her, but she didn't know Fitch. It would be so easy for him to trick people into hiding him. And who knew what he would do to them when he was ready to move on?

Detective Tyrone was eager to take Matt home to his parents, and to reunite me with Gram. But I wasn't quite ready. As the ambulance arrived to take Abigail to Shoreline General, it backed into the parking lot, making that beep-beep-beep sound.

I grabbed Matt's hand. "I think I know where he went," I said.

"Fitch?"

I nodded.

"I think I do, too," he said. "Let's tell Detective Tyrone."

"Not yet," I said. "Let's just drive by—to see if he's there. Then we'll call her."

Matt gazed at me for a few seconds. He might have wanted to talk me out of it, but he saw in my expression that it would be futile.

We took advantage of all the police activity to climb into Matt's Jeep. Minerva stayed at the hotel with Daphne, Abigail sped off to Shoreline General with lights and sirens going. Iris and Hayley were surrounded by police and medical personnel, being questioned and taken care of, waiting for their parents to arrive.

No one even noticed us leaving.

Matt drove us to the Braided Woods.

thirty-one

I felt tense the whole way there, but my pulse slowed when we turned onto the lane that led deeper into the boulder-strewn forest. This was sacred territory. My sister had been here. I had visited her grave. I had spoken to her, heard her voice.

I looked around for Fitch's car but didn't see it.

It was just past sunrise on this early summer day. In the attic, I'd somehow forgotten that it was the season of the beach, of carefree fun, of sea breezes. Sunlight came through the green leaves and pine needles, creating shadows that danced across the ground as the soft wind ruffled branches overhead. Matt and I drove slowly along the forest road, not saying a word.

That's when I saw it.

The trees had shaded the spot where Fitch had parked. His car had merged into the low foliage of rhododendrons and mountain laurel, and it had been invisible at first.

"He's here," I said.

"You knew it," Matt said.

Matt parked. I started to open the Jeep door, but Matt grabbed my wrist.

"Wait," he said.

My heart was pounding now, and there would be no waiting. But he kept talking, trying to reason with me.

"I don't know what he might do," Matt said. "He's hurt you enough already. I know him better than you. You know that, Oli. He is—he was—my friend. Let me go talk to him, get him to turn himself in."

"He was my friend, too," I said. "I have to do this, Matt. For Eloise."

Matt hesitated, then nodded. "I get it," he said.

He and I walked along the trail. Matt reached out, took my hand. I felt a charge go through me—a tiny lightning bolt, like a burst of magic. So much of the day had felt enchanted, taking me beyond the terror of Fitch: the presence of Eloise, the protection of Daphne, and, now, the touch of Matt.

He turned to me then, as if he felt my gaze, and I saw that familiar smile. The space between his front teeth had always melted my heart. It wasn't perfect, but it was his. How could I have ever believed he was on Fitch's side, that he would ever hurt me? This was the Matt I had always known. A boy who had given me his rope bracelet, who I still hadn't kissed, but it didn't matter: He was the love of my life.

Sometimes you just know.

Sometimes you just know.

We kept walking. The last time I had come here, I'd been carrying a bouquet of sweet peas for my sister. I had approached her grave, and a voice had called out from the dirt. It had been Iris. And now, slowing down, Matt and I could hear the digging—shovel hitting rock. Rounding the bend, we saw Fitch.

He was standing in the granite crevice that had been Eloise's— and almost Iris's—grave. He seemed to be scraping away bits of dirt, leaves, and moss that the wind had blown in. Nature had done most of the digging for him—it was a five-foot deep fissure scored in the rock ledge by the last glacier. But there he was, excavating the grave, ready to bury his notes and equipment. Evidence.

"Hi, Fitch," I said.

He looked over at us, barely any expression on his face, and kept working. Why had he come back here? Didn't he realize this would be one of the first places law enforcement would look for him? Now that Iris's story was out, this would be a crime scene again, as it had been after Eloise's murder.

"You shouldn't bother with burying all that," I said. "The police are going to find everything."

"I don't care," he said. "Nothing matters now."

"Give it up, Fitch," Matt said.

"You've destroyed everything I've worked for," Fitch said to me bitterly. "It was all for my sister."

"What about *my* sister?" I asked.

"I told you, I am sorry for what happened. But I was doing something important, that would have saved people."

"Are you thinking of Eloise right now?" I asked. "How you

263

buried her right in that very spot, where you're digging?"

"I'm thinking of Gale."

"What about Iris? How you put her in that hole while she was still alive?" I asked.

He stopped and leaned on the shovel.

"Don't you get it, Oli? Other girls were casualties that couldn't be helped."

"Other girls?" Matt asked.

My blood ran cold. "How many people have you murdered? You're a serial killer?" I asked. "Or are you talking about the future? Girls you *would* have murdered?"

Fitch glared at me.

"I couldn't stand seeing what Gale was going through," he finally said. "She was in pain. She couldn't rest, couldn't have healthy sleep, couldn't look forward to a normal life. Every minute of every day she's worried that she might not survive the night . . ."

For a minute, I heard what I thought was compassion. But Fitch quickly changed direction, made it about him.

"It was unbearable for me. Do you know how it felt, to see her that way? No one could revive her until the spell ended—that's what the stupid doctor in Boston called it at one point, when she was just twelve! As if she was Sleeping Beauty. As if a witch had cast a spell on her."

"Is that why you turned to the *Hammer of Witches*?" I asked. "And the gold dust? The feather? Covering all your bases?"

He reddened then, as if ashamed he'd gotten caught deviating from the path of pure science—his excuse for everything. But rage overcame embarrassment.

"I think of the sibyls as witches," he said. "And all the girls who brought this on our *family*. Daphne, Circe, Athena. My sister. My mother. So I went out of my way to find the perfect ones. The AB negative girls who'd escaped parasomnia. Who managed to sleep through the night without *dying*. Like you, Oli. Like Eloise."

I felt fury, hearing him say her name. But I needed to hear him continue, talk more about why he'd done this.

"I could have gotten you both that morning, if you hadn't caught the early bus," he said. "That had been my plan. Seeing Eloise alone at the bus stop messed me up so bad. It made me overreact, if you want to know the truth. I hurt her worse than I would have if you had been there."

His eyes glinted. I could see he was trying to bait me, so I forced myself to stay calm.

"I really should have grabbed you both when we were birdwatching at the blind," he said. "You were so excited about the black-throated blue warbler. You and Matt. It was almost cute. And then Chris asked Eloise to track owls that night, and she swooned, she couldn't wait for it. And Oli, you were so big-sister-y, all 'are you rushing it'?"

"You heard us?" I asked.

"I know how to listen," he said.

I felt Matt wanting to charge at him, but I took Matt's hand to hold him back.

"This place must mean a lot to you," I said to Fitch. "To come back here today."

He nodded, glaring at me.

"Why here?" I asked. "Why did you take Eloise and Iris here? And why come back here now?"

"My parents' marriage fell apart because of Gale," he said, a total non sequitur. "They just gave up. My dad left, and my mom stopped bothering with either of us. Because she's a doctor, and how do you think it made her feel, Gale having this condition?"

"Pretty terrible," I said.

"Fitch, you're sick," Matt said. "Come on, Oli, let's go—the cops can get him."

"*I* was going to make it all better, come up with a cure," Fitch went on, ignoring Matt. "If I'd just had more time. We could have been famous, Fitch and Abigail Martin, the brother-and-sister team. She had the disorder, I was going to find the cure. That would have shown my mother." He took a deep breath. "And that's why I came here those times . . . to show my mother."

"What do you mean?" I asked, feeling the back of my neck tingle.

"This place," he said, waving his hand. "This beautiful, scenic spot in the Braided Woods. She used to bring us here when we were little. My dad was still with us then. She'd pack a picnic, and she'd set it up right over there . . ." He pointed at the clearing just beyond the crevice, where I had found the charm. "We'd eat sandwiches and fruit salad, and drink lemonade, and play hide-and-seek."

"Where would you hide?" I asked, feeling sick because I already knew.

"In there," he said, pointing at the crevice where he had buried Eloise and Iris. "And guess what? No one ever found me."

He stood right there leaning on his shovel, next to the open grave, staring defiantly at me and Matt.

"Matt, if not for you, the girls would still be in the attic," Fitch said. "You turned everyone against me. And if the cops catch me, you're going down, too. I'll lie, I'll tell them you were part of it."

"Go ahead," Matt said. "As long as you're in prison, it will all be worth it."

Fitch muttered something under his breath and bent back into his work, digging faster. It seemed that he was done listening and talking, and he wanted to bury his material.

I heard Matt talking, trying to convince Fitch to give up, telling him that he had no hope of avoiding the police. But I tore my hand away from Matt's, running as fast as I could, flying toward Fitch in a tackle. Fitch had barely a second to turn around, but it was just enough time to raise the shovel over his head and bring it smashing down toward me.

"No!" I heard Matt shout.

I ducked just in time, and the shovel's blade missed my head and hit rock instead. Fitch tried to scramble away, but I grabbed hold of him and held on. My fists clenched his shirt so tightly, it tore as he tried to wrench himself away. The harder he tried to get me off him, the tighter I held on. He knocked me off for a second, but I jumped onto his back, and we rolled to the edge of the crevice.

"Let go, Oli," he yelled.

"No, this is it, Fitch," I said, out of breath.

He tried to hit me, but I ducked again and he barely caught my shoulder. He used the moment to wriggle away. I wasn't going to let that happen—it just made me more determined. Matt came running and grabbed Fitch. I still had hold of Fitch's arm; the momentum of Matt's running jump and my yanking Fitch's sleeve sent Fitch tumbling into the crevice.

I stared down, saw him lying in the dirt.

My heart skipped. For a moment, I thought he was dead. But then I saw his eyes open. He had thrown girls into that fissure, and it had become their graves. It wasn't his, though. I saw his chest rise and fall. He was still breathing.

"Oli," Matt said, putting his arm around me. "Are you okay?"

"I'm fine."

"You got him, Oli," Matt said. "You did it."

"For Eloise," I whispered.

Fitch sat up, looking toward me and Matt. There he was in that crevice where he had hidden as a child, where he had thrown my sister and Iris as if they were trash. There was no way he was going to climb out with me and Matt guarding him. There was no way he'd ever hurt another girl.

Matt handed me his cell phone, and I texted Detective Tyrone's mobile number. She had given it to me last October, when she first started investigating my sister's murder.

I told her where we were. And I knew she would come right away.

While Matt and I stood watch over Fitch, I looked up at the sky.

Hardly any time passed before we heard sirens. A stream of police cars drove into the Braided Woods, up the road past our birding blind, the owl trees, all the way to this place that had become my sister's grave.

The officers surrounded Fitch, hauled him onto his feet. I heard the click of handcuffs go around his wrists. I watched Detective Tyrone come toward me, concern in her eyes, as if she knew what this moment meant to me.

But she couldn't know, not really.

"It's over," I said out loud, and Detective Tyrone nodded.

"It is," Matt said, but I wasn't talking to him.

I was talking to Eloise, who had been buried here in this very spot, who had seen me through, who had brought us to this moment. I think Matt understood. Because he put his arms around me.

And I heard him whisper, as if he felt her spirit just as strongly as I did:

"Eloise Parrish, you have the best sister in the world." And then, "Oli, that's you. That's you."

He was wrong, though.

Eloise was the best sister in the world.

No contest.

Thirty-Two

Detective Tyrone took us to the Connecticut State Police barracks. I had driven past this place, just off the highway, so many times in my life. Eloise and I had gone to the shopping outlets at the next exit. We'd had clam rolls at Patrick's Seafood Shack down on the waterfront. Adalyn's aunt's beach house was less than a mile away. Never in my life would I have dreamed that the police barracks would become familiar to me . . . but ever since Eloise's murder, they had. This was the epicenter of the investigation.

Instead of the stark interrogation room, Detective Tyrone told Matt to wait near the entrance, in a chair across from the police sergeant's desk. She brought me into her office. I had been in here before, when Eloise first went missing.

She had a wide desk covered with neat stacks of papers, a couple of law books, and a nameplate that said DETECTIVE EILEEN O. TYRONE. The shelf beside the desk held medals and commendations she had received through the years. There was a framed photo of her in uniform with a group of other police officers, one with her dressed in the dark pantsuit I'd always seen her wear as a detective, and of her shaking hands with the current governor of Connecticut.

Tilted toward her chair, out of visitors' views, were two framed photos of children. I craned my neck and saw that one was of a boy and a girl, teenagers, and the other was a family with Detective

Tyrone, a man, and the two kids. In spite of how often she and I had spoken since last October, she had never mentioned her family to me.

She had a whiteboard on the wall beside a big window. I stared and saw that every inch was covered with details about Eloise and her case. A timeline of the crime, clues that even I hadn't know about—she had found gold dust at the scene and held that back from the press, even from me. Eloise's life list of birds. She had taped photos of my sister to the board—Eloise as a child, her eighth-grade graduation portrait, and a photo with me taken at the beach last summer.

I sat on the other side of the desk from Detective Tyrone. I was dusty and dirty from fighting Fitch. She brought me a bottle of water, and I drank it down. I had been so frustrated with her at first, when the investigation had been stalled. But I kept glancing at the bulletin board, realizing how much she cared, and how much she had been working these last months. She saw me staring at the board, but neither one of us mentioned it.

When I finally looked away, I asked about Iris and Hayley.

"Are they okay?" I asked. "Did their parents get them?"

"Yes, the girls are doing well," she said. "Their parents came straight to the hospital from Newport, and they are all together."

"The hospital?" I asked, my heart skipping.

"Nothing too serious," she said. "Both girls had to be checked over, and Iris is having X-rays and an MRI."

"Because of her head injury," I said. That choked me up. "We wanted her to go to the clinic, but she couldn't—Fitch had said he'd kill Hayley if she told anyone. That's why I didn't call you," I explained.

"You were in a tough position, Oli," Detective Tyrone said. "Of all the people in the world, you knew what Fitch Martin was capable of."

I nodded. She was right about that.

My backpack was under my chair. I pulled it out, opened it, and put the Ziploc bags on the detective's desk.

"What are these?" she asked, bending over them.

"Evidence I collected after I pulled Iris out of the crevice," I said, pointing out the leaves I had combed from her hair, the feather, the fingernail scrapings, the traces of gold dust, and the delicate little charm.

"Good thinking to do that," she said, peering at them.

"The charm was made by Minerva Morelock," I said. "And the gold dust came from her jewelry shop. Fitch used it. It was part of his ritual."

"Tell me what you know about that," Detective Tyrone said.

"He sprinkled gold dust on Eloise and Iris before he buried them," I said. "He pretends to be a researcher, all about science, but he also uses alchemy. It's part of their family history. He has a book of magic—the Sibylline version of *Malleus Maleficarum*—the *Hammer of Witches*."

"Yes," Detective Tyrone said. "We found it in the attic."

"It belonged to their great-aunt Daphne Agassiz.

"Daphne," Detective Tyrone said. "What a life she has led. A hundred years old, incredible. And one of the original Sibylline sisters."

"You'd heard of them before?" I asked.

Detective Tyrone nodded, with a smile and a far-off look in her eyes. "Oh, yes," she said. "I think everyone who grew up on the shoreline has. We'd drive past that faded sign down by the New London waterfront and wonder who those girls were."

"It's called a 'ghost sign,'" I said. I hesitated, wanting to be respectful of her privacy, but I had to know. "You said 'we' . . . Who did you drive by with?"

"My sister," Detective Tyrone said.

"You have a sister," I said. I felt a tingle that went all through my body.

"I do," she said. "Jenny."

I closed my eyes for a minute. When I opened them, I saw her watching me with incredible kindness. "I'm not at all surprised," I said. "I felt how much you understood Eloise and me."

"Sisters," she said. "There's nothing like it."

"Is she older or younger than you?" I asked.

"Younger," she said. Like Eloise.

Then she did something I didn't expect. She came around the desk and pulled a chair next to me. She held my hand, gazing into my eyes.

"You've been so strong, Oli," she said, and paused for a long time. "I'm not sure I could have been that strong."

"If you lost Jenny," I whispered.

"Yes."

We sat there in silence for a few minutes. She didn't let go of my hand, and I knew we were both thinking of our sisters, of how happy I was that she still had Jenny, and how much we both wished that I still had Eloise.

"I know how hard this year has been for you. As many cases as I've worked on, this has meant . . . so much to me. I wanted to catch him for you. I wanted to find the person who killed Eloise."

"I know you did," I said.

"But you caught him, Oli. You solved this crime."

I nodded. With the help of my friends, it was true.

"You even thought to collect evidence. You're a good investigator," she said, letting go of my hand.

"Thank you," I said. I held back for a few seconds, then blurted it out: "I think I want to be a detective someday."

She didn't look taken aback at all; she looked happy. "Well," she said, with a wide smile. "I'm not surprised. I'm not surprised at all. You'll make a good one."

"Really?" I asked.

"Absolutely. You like to figure things out, and you're good at it. When the time comes, I'll help you."

That meant a lot to me. My grandmother was slipping away too fast to appreciate what I wanted to do and why. Only Detective Tyrone got it. Well, her and Eloise. It might have been weird to say this, but I suddenly felt as if I had family again. A person who cared about me, who knew me.

"A lot of families just want to move on from what they've been through," she said. "The loss, the investigation. We haven't gotten to trial yet. That will be hard on you, Oli. It might change the way you feel about joining the police."

I hadn't let myself think about a trial yet, but I was ready for whatever happened, whatever it took to put Fitch in prison. "It won't change what I want to be," I said. "I am positive about that."

"The trial will bring it all back," Detective Tyrone said. "There will be a lot of testimony, forensic evidence, and crime scene photos that will be painful for you to see. You'll be called on to testify. You'll have to be up there on the witness stand with Fitch at the defense table, watching you. His lawyer . . . won't be easy on you or anyone."

"I don't care," I said. "I won't be easy on him, either."

She actually laughed at that.

It was time for me to leave the State Police barracks and to say goodbye to Detective Tyrone. Not forever, that was for sure. But our connection would be different now. We knew who had killed my sister, and he was in custody. I hoped Detective Tyrone would be my mentor when the time came.

She put out her hand to shake mine. I couldn't help myself. I stepped forward and gave her a hug instead.

Then I left her office, went into the outer area, and found Matt.

"Ready to go?" he asked.

"Yes," I said, giving him a genuine smile, because the weight of the world—or at least a large part of it—had been lifted from my shoulders. Together we walked outside, down the steps, and into his Jeep. He reached across the seat and touched my Turk's head bracelet. It was no longer white; dirt from the Braided Woods had turned it dark and dusty brown.

"I'm going to make you a new one," he said.

"No way," I said. "I'm never taking this one off. Sailor's knot. It symbolizes . . ."

"Us," he said, smiling. "It symbolizes us."

"It does," I said.

He leaned forward, and every inch of my body shimmered because I was sure he was going to kiss me. Then a group of police officers walked into the parking lot and stood a few feet from the Jeep—not paying attention to us, just talking and laughing. But we felt self-conscious, so we both smiled and pulled apart.

And then Matt shifted into drive.

And we headed out of the parking lot and left the police barracks in the rearview mirror as he drove me home.

Thirty-Three

When I got home, Noreen was sleeping but Gram was sitting on the sofa, her memoir notebook in her hands. I rushed over to hug her.

"Hi, Oli," she said, as if nothing was wrong.

She had hardly noticed I had been gone, but that's just how she was now. She never had found that note I'd left her, and neither had Noreen. All this time, they must have thought I'd just gone away with my bird-watching friends or something.

I found the note where I had left it, and I reread what I had written:

IF ANYTHING HAPPENS TO ME . . .

And so much had happened.

In a way I was glad Gram didn't know it all.

And, in another way, I knew that what had happened to me was as much a part of her story as it was mine. My grandmother had stepped up as soon as Eloise and I had needed her. She became both our mother and father—while keeping our parents' memories alive for us. I knew she would have done anything she could to protect Eloise and me from Fitch.

Yes, Gram. A few things happened to me.

I set those thoughts aside, but I knew I would return to them soon.

Detective Tyrone had said that I liked to figure things out, and she was right. There was still a lot to unravel.

I texted with Iris and Hayley many times a day. They were so happy to be reunited with their parents, and all the kitties in the Cat Castle. It felt weird to have been so close, to have been through life and death with them, and to now live in separate states, over an hour away from each other.

Minerva came to visit me, and I had questions for her about the gold charms I had found attached to the panels. In those desperate moments, I had thought maybe Minerva had put the charms there, that they were part of a bizarre family ritual—like Fitch spreading gold dust over his victims.

"That's not it at all," Minerva said. "I'm sorry you had doubts, but I can understand it. Everything was happening so fast, and it took ages for me to get back to the Miramar."

"What kept you?" I asked.

"That brochure," she said. "I was racing around trying to find it. I ran into Matt outside the library, and that's when we put everything together. I headed straight back to the hotel, following Matt. But by the time I got to the front porch, Daphne didn't know where you'd gone."

"Up to the attic," I said. "Fitch drugged me and took me up there."

"That's where Iris thought he'd probably taken you," Minerva said. "I managed to find both Matt and Iris, and together we started planning how to help you all. Of course Daphne had no idea what Fitch was up to, but she had lived in the Miramar so long, she knew a few secrets about it. She told us about the crack in the hurricane window, and she helped us figure out which room Fitch was most likely using to sleep in and keep his surveillance equipment. My job was to distract Fitch in the hallway once he realized Matt wasn't on his side."

"And that Matt and I had disabled the cameras," I said.

She nodded.

"Sometimes I think we could have just overpowered him," I said. "Tackled him when he came rushing through the door. With Hayley and Abigail, it would have been four against one."

"But your instincts told you not to, right?" Minerva asked.

"They must have," I said. "Because all I knew was that we had to break that window and get down the fire escape, away from him, as fast as we could."

"That was good thinking," Minerva said. "Fitch is dangerous, and there's no telling what he would have done in response. Maybe a little of our family clairvoyance rubbed off on you," she added with a twinkle in her eye.

Maybe I *was* a little clairvoyant. I didn't really believe it was true—I was a detective, not a sibyl. Still, coming from Minerva, the idea meant a lot to me.

"So what about those gold charms?" I asked. "Attached to the paintings? What was the symbolism? Did Fitch put them there?"

"Far from it," Minerva said. "Those panels date back to the 1930s and 1940s, when the Sibylline sisters would give their shows in theaters. They needed stage sets, so the three girls painted panels. Each one did a portrait of one of the others."

"I love that," I said.

"Daphne was always avant-garde, and she wanted their work to be more than just paintings. She had seen 'assemblages' at a museum in Boston, so she inspired the other sisters to create small charms engraved with images from their dreams, their visions."

"But how did they create them in gold?" I asked.

"That was Daphne, too," Minerva said. "Many admirers went to see their shows, and there was one man—Serge Gault, a wealthy jewelry maker from Providence—who imported gold for his work."

"And he fell in love with Daphne?" I asked.

"Actually, her sister Athena," Minerva said, with sadness in her eyes. "But Athena died of parasomnia before they could get married. So Serge wanted to make a series of gold charms in her honor. It was Daphne who urged him to enamel them with the images that the sisters, especially Athena, loved." She paused, smiling. "And he not only did what she suggested, he taught her how to work with gold."

"So Daphne started the shop in New London?" I asked.

"She did. And she is the one who taught me her trade."

"But what about the panels? And the charms?" I asked.

"Like I said, Daphne was always thinking of new ways to create," Minerva said. "She was the one who installed the charms on the panels that she and her sisters painted, as a way of honoring them.

They were sea witches, mermaids, seers, sibyls. And each charm represents the most magical parts of their sisterhood."

I smiled at that. Sisters were indeed magic.

As the week went on, I knew I had to see Abigail. I steeled myself to ask her questions and listen to whatever she had to say. Or maybe she would decide not to talk to me. Maybe there were answers she didn't want me to know.

I knew from Detective Tyrone that Abigail was considered a suspect—because she had known about Fitch's activities and not done anything.

That bothered me. Was there a point where she could have stopped him? If she had turned him in, would that have prevented him from kidnapping Eloise, Iris, and Hayley?

Abigail wasn't in custody, but she was still at the hospital for evaluation and treatment. Her mother cut short the European leg of her lecture tour to return home and face the reality of what her children had done. Reporters and TV crews surrounded Shoreline General Hospital, wanting news about the case.

I had watched footage online, seen reporters stick microphones in Dr. Constance Martin's face every time she walked in and out of the hospital lobby, but Dr. Martin refused to be interviewed.

When I went to visit Abigail, the press did the same to me.

"Olivia!" they called as I shouldered through the crowd standing across the sidewalk from hospital property. "Tell us how you feel about Fitch Martin being arrested! Was he your friend? Was he Eloise's? Tell us about the attic, what happened in the attic?"

Every question they yelled was too private for me to answer, so I just put my head down and entered the hospital. They weren't allowed inside, and it was nice and quiet in there.

When I got to Abigail's room, Dr. Martin walked past without even saying hello to me. I stepped through the door, saw Abigail in bed. She was wearing a blue-and-white hospital gown. She was attached to a heart monitor and blood oxygen sensor. Two bags of clear fluid hung from an IV pole.

"Sorry my mother ignored you," Abigail said. "Don't take it personally. This just isn't her kind of thing."

"'This'?" I asked, as if I cared about her mother ignoring me.

"Yeah. Having everything come out. All our family secrets. Fitch being arrested for kidnapping and murder, me in the hospital and our family disease splashed all over the news."

"Right," I said a little sarcastically. "That must be really hard."

"Oh, Oli," she said. "I don't mean it that way. It's nothing compared to what your family has gone through. And the Bigelows."

I was silent, waiting to hear what else she would say.

"My lawyer told me not to talk to anyone." Abigail paused. "Especially not you or any other family members of Fitch's victims. But Oli, you're the one I most want to talk to. I don't have any excuses.

I know that saying I'm sorry isn't enough, doesn't mean anything to you . . . but it's true. If I could go back in time, everything would be different."

"You knew what Fitch was doing?" I asked. "The whole time?"

"I didn't know. Not right away, not with Eloise."

"But you were right there, in the attic," I said. "What did you think was going on? You told me you saw her, that she talked to you, that she wanted to go home to me . . ."

"I kept thinking he would let her go," she said.

"But he didn't. And then he took Iris and Hayley."

"I hate myself for it," Abigail said. "Oli, as awful as the things Fitch did, I felt more loved by him than I do by anyone else. He cared about me so much. He did it for me. I can't stand that. It's unforgivable."

"It is," I said. But I could see the anguish in her face, hear the guilt. I couldn't imagine what it must be like to be her—neglected by her mother when she was sick and scared, loved only by Fitch. Her brother who had done such terrible things.

"The police are not going to arrest me," she said. "But I think they should."

"Abigail . . ."

"It's true. That's why my lawyer told me not to talk to anyone. He says I'm lucky not to be prosecuted, and he doesn't want that to change. But I want it. You do, too, I'm sure. You want to see me punished."

I stared at her. She was so pale, it was almost as if I could see her blood running through her veins. I saw the grief pouring off her, and I knew that she was being crushed by remorse.

"You're already being punished," I said. "I can tell. You're doing it to yourself, Abigail. Arresting you won't change anything. And . . ." I thought it would be hard for me to say the next part, but it wasn't. "I don't want that for you."

"You don't?" she asked, her voice breaking.

I shook my head. "I really don't. I want you to get help. You need it—not just because of the parasomnia, but because of what he did to you. He hurt you, too, Abigail. He manipulated you. He knew all about your condition, and he tried to make you an accomplice. But you weren't."

"But I . . ."

I interrupted her. "You're the reason we were able to escape. You did everything you could to help. It wouldn't have been possible without you."

She looked shocked for a minute, that I would say that. The remorse was still in her eyes, but I saw a little relief beginning to shine through.

"Thank you, Oli," she said.

"You're welcome. What's next for you? What are the plans, now that your mother is home?"

"Not for long," Abigail said. "She can't wait to get away from me— and from what Fitch did. She is planning to get back out there, on

285

the road after the trial. She had to cancel some dates in Europe, but Barcelona awaits. Geneva and Brussels, too."

I didn't know what made me do this, but it wasn't hard at all. I guess you could say it came straight from my heart, because it seemed I didn't have control over my words or actions, they just happened.

"You have me, Abigail," I said, leaning over to hug her. "It's not the same as family, but . . . we're a different kind of family. We were in the attic together. We understand each other."

"I think we do," she said.

"You're going to get better," I said.

She shook her head with discouragement, but I believed that to be true.

And as time went on, it seemed that I might be right.

The news was full of stories about the case. Some reporters had delved into the Sibylline sisters. They had tried to interview Daphne, but she had seemingly disappeared. Not really, though. Minerva was hiding her in an apartment upstairs from Mermaid's Pearls, protecting her privacy.

Other journalists focused on the medical aspects of parasomnia. They uncovered other cases, wrote about its rare and devastating effects. How no one really knew how it started, how some people died from it and others survived.

The national attention given to the Martin and Agassiz family, to the long history of parasomnia, caused several doctors to come forward. It turned out that more research than anyone in the family had previously realized was being done on the genetic factors behind the condition.

Abigail was going to be under the care of a young neurologist at Rhode Island Hospital. Dr. Melanie Aguilar was also on the faculty of Brown University, where she was overseeing a study on this rare cause of seizures. Providence wasn't far from Black Hall; I knew that I would pitch in, driving Abigail to her appointments whenever her cousin Minerva couldn't, and when I had the time.

thirty-four

I had a lot of visitors that summer. Iris and Hayley came to Black Hall to see me on some weekends, and Abigail did, too, once she got out of Shoreline General, and between visits to her new doctor in Providence.

Detective Tyrone would visit with updates. Fitch had been arraigned for murder, attempted murder, and kidnapping. His mother had hired him one of the best lawyers in Connecticut, but there was no chance of him being free anytime soon—in fact, probably not even in his lifetime. He was being held without bail, as an adult, in a prison near the Massachusetts border. There would be psychiatric tests to determine if he was sane. Detective Tyrone warned me that he would probably try for an insanity defense. But she said that was unlikely to work. Fitch had known exactly what he was doing.

Abigail would testify to that.

Minerva came over, too, bearing news of her great-aunt. It totally delighted me that Daphne, soon to be 101 years old, was swept away with a whole new flood of inspiration, based on what she called "the new sisters": Iris, Hayley, Eloise, and me. She was designing a charm for each of us, and I couldn't wait to see them.

One day, when only Abigail was over at my house, we were having lemonade and cookies on the couch. Gram was still sleeping, and

Noreen came into the living room with Zoey. She walked the dog straight over to Abigail.

"How are you doing?" Noreen asked.

"Okay," Abigail replied. At this point, with her unwanted notoriety, she was used to being approached by practically anyone.

"Do you like dogs?" Noreen asked.

Abigail nodded. "All animals," she said, petting Zoey and impetuously hugging her neck. Zoey wriggled with pleasure.

"Because I have an idea," Noreen said, crouching down in front of Abigail, kindness in her voice. "I've heard you girls talking in here. Not eavesdropping exactly, but you know, working in the other room. And, Abigail, I've read about how you have that condition where you stop breathing and can't wake up."

"Yeah," Abigail said.

"Dogs can be trained," Noreen said to her, "to do almost anything. They're so smart, Abigail. They really are. Now, Zoey here is spoken for. I've been training her to comfort Oli's grandmother. Because, you know, Oli has had too much responsibility."

I blushed. Why was Noreen saying that?

"Oli's lost her parents and her sister. She's just sixteen, and I don't want her worrying anymore—all that grocery shopping and housekeeping and looking after her grandma. That's what I'm here for. Me and Zoey. Zoey's going to be her grandmother's support animal. No argument from you, Oli. Okay? You hear me? You've got to be a kid. That's your job."

I was stunned, but I felt a big smile on my face. I hadn't seen this coming. Noreen caring about us? I'd thought of her as an employee sent by the agency—good at her job, but not really engaged with my family. Now it seemed she really saw us, really cared. And it meant so much to me, all I wanted to do was throw my arms around her. Because sometimes being seen was all it took. Sometimes it was everything.

Noreen didn't wait for a response from me. She was completely focused on Abigail, staring straight at her.

"I am very good at what I do," Noreen said. "A caregiver for humans, and a trainer of dogs. And I can help you."

"You can?" Abigail asked. She gave a quick, nervous laugh. "You can wake me up before I die?"

"I know someone who can."

"Who?"

"Zoey's sister," Noreen said. "Bella."

"Excuse me?" Abigail asked, looking confused.

"Bella is just as sweet as Zoey. I've been training her, too. I am a home health aide, and I specialize in geriatric care. So I'd been planning to place Bella in the home of another elderly person. But now I am going to change direction. See, dogs have the greatest instincts in the world. They're descended from wolves, Abigail, and the most important thing for a wolf is to survive."

"Okay," Abigail said, listening.

"A dog can pick up on brain waves through scent," Noreen said.

"Detect chemical changes before they have a chance to trigger physical responses."

"You mean a dog can smell when I'm about to have an episode?" Abigail asked.

"You bet," Noreen said. "That's a known fact among dog trainers and behaviorists. Beyond that, I've been reading up. Ever since hearing about you, knowing you're Oli's friend, I've wanted to find a way to help. And I think I have."

"How?" Abigail asked, her voice a combination of eagerness and desperation.

"There are seizure assistance dogs. Not only do they respond to the scent of chemical changes, but their presence can actually lower seizure activity. Not sure why. Probably because of trust—the bond. An understanding. Empathy. Connection. All those things alleviate stress."

"Really?" Abigail asked. "It's been proven?"

Noreen smiled at Abigail. "It's a fact known to trainers like me, but does that mean it's made its way into the medical literature? To tell you the truth, I have no idea. But Bella and I would love to work with you on it. What do you say, want to give it a try?"

I stepped over to Abigail. I put my hands on her shoulders to let her know that I was with her, every bit as much as Bella and Noreen would be. I wished I could have had the instincts of a dog, of a wolf, and helped her when we were in the attic. I wished there could have been a canine breakthrough when she was just a child.

So that Fitch wouldn't have had her to use as a subject. So he wouldn't have had to hurt any of us. So Eloise would still be here.

"Yes," Abigail said, petting Zoey's head. "I would like to work with Bella." She raised her eyes to Noreen. "And you, Noreen. I'd like to give it a try. Thank you."

"Okay, then," Noreen said, her eyes twinkling. "We have a plan."

thirty-five

And then there was the best visitor: Matt came over every day.

It was July now, with plenty of summer left. We carried the sails and rudder down to the JY15, rigged the dinghy, and sailed out from the beach. We sat side-by-side. I had the tiller, and we kept the sails tight and the rail in the water, sailing fast and gulping air as we rushed along. Eventually we headed to the raft. I wrapped the line around the cleat, and he and I climbed out of the boat. We lay on the salty, splintered wood, just as we always had during summers gone by.

In September, we would be juniors. I felt so much older than that, as if I'd lived a whole lifetime already. I looked at Matt and wondered if he felt the same way. He looked inscrutable, his eyes squinting in the bright sun.

"What was it like?" I asked him.

"What was what like?"

"Having to trick Fitch into believing you were with him," I said.

"It was the hardest thing I'll ever have to do in my life," he said.

"How do you know?" I asked. "You haven't lived your whole life yet, there could be much worse things."

"Worse than having to pretend to go along with someone who was hurting you, Oli? No, I don't think so. Nothing will ever be harder than that." He paused. "What did you really think, when you saw me with him?"

I wished I could lie, tell him that I knew all along that he was good: that my old friend Matthew Grinnell would never be anything like Fitch Martin. But gazing into his clear, serious, blue eyes, I knew that everything between us was true and real, and I had to tell the entire truth, no matter how hard it was.

I had to sit up to say this. He could tell I was about to say something difficult, and he sat up beside me, so we were at eye level with each other.

"I was scared," I said.

"Of me?" he asked.

"Yes."

He looked away. I saw I'd said something to him that I could never take back. I wanted to make excuses, erase or at least mitigate the effect of my words: backpedal and tell him that I had been terrified, that my world had been turned upside down, that my senses were skewed, that trust in everyone and everything—not just him—had exploded, and, especially, that I had known all along that he was good.

I regretted how terribly I had misjudged him, even for so short a time. But I had had no choice—I had been afraid for my life. And Matt had been playing a role designed to trick Fitch—he had also fooled me.

Right now, looking at Matt and seeing how affected he was by my saying I'd been scared of him, I knew that more words would be inadequate. Sometimes hurt is so deep, apologies can only make it worse. Actions were all that counted. Way more than thoughts, memories, even wishes.

So I reached for Matt's hand. His skin was warm from the sun. We laced our fingers together, but he still hadn't looked at me. He was still upset. The waves rocked the raft. We sat there, our legs dangling into the salt water.

"You, Matt," I said after a long time.

"You, Oli," he said.

He turned toward me with that mischievous smile that showed me we were okay. He squeezed my hand, and I squeezed his. The sun beat down, and the salt crystals dried on our skin.

My whole body tingled, and I felt as if something was going to happen.

And it did. But not what I thought it would be.

He didn't kiss me.

"Feel like seeing some birds?" he asked.

"Always," I said.

"I know somewhere we can go. We have to turn it back into the place we always loved. The place we know better than anyone," he said.

He didn't have to tell me where it was. I just knew, as surely as I had ever known anything before. We climbed into the dinghy and set the sails. The wind was at our backs, and long and slow, we sailed downwind back to shore. We went to my house, and I ran upstairs to change. I grabbed my Sibley birds guide, my binoculars, and a sun hat. I had hardly used them in months.

Twenty minutes later, we drove into the Braided Woods.

We had to drive past the grave. It was unavoidable, in order to get to our real destination. I was relieved to see that the yellow crime scene tape had been taken down—for the second time. It had been there for three investigations—Fitch's murder of Eloise, his attempted murder of Iris, and his eventual capture. Now those rock croppings, the stately boulders, that granite crevice, the white pines, and the red oaks could return to their ancient loveliness. The terror was over.

Matt drove the Jeep to the place we had always gone, the site of endless birding happiness: the location of the blind. Sunlight shimmered through the leaves overhead. July was beautiful in its own way, but most people would say it wasn't the most exciting time for birding. Nesting was over; the first broods had been hatched. Fall migration was at least a month from starting—that would begin in August, a good month before it was fall on the calendar. There weren't too many rarities around now; the possibility of seeing a life bird—a first-time sighting—was low.

But summer birds were alluring, too. Two different osprey families had built nests at Hubbard's Point. But here in the woods, this was an excellent time to concentrate on identifying sparrows and finches, the less-flashy "backyard birds" that tend to look so much alike.

At first, their dun-colored plumage looked dull. But the more you gazed, the more you saw shades of chestnut, mahogany, silver-gray, molten gold. You'd notice white eye rings and wing bars, black masks, pointed bills, cone-shaped bills. When Matt and I entered the blind, sat down on two of the tree stumps that we had always used as makeshift benches, I was looking forward to settling in, focusing on learning more about species I had been seeing forever.

"Hey," he said, reaching for a piece of paper wedged into the blind's weathered wood.

"What is it?" I asked.

Matt unfolded the paper. It was unlined, three-by-five inches, torn from one of the Moleskine notebooks most of us used to keep notes about our birding excursions. I leaned closer and saw Chris's handwriting.

Oli, Matt, both of you.

I'm sure you're going to see this sooner or later. I know our main birding time is during migration. We did it in spring, and we will do it this coming fall. That's going to remind me of last year. It'll remind you, too.

It's when we were all together for the last time. You two, me and Eloise, Adalyn, and Fitch.

"Me and Eloise"—Hurts to write that.

Hurts to write "Fitch," too.

I know I haven't been around much. I wasn't there for you, with you, when the stuff with Fitch went down. I still can't believe it. Did you have any idea about him? I didn't. I drove to the prison yesterday and sat outside for a long time. I wanted to visit him, ask him why he did it. Can he even have visitors? I have no idea.

He killed Eloise, that's the thing. So why would I ever want to sit there and listen to him say anything?

It's hard with friends, to see the worst in them when you've always seen only the best. When that's all you thought there was. I don't want to say I held him on a pedestal, but I imagined us going through school together. Black Hall, but maybe even college and med school. I pictured us becoming doctors and supporting each other's practice and research.

I thought we'd be birding together our whole lives.

All of us—I thought we'd be hanging out in this blind for a million more migrations. I am dreading fall—next time I'm here, it will remind me of last October. The ninth. The last time I saw her. Can we come here together that day? Can we look for owls? She loved owls. That might make it better. If anything can make it better.

See you,

Chris

Matt and I sat in the blind, not speaking for a long time. I thought about October. It was still months from now. October 9 was an anniversary that would come every year. I had been pushing the thought away, dreading it, but somehow Chris's note made it possible for me to let it in. Days ticked by, month after month. That was the way of life. Good memories, unwanted memories. Eloise and I had learned that when we had lost our parents.

Now I was learning it all over again, and so were our friends.

"I like his idea," Matt said. "Meeting him here that day."

I nodded. "He's right. Being together might make it better."

"If anything can make it better," Matt said, watching me, to see if I really believed that. I wasn't sure I did, but I was willing to give it a try. I pictured us here, the core group that was left: Adalyn, Chris, Matt, and me. There would be owls, and I would bring something that Eloise had loved. I would carve a pumpkin for her. Instead of a jack-o'-lantern, it would be the face of a great horned owl.

"We could have cider," Matt said, sitting beside me as I held the note. "Hot, in a thermos."

"Apples, too. Or a pie," I said. "Our grandmother used to bake great apple pies. Maybe she'll be up to baking another one this year. I can help her."

"Yes," Matt said. "That would be great."

The leaves on the maples, oaks, birches, and sassafras all around the blinds would change color. They would turn scarlet, crimson, orange, bright yellow, and they would twinkle down from the branches to the ground. The Braided Woods would smell like spice—black walnuts, bayberry, bittersweet, the last of the goldenrod. Dusk would fall, and owls would call.

But still, for now, it was summer.

Just then I heard an unusual call, but I knew it right away: a cedar waxwing. A favorite bird of mine and Eloise's, pale gray with a yellow tinge, a red wing-stripe, a subtle crest, a dashing black mask. Delighted, I turned to Matt, assuming he would be focused on the direction in which the call had come. But instead he was gazing at me.

"Did you hear that?" I asked.

"Yeah," he said.

"A cedar waxwing," I said.

"Oli," he said.

"Matt."

"When we were just out on the raft," he said.

I nodded, thinking back to earlier that afternoon.

"We almost," he began.

"I know," I said, feeling heat rising in my chest. I was almost too overwhelmed to look at him, but at the same time, I couldn't look away.

Some things had already happened, weeks or months in the past: We had hugged, he had brushed his lips across my cheek, held me while he whispered in my ear. We had held hands. He had given me the rope bracelet that I still wore—now worn and frayed, still brown from that day.

But until now, one thing hadn't happened.

And then it did.

We were looking straight into each other's eyes. He put his arms around me and pulled me even closer. I always thought people closed their eyes. I was sure of it. But we didn't, not at first. And I'm glad. Because I wanted to see him. I wanted him to know, to read in my eyes what I was feeling when . . .

When he

When he kissed me

And he did: He kissed me

Or maybe I kissed him

Or we both, or we both, or we both . . .

Either way, we kissed.

It was my first kiss. And I closed my eyes. All of me tingled. I wanted the kiss to go on forever. I reached up to touch his face, and he touched mine. And then we opened our eyes again.

"Oli," he said.

I tried to say "Matt," but my voice wouldn't work.

It was summer.

I had just had my first kiss.

I was wearing Matt's bracelet.

And we were here.

It wasn't an accident that we had come back to the Braided Woods. This was my place. This was where I had loved birds. Had loved looking for owls after sunset. Had loved coming with my sister. This was where I had loved life. I thought I had lost it, but now I had it back. I'd reclaimed this magical spot. I'd reclaimed myself.

My life could begin again. Not the same as it had been. Not better, not worse, but different. I knew more. My heart was bigger. For a while it had seemed my world had gotten very small, but now it was wide open, and it was mine.

Matt had been holding Chris's note, but I gently took it from his hand. I stared down at it—not at his handwriting, not at what he had said. It made me think of that other note, the one I had written to Gram. *If anything happens to me . . .*

Writing was so powerful. Gram's memoirs, Chris's note, the way writing can make us feel, make us look at what we have, at what matters more than anything.

I thought of Gram's journal, the book of her memories that were fading so fast. Maybe I could help her finish her memoir. I could keep listening, and I could pull up all the stories she had told me and Eloise over the years. I could write them down for her. Maybe I could write my own story, too. I began to think of a title. *If Anything Happens to Me . . .*

A whole lot had happened to both me and Gram. And it had made us stronger. It had brought us closer.

I knew my way now.

I looked up at the sky. It was so blue, a blue that would forever be my favorite color. I wished I could tell Eloise. Not just about the kiss, not just that I was wearing Matt's bracelet, not just that Gram and I were going to be okay.

But I wished I could tell her everything. Everything that had happened, that would ever happen, for the rest of my life. For the life I wanted to share with her, for all the happiness, all the adventure, all the sadness.

Not just anything, but all the all and the all the all.

And sitting right there, next to Matt, holding his hand, I did just that.

I whispered to the blue sky, to my favorite color, to my sister.

"Everything," I told Eloise.

"What?" Matt asked. "What did you say?"

I turned to him, looked into his eyes, saw his beautiful smile with the space between his front teeth. Matt, the boy I loved.

I smiled at him and I said:

"Everything."

ACKNOWLEDGMENTS

I am very lucky to have grown up in a world of books and writing. My mother was an English teacher, as well as an artist and writer. She wrote short stories every night after my sisters and I went to bed, and my lullaby was the sound of her typing at the dining room table. She believed in me so much and sent out my poems and short stories without my even knowing it. When my first poem was published in the *Hartford Courant* when I was eleven, I thought it had appeared there by magic.

My father sold and repaired Olympia typewriters. He gave me my first Olympia SM-9 when I was in fourth grade. He told great stories about when he was a boy at Hubbard's Point and swam to the big rock, over half a mile away; about climbing the rickety ladder to the top of the water tower; about being a navigator-bombardier in World War II, tales of his leaves in London, how he would always find the closest bookstore and lose himself in stories.

With parents like that, no wonder I became a writer. Thanks, Mom and Dad. I miss you and wish you could know how much your love and encouragement mean to me.

They would be so happy to know I have a literary life and have found such wonderful, inspiring people to share it with. I am so grateful to my wonderful team at Scholastic:

Aimee Friedman, David Levithan, Ellie Berger, Janell Harris, Elizabeth Krych, Erin O'Connor, Maeve Norton, Elizabeth Parisi, Cianna Sanford, Erin Berger, Seale Ballenger, Lia Ferrone, Rachel Feld, Lizette Serrano, Emily Heddleson, Jana Hausmann, Elizabeth Whiting, Jackie Rubin, Dan Moser, Savannah D'Amico, Priscilla Eakeley, Starr Baer, and everyone else who contributed to this book. A very special shout-out to Betsy Politi, Sue Flynn, and Nikki Mutch—can't wait to see you again!

I count my blessings for having an agent who has also been my friend since the beginning of our careers—Andrea Cirillo. I'm so thankful to her and everyone at the Jane Rotrosen Agency:

Jane Berkey, Meg Ruley, Chris Prestia, Jessica Errera, Annelise Robey, Rebecca Scherer, John Achilla. Nancy Russo, Kate Fraser, Kristen Comeaux, Maria Burfield, Casey Conniff, Jack McIntyre, Julianne Tinari, Kathy Schneider, Hannah Strouth, Tori Clayton, Allison Hufford, Amy Tannenbaum, Logan Harper, and Don Cleary—wizard emeritus of JRA.

Thank you to my friend and film agent, Ron Bernstein.

Wherever life takes us, William Twigg Crawford has provided deep friendship and magical inspiration for as long as I can remember.

Many thanks to Carl Safina. He is a wonderful writer and

scientist, and he speaks owl better than anyone I know, including most owls.

I am grateful to friends at the Ocean House, the real location of the Tower Suite and the merlin's lair. Special thanks to my good friend Deborah Goodrich Royce—superb writer and founder of the Ocean House Author Series—who has made the hotel a literary destination for authors and readers. It has inspired me so much over the years and is one of my favorite places to write.

ABOUT THE AUTHOR

Luanne Rice is the *New York Times* bestselling author of thirty-eight novels that have been translated into thirty languages. Several of Rice's novels have been adapted for television, including *Blue Moon* for CBS, *Follow the Stars Home* and *Silver Bells* for Hallmark Hall of Fame, and *Beach Girls* for a mini-series on Lifetime. She is a recipient of the Connecticut Governor's Arts Award for Literary Excellence. She lives on the Connecticut shoreline. Learn more at luannerice.com.